*Be seduced and swept away
by these desert princes!*

You won't want to miss this new,
thrillingly exotic quartet from Marguerite Kaye!

First, exiled Prince Azhar must decide whether
to claim his kingdom *and* beautiful
unconventional widow Julia Trevelyan!

Read
*The Widow and the Sheikh*
Already available!

When Sheikh Kadar rescues shipwrecked
mail-order bride Constance Montgomery,
can a convenient marriage help him
maintain peace in his kingdom?

Find out in
*Sheikh's Mail-Order Bride*
Already available!

To secure his kingdom's safety,
Sheikh Rafiq must win Arabia's most dangerous horse
race. His secret weapon is an English horse whisperer...
whom he does *not* expect to be an
irresistibly attractive woman!

Read
*The Harlot and the Sheikh*
Available now!

And don't miss *Claiming His Desert Princess*,
coming soon...

Daredevil Christopher Fordyce has always craved
adventure. When his travels lead him to the kingdom of
Nessarah, he makes his most exciting discovery yet—
a desert princess!

## Author Note

Stephanie is the third English heroine in this series to find herself in deepest Arabia at the start of the nineteenth century. Preposterous, right? Maybe not as fanciful as you might think. Lady Hester Stanhope, who inspired my first desert book, *Innocent in the Sheikh's Harem*, lived in Arabia from 1815. The last of Lady Jane Digby's four husbands was a sheikh. She settled permanently in Arabia in 1853. Lady Anne Blunt, a breeder of Arabian horses and part inspiration for Stephanie, met with Lady Jane Digby in Damascus in 1877. And Gertrude Bell traveled to the Arabian desert in the early twentieth century and was instrumental in the foundation of Iraq. So my intrepid heroines do have a sound foundation in historical reality.

I have, however, chosen to avoid some of the more contentious aspects of nineteenth-century Arabia. My fantasy Arabia is free of the controversies of religion, imperialism and world politics, which affected it then and, unfortunately, continue to do so to this day. This series is quite a departure for me, but it's been creatively liberating. I hope you enjoy my fantasy kingdom as much as I enjoyed dreaming it up.

I'll end with a small confession. Before I started this book, I knew absolutely nothing about horses. I've ridden two. A donkey on the beach on the Isle of Bute, Scotland, and a carousel horse in Glasgow. I fell off both times. So please forgive any inaccuracies relating to equine matters; they are entirely my own doing.

# MARGUERITE KAYE

---

## *The Harlot and the Sheikh*

Don't Give Up
You're Not Alone
You're Going To Be Ok
I Deserve To Live

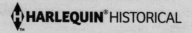

**H**ARLEQUIN® HISTORICAL

Recycling programs
for this product may
not exist in your area.

ISBN-13: 978-0-373-29916-4

The Harlot and the Sheikh

Copyright © 2017 by Marguerite Kaye

Printed in U.S.A.

HARLEQUIN®
www.Harlequin.com

**Marguerite Kaye** writes hot historical romances from her home in cold and usually rainy Scotland. Featuring Regency rakes, Highlanders and sheikhs in her stories, she has published almost thirty books and novellas. When she's not writing, she enjoys walking, cycling (but only on the level), gardening (but only what she can eat) and cooking. She also likes to knit and occasionally drink martinis (though not at the same time). Find out more on her website, margueritekaye.com.

### Books by Marguerite Kaye

#### Harlequin Historical
#### and Harlequin Historical *Undone!* ebook

#### *Hot Arabian Nights*

*The Widow and the Sheikh*
*Sheikh's Mail-Order Bride*
*The Harlot and the Sheikh*

#### *Princes of the Desert*
#### (linked to *The Armstrong Sisters*)

*Innocent in the Sheikh's Harem*
*The Governess and the Sheikh*
*The Sheikh's Impetuous Love-Slave* (Undone!)

#### *The Armstrong Sisters*

*The Beauty Within*
*Rumors that Ruined a Lady*
*Unwed and Unrepentant*

#### Stand-Alone Novels

*Never Forget Me*
*Strangers at the Altar*
*Scandal at the Midsummer Ball*
"The Officer's Temptation"

Visit the Author Profile page
at Harlequin.com for more titles.

# Chapter One

*Kingdom of Bharym, Arabia—June 1815*

Dawn was gently breaking as Rafiq al-Antarah, Prince of Bharym, trudged wearily out of his stables after another tense all-night vigil. The outcome had been tragically predictable: the loss of another of his prized Arabian thoroughbreds to this mysterious new sickness. Inas, on this occasion, a beautiful chestnut mare, her suffering brought mercifully to an end when it had become obvious that there could only be one outcome. Eight of his priceless breeding stock lost in just six months, and the only mare to have contracted and survived the seemingly random infection left utterly debilitated. Would there be no end to this torment?

Leaning against the wooden picket fence which bordered the empty paddock, Rafiq surrendered momentarily to the fomenting mixture of grief, rage and frustration which consumed him. It was enough to bring the strongest of men to their knees, enough to make even the most stoic weep. But a prince could not countenance displaying human weakness. Instead, he clenched his fists, threw back his head and roared impotently at the fading stars. His beautiful animals were innocent victims, punished for his crime. He was certain of it. In this darkest hour which was neither night nor morning, when he felt himself the only man alive in this vast desert region, he had no doubt at all. The fates had visited this plague upon him in retribution, making a mockery of the public pledge he had made to his people, the private vow he had made to himself. Reparation, in the form of restored national pride and a salved personal conscience, were both in danger of slipping from his grasp.

He had to find a cure. If nature continued to wreak her havoc unrestrained, it would destroy everything he had worked so tirelessly to achieve. He and Jasim had come to recognise the tell-tale symptoms, but even his illustrious Master of the Horse, whose claim to be the foremost trainer of Arabians in all of the East was undisputed, even he had been powerless.

Turning his back on the paddock, Rafiq rubbed his eyes, which were gritty with exhaustion. When he had inherited the kingdom from his father, the stable complex had been quite derelict, Bharym's legendary Arabian horses, whose blood lines could be traced back through ancient scrolls and word of mouth to the purest of antecedents, long gone, lost in the course of one fateful day. A day that destroyed his father personally and sullied the honour of the entire al-

Antarah royal family. A day that his people believed to be the blackest in their kingdom's long and proud history. A day of humiliation that dealt a fatal blow to their sense of national pride, and his own. The day that the Sabr was lost.

Rafiq had been sixteen, on the cusp of manhood, as he stood amidst the smoking wooden embers that were all that remained of Bharym's stud farm. He had sworn then that when he eventually came to power, he would make good the loss. For six more years, he had been forced to witness his father's slow but terminal decline, and the resultant decline of his kingdom's fortunes.

Eight years ago, just days after his twenty-second birthday, he had inherited the throne and a kingdom that seemed to have lost its way and its sense of identity. He had promised then to make Bharym a better place, a richer place, a kingdom fit for the new century, but his changes, improvements, renovations, were met with apathy. Nothing mattered save the restoration of the Sabr, the tangible symbol of Bharym's pride and honour. Until the Sabr was won, his people would not fully embrace the bright future he wished for them. Until the Sabr was won, it seemed that Bharym had no future worthy of mention.

And so, five years ago, he made a solemn vow to deliver the one thing his people longed for above all else. He had been certain that his honourable intentions more than compensated for the cold bargain he had struck in order to deliver on that promise. Only later, when the true, tragic price had become clear had Rafiq's resolve faltered. To continue on a path that had extracted such a terrible cost went against every tortured instinct in his being. But as darkness segued into a grey, gloomy morning on that tragic day, he knew he had no choice but to carry on. The return of the Sabr was not irrelevant in the face of such loss, it was doubly important. To give up would make the tragedy utterly futile.

A soft whinny carried on the breeze through an open window. Above him, the sky was turning from grey to the milky-white shade which heralded sunrise and a new day. Rafiq drew himself upright. He would not concede defeat now, or ever. He was Prince of Bharym, ruler of all he surveyed, one of the most powerful men in Arabia, and not yet entirely helpless. There was still time to hear word from the renowned English expert to whom he had turned in desperation—more in hope than expectation, if truth be told. Perhaps even now Richard Darvill was on his way, the royal travel warrant which Rafiq had enclosed with his letter helping to speed him towards Arabia. Even Jasim, fiercely resistant to any outside interference in what he considered his personal fiefdom, grudgingly conceded the English horse doctor's reputation was unimpeachable, his fame well earned.

It was reputed the man could work miracles, bring horses back almost from the dead. Rafiq certainly needed nothing short of a miracle now. These stables, the thoroughbred racehorses within, had to be protected at all costs. He owed it to his people to be the Prince they believed him to be. He owed it to his father's memory to repair his family's reputation. Most importantly of all, Rafiq owed it to himself to honour the debt he had incurred. He had carried the burden of his guilt for so long, he would not permit the fates to extend his punishment any longer. His atonement would be made. He could not alter the past but he would ensure something positive emerged from the darkest chapter in his life. It could never be enough, but it was all he could do.

*Two weeks later*

The end of Stephanie's long journey was finally in sight. The dhow in which she had sailed the length of the Red Sea from Egypt docked at the closest port to her landlocked destination just as dawn was breaking. On the quayside, a tall, austere-looking man scrutinised her papers before beckoning her to follow him.

A small train of camels awaited them at the end of the quay. Stephanie's cumbersome baggage was secured on the accompanying mules while she was assisted into the saddle of a camel with brusque efficiency. The official then took the reins, indicating by means of hand gestures that he would lead her mount. His inscrutable expression faltered only when she spoke to him in his own tongue, informing him that she understood him perfectly well and was grateful for his assistance. But if Stephanie imagined that her command of his language would encourage the man's demeanour to soften, she was mistaken. The official responded to her overture with a formal bow before turning his attention back to the four men who accompanied them. His short, sharp instructions were immediately and efficiently obeyed. Within half an hour of setting foot on land, Stephanie was once again aboard a ship. Only this time, it was a ship of the desert.

They traversed the bustling port, a chaotic melee of people, camels, mules and goats. Wagons piled high with goods fought for space on the stone jetties. A cacophony of bleating and braying and shouting filled the air, the clatter of hooves and wheels on the rough-hewn roads competing with the cries of the drivers and riders, the sailors and dock hands, and the excited knots of children who followed anything and everything, for no other reason, it seemed to Stephanie, than for the simple joy of adding to the noise and the crush.

As they left the coast the sea breeze quickly died and the briny air gave way to a burning heat. The sun rose and the wide road which led them inland narrowed to a rocky track which opened up on to an expanse of true desert, as the air around her grew hotter and drier. Her face protected from the worst of it by her wide-brimmed hat, Stephanie nevertheless began to feel as if she were sitting inside a huge kiln. Occasional gusts of wind blasted red-hot sand on to her face like the fiery breath of a lion. The light cotton jacket and blouse she wore felt like they were made of thick pelts of bearskin. Perspiration trickled down her spine, pooling in the small of her back where her wide belt cinched her waist. Her undergarments and stockings clung unpleasantly to her damp skin. Her eyes, her mouth and her nose were gritty with sand and dust. Inside her long riding boots, her feet throbbed.

Some time around noon, when the sun had reached its zenith, her guide informed her that they had crossed the border into the kingdom of Bharym. Here, they made the latest in a series of stops for refreshments, just at the point where she thought she might die of thirst. She, who had refused to wilt under the blazing heat of the Spanish sub in the height of summer, was struggling not to drink the entire contents of her goatskin water flask down in one gulp. This furnace-like heat, this desert terrain, should not be alien to her. It was in her blood, for goodness sake, she had reminded herself at the second stop, trying in vain to mimic the measured sips taken by her escorts. But the heat in Alexandria and Cairo had not prepared her for this. She shook her flask, aghast to find it almost empty. When the silent but obviously observant official handed her another, she was too grateful to be embarrassed.

As the day wore on and the rolling gait of the camel took its toll on her stomach and her head, Stephanie ceased to care what he thought of her. All she wanted was for the journey to be over, for then she could clamber down from this animated fairground ride and out of the blazing sun. Yet on they travelled.

Finally, the imposing walls of a city reared up, nestled snugly in the foothills of a range of flat-topped mountains. Constructed of red stone decorated with paler swirls which reminded Stephanie of an elaborate cake, and surmounted by wide ornate battlements, the parapets were triangular in shape rather than the more traditional rectangular design. Like ravening teeth, she thought with a shudder.

The city gate was an enormous, soaring stone arch with a fortress-like tower set on either side, like two impassive sentries. Though every other camel and mule and cart on the road passed through it and into the city, Stephanie's caravan continued onward, following the contour of the city walls before beginning to climb the wide, clearly marked route which led upwards, where her final destination came into view.

The edifice which could only be the royal palace stood on the plateau of a hill overlooking the city below, enclosed entirely behind a set of soaring square walls. Tiny rectangular windows were inset at regular intervals on the lower level and seemed to monitor her approach, making Stephanie feel distinctly uncomfortable. The excitement which had gripped her since this undertaking had first been proposed gave way to acute apprehension. She was not expected here. Would she be welcome? Behind those shadowed windows, many pairs of eyes might be watching her arrival. Her presence must inevitably be giving rise to speculation.

The shame which had been her constant companion for the last year crept stealthily up on her. She caught herself as, instinctively, she bowed her head.

She had travelled halfway across the world in order to leave it behind. Here in far-flung Arabia, whatever else might become of her, she would not be publicly branded a scarlet woman, a harlot.

Stephanie sat up straight in the saddle and turned her attention back to the present. Much larger arched windows were set higher into the walls of the palace, which replicated the design of the city walls. A decorative band was cut into both the walls and battlements, formed from what looked like dazzlingly white stone. Alabaster? The fang-like battlements took on an air of menace as she drew nearer, the many hooves of the caravan resounding over the piazza, where the marble floor was veined with something that glimmered like gold, but couldn't possibly be. Well travelled as she was, she had seen nothing to compare with this palace. It was intimidating, stark, yet utterly exotic and magically beautiful.

As the double doors swung open her stomach knotted with nerves, making her forget her travel weariness and discomfort. The Prince who lived behind these walls must be wealthy beyond her comprehension. Of the man himself, she knew only what she had gleaned from those who considered themselves experts in such matters, that the Prince bred and sold his thoroughbreds only to a privileged and chosen few, personally vetted by him. To own one of Bharym's Arabians was fast becoming an honour which no amount of gold could buy. A clever and cunning prince, she had thought cynically. Men, especially rich and privileged men, always wanted what they were told they could not have, be it horse or woman. Was she not living proof of that? And proof too, that once obtained, the object of desire quickly lost its lustre.

No more, Stephanie reminded herself sternly! There would be no more looking over her shoulder. She had had a year, time enough to come to terms with her shame and her guilt, to curse the lack of judgement which had led to her downfall. She had paid a high price for her sin, and inflicted a great deal of pain on the two people in the world she loved most. Now it was time to make amends by taking control of her own life, mitigating the effects of her foolishness by putting the past firmly behind her.

If, that was, the Prince accepted her proposition. Stephanie shuddered, reminding herself that the Prince knew nothing of her disgrace, and nor did he need to. The parting words of encouragement spoken to her rang in her ears, reinforcing her determination to live up to those expectations and by doing so repair some of the heartache she had caused. She was here now. It was up to her to grasp the opportunity and make of it what she could.

In the central courtyard, Stephanie's escort handed her over to another intimidating official after a prolonged and, as far as she could discern, acrimonious dispute. There was much gesticulating, many pointed looks in her direction, and several minions sent scurrying. As this new official finally made her a formal bow, he eyed her from below beetled brows as if she might at any moment metamorphose into a brigand, or perhaps explode like a cannonball.

It was growing dark as she followed the man across the now deserted courtyard, the servants, the official who had escorted her here, the camels and mules bearing her luggage having all melted away in the gloom. A hazy half-moon swathed in thin cloud hung in the sky as she followed the official through a door at the far side.

Long narrow corridors with marble floors, tiled walls, their double-height ceilings supported with soaring arches, were lit at regular intervals by flickering sconces. Guards stood impassively at each door, their short-sleeved black *abba* cloaks worn over white *dishdasha* tunics doing nothing to disguise their muscular bulk. On their heads chequered red *keffiyeh* headdresses were held in place with an *igal* formed by a twisted black scarf. A lethal-looking scimitar hung from one side of a belt, from the other a *khamjar*, or dagger, the sheath emphasising its vicious curve. As the official passed, each guard solemnly bowed his head. As Stephanie trailed in his wake, she could sense their eyes boring into her back. By the time she arrived at a huge set of doors, she was out of breath and bristling with nervous anticipation.

Two particularly menacing guards manned this portal. Her escort announced her in a tone that clearly indicated his desire to wash his hands of her. 'Most Royal Highness, Prince Rafiq al-Antarah of Bharym, I present to you, the English Woman.'

A small but determined shove to the small of her

back propelled Stephanie from the spot where she had temporarily taken root, forcing her to step into the magnificent chamber with its high vaulted ceiling. Quite overawed, she gazed around her at the dark marble pillars veined with gold. More gold was evident in the richly painted friezes and cornicing. The tiles on the high walls dazzled with multi-hued jewel colours. The stained glass reflected the light from the star-shaped chandeliers. Rich silk rugs covered the massive floor, and heavy embroidered brocade drapes fell in lustrous folds from the only piece of furniture in the room. A gilded throne. On which, imperiously, sat the Prince.

The doors behind her closed with a soft click. Glancing back over her shoulder, Stephanie discovered that she was quite alone with the royal personage. She had no idea what to do. Should she approach him? She took a tentative step. Curtsy? She hesitated. Or would he expect her to fall to the floor in obeisance? Completely unable to decide, she was still poised to perform any or all of these acts when the Prince rose from the throne, and she froze.

He was very tall. And extremely forbidding. And quite the most stunningly handsome man she had ever seen. Stephanie stared, round-eyed and open-mouthed. It was rude of her, and it was gauche, but she simply couldn't take her eyes off him.

Prince Rafiq was dressed from head to foot in white and gold. A white silk tunic high at the neck and tight at the sleeves, clung to a well-muscled body, long legs, a broad expanse of chest and wide shoul-

ders. The heavy belt slung over his slim hips was
studded with precious stones. The sheath of his scimitar was similarly jewelled. The thin cloak which covered his tunic seemed to be spun from silver and
scattered with tiny diamonds. His *keffiyeh*, made of
the same material, was held in place with what looked
like rope woven from gold.

But it was the face framed by the headdress which
held Stephanie's attention. She had encountered some
handsome men in her time, but this man could have
served as a model for perfection. Skin the colour of
sand in shadow. Sculpted cheeks, a nose verging on
the aquiline, offset by a mouth that managed to be at
the same time both utterly sensual and completely un-
forgiving. Under his high-arched brows, his eyes were
such a dark brown shade as to be almost black. She
could not see his hair, but she was willing to bet that it
was the colour of night. A fallen angel steeped in sin.
She had no idea where that fanciful notion came from,
but sinful in every way exactly described this man.

And sinful in every way exactly described her
thoughts. For goodness sake! She of all people should
be wary of harbouring such dangerous notions. It
was not the Prince's handsome looks which should
be occupying her mind. Though his lids might be
heavy, his gaze seemingly merely languidly contem-
plative, his expression almost one of dignified lassi-
tude, Stephanie was not deceived. Here was a man so
accustomed to power he needed no ostentatious dem-
onstration of it. Prince Rafiq could be wearing tat-
tered rags, and still she would have been in no doubt

of his status. It was in his eyes. Not arrogance but a sense of assurance, of entitlement, a confidence that he was master of all he surveyed. And it was there in his stance too, in the set of his shoulders, the powerful lines of his physique. Belatedly garnering the power to move, Stephanie dropped into a deep curtsy.

'Arise.'

She did as he asked, acutely conscious of her dishevelled appearance, dusty clothes, and a face most likely liberally speckled with sand. Those hooded eyes travelled over her person, surveying her from head to foot with the dispassionate, inscrutable expression she had seen the Duke of Wellington adopt when inspecting his troops. It was a look which could reduce the staunchest, most impeccably turned out of officers to blithering idiots.

'Who are you, and why are you here?' Prince Rafiq asked, when the silence had begun to stretch her nerves to breaking point. He spoke in English, softly accented but perfectly pronounced.

Distracted by the unsettling effect he was having on her while at the same time acutely aware of the need to impress him, Stephanie clasped her hands behind her back and forced herself to meet his eyes, answering in his own language. 'I am here at your invitation, Your Highness.'

'I issued no invitation to you, madam.'

'Not as such, admittedly. Perhaps this will help clarify matters,' Stephanie said, handing him her papers.

The Prince glanced at the document briefly. 'This

is a royal warrant, issued by myself to Richard Darvill, the renowned Veterinary Surgeon attached to the Seventh Hussars. How do you come to have it in your possession?'

Stephanie knitted her fingers more tightly together, as if doing so would stop her legs from trembling. 'I am Stephanie Darvill, his daughter and assistant. My father was most concerned to read of the malaise which has afflicted your stud farm but he could not, in all conscience, abandon his regiment, with Napoleon on the loose and our army expected to go into battle at any moment.' Which was the truth, though far from all of it.

'And so he saw fit to send his daughter in his place?'

The Prince sounded almost as incredulous as she had been, when Papa suggested this as the perfect solution to her predicament. The enormity of the trust her father had placed in her struck her afresh. She would not let him down. Not again.

'My father tutored me in the physiology of horses and the treatment of their various ailments,' Stephanie said more confidently. 'From a very early age, I have worked at his side, learning from him. In addition, for the past year I have been working at one of England's largest stud farms, located near Newmarket racecourse. So I do have relevant expertise, Your Highness, though I would never claim my father's vast experience.'

'Richard Darvill has the reputation of being the

foremost equine expert in the world. His fame has spread even here, to Arabia.'

'It is a fame well earned,' Stephanie said proudly. 'In fact, it would be no exaggeration to say that my father is something of a visionary. He has fought tirelessly over the years to bring the practice of veterinary medicine out of the dark ages, to persuade the army farriers to abandon their unnecessarily cruel and largely futile treatments. To introduce new methods, new ideas based on the principles of that radical surgeon, the great Mr John Hunter himself. My father—'

'I am aware of your father's achievements, Miss Darvill,' the Prince interrupted her. 'It is the reason I requested his help and not his daughter's.' He eyed her with another of those cool looks of his that were beginning to get under her skin just a tiny little bit. Though not as effectively as his next words. 'Apart from anything else, you are a woman.'

'Daughters usually are.' Stephanie gritted her teeth. It was hardly the first time she had encountered such prejudice. 'I find it is not a factor which weighs heavily on my animal patients' minds.'

'Perhaps, but I cannot believe it is a factor their masters so readily ignore.'

'One of the many reasons why I prefer horses to men,' Stephanie retorted. Her headache was intensifying. She pulled off her hat, raking her hands through her sweat-damp hair. No point in antagonising the Prince. It was far more likely to get her thrown out into the desert than gain her entrance to the stables.

'Your Highness,' she said, striving for a more conciliatory tone, 'I understand that my arrival here has come as a surprise, to put it mildly, but I assure you I possess the necessary expertise to be of assistance to you.' Rather belatedly she remembered the letter her father had written and handed it over. 'This should provide you with the reassurance you seek.'

The Prince broke the seal and scanned the note, written and signed in Papa's precise handwriting. 'A most impressively effusive testimonial. One that I trust is not distorted by a father's benevolence.'

Taking the letter back, Stephanie refused to lose heart. 'My father is a man of science. He prefers to deal in facts, not emotion, as do I. The fact is, Your Highness, you would not have sent all the way to England for assistance if the situation was not dire, or if you had anyone else who could help you. I am not my father, but I am here with his blessing, I am an excellent veterinarian, and I promise you I will do my utmost to help you. So why don't you forget that I'm a woman and permit me to attend to your sick horses?'

He ought to be outraged by her temerity in addressing him thus, but Rafiq was, reluctantly, impressed by the petite female glowering up at him, her big brown eyes defiantly challenging, seemingly oblivious of the fact that she had broken almost every rule of propriety, breached all etiquette and ignored every protocol.

She was not as young as he had taken her for—twenty-five or six, perhaps. Though her hair was streaked with gold by the sun, he guessed it must be naturally darker, for her brows and lashes were a very dark brown. Her skin was not that of an English rose but more olive in tone, flushed by the sun but not burnt. She was not beautiful. Her cheeks were too round, her eyes far too bold, her chin too decided. She had far too much strength of character to be anything so insipid as pretty, but there was something very attractive about her, an indefinable allure he could not name. Despite the evidence of her long day's travel, despite the fact that there was nothing remotely provocative about either her appearance or her demeanour, she gave him the impression that she had just risen languorously from a night of tumultuous and highly satisfying lovemaking.

He doubted that he would ever be able to do as she bid him, and forget that she was a woman. Looking at those pink lips, plump as pillows, he could not think of anything other than kissing them, of stripping the masculine attire from that very feminine form to discover if her nipples were the same shade of pink. Was her waist, cinched by that belt which looked as if it was meant to holster a gun, really as small as it seemed? Did those riding boots of hers stop at her calves, or her knees, or reach up to the soft flesh of her thighs?

Forget she was a woman! No, he could not do that, but he could remind himself that it was not the most salient fact about her, Rafiq thought grimly, and he could acknowledge that there was one thing on which they were agreed. He needed someone to save his horses. Could that someone really be this woman?

'My scepticism as to your abilities is understandable, Miss Darvill,' he said. 'I am sure even you would concede that a female practitioner is extremely rare, if not unique, in your chosen field.'

It seemed she would concede no such thing. 'Why would I make a false claim to skills and expertise I do not possess,' she demanded of him, 'when I can so easily be proved wrong? I have no desire to be thrown into your dungeons or cast out into the desert for being an imposter, I assure you.'

She threw back her shoulders as she spoke to him, looking him straight in the eye—or at least as straight as she could, given that she was a full head smaller than him. He admired her nerve, though her lack of deference was beginning to get under his skin. 'You forgot to mention the option of being escorted to my harem, Miss Darvill, and incarcerated in luxurious surroundings to await my bidding.'

He had meant only to put her in her place. Her re-action to this sally took him completely aback. Her eyes flashed in anger. Her hands curled into fists. 'I am not that sort of woman,' she said, through gritted teeth.

Her words piqued his interest. What type of woman was she? The challenge in her eyes, the defiance in her stance made it clear she was accustomed to fighting her corner, but why choose such a difficult fight in the first place? And how had such an attractive woman, one who, it seemed, had spent her life surrounded by elite English army officers, managed to remain defiantly unmarried? Sultry, that was the word he had been searching for. Stephanie Darvill was sultry, and she was either wholly oblivious, or wholly indifferent to this fact.

Not that it was in any way relevant. It was not her appearance but her sex that was the issue. If by some miracle she was the skilled veterinarian her father's letter claimed, she was going to have to work in his stables, with his men. Her very presence there would be seen by many as close to sacrilege. And as for one man in particular...

But he was getting ahead of himself. 'While I appreciate your father's good intentions, you must understand that your arrival here in his stead is a rather mixed blessing. Loath as you are to accept the fact that your sex is irrelevant, the fact of the matter is that it would make your appointment as Royal Horse Surgeon problematic. You will excuse me for a moment, Miss Darvill, I need to order my thoughts.'

Rafiq stalked over to the row of windows at the far end of the Royal Receiving Room and gazed out on the Courtyard of the Mirrored Fountain. The situation was, as the redoubtable Stephanie Darvill had rightly pointed out, dire. The plague would strike again and again, until it struck at the very heart of his ambition, wiping out the racehorses in which he and his people had invested all their hopes. This year was to be their year, the year the Sabr was recaptured.

Yes, the situation was dire indeed, but did it warrant the undoubted risk of appointing this woman? He turned from the window to study her. She stood with her arms crossed, her expression an endearing mixture of defiance and supplication. For weeks, months, Rafiq had been struggling to keep himself from the pit of despair. Could this female prove to be his unlikely saviour? Even if her spirit and her courage were sufficient to the challenge of working in the exclusively male preserve of the stables, her claims to expertise could still prove to be exaggerated.

He wanted to believe her, though he must be careful not to allow his hopes to override his caution, nor indeed her disconcerting allure to cloud his judgement. 'You speak our language exceedingly fluently,' Rafiq said, re-joining her. 'How does an Englishwoman come to be so proficient?'

'My mother is Egyptian, Your Highness.'

Which explained her colouring, he thought, careful not to allow his surprise to show. 'Your command of Arabic would certainly be an advantage if I did appoint you.'

'Though it is hardly the decisive factor. I do understand that.'

Her words had just the faintest hint of irony in their tone. Not something he was accustomed to encountering, which gave him pause for thought. 'The decisive factor, Miss Darvill,' Rafiq said coolly, 'is whether you can promise me that you will save my horses?'

Her face fell comically. 'No, I cannot, Your Highness. If such an assurance is a condition of my remaining here then I must reluctantly take my leave.

My father taught me never to offer any such guarantees. Even in the most routine of cases, the vagaries of nature cannot be discounted. From the details of the sickness you gave in your letter to my father, it sounds as if it is something quite new and undiagnosed. You have been very unfortunate.'

'My misfortune is entirely of my own making, Miss Darvill.' She frowned at the bleakness evident in his tone, and Rafiq, knowing enough of her already to guess that she would pursue the matter, unaware or careless of the fact that to do so amounted to gross impertinence, forestalled her. 'What matters is not how this plague came to visit the Bharym stud, but whether you can put an end to it.'

Most men would furnish him with a blustering affirmative. No man would dare reply in the negative. Stephanie Darvill was silent for a long time, biting her lip, when she eventually spoke, choosing her words with care. 'I can promise that I will do my utmost to save your horses, but I can offer no absolute guarantees that I will be able to do so. Perhaps that is not the wisest response to your question,' she added with a grimace, 'but it is the most honest one I can give you.'

She could not have given him a better one. Rafiq permitted himself a small smile. 'Your honesty is refreshing, and strangely reassuring. I am surrounded by people who tell me what they think I want to hear, rather than what I need to know.'

'Does that mean you will permit me to examine your horses?'

Her eagerness was touching. 'None of my blood-stock is at present infected by this plague. The affliction takes hold suddenly and violently. We lost Inas, a four-year-old mare, two weeks ago. Since then there has not been another occurrence, but that has been the pattern. I don't doubt there will be another, and another, in due course. Tomorrow I will introduce you to my Master of the Horse.' Rafiq paused, wincing at the thought. If only there was a convenient way of removing Jasim temporarily from the stables.

Once again, he was getting ahead of himself. Jasim was a problem only if he decided to appoint the intriguing Miss Darvill. 'We will talk more when you join me for dinner. You have endured a long and gruelling journey and will no doubt wish to bathe and refresh yourself first.'

His invitation clearly startled her. 'Join you? But I have not the correct attire. I thought—that is I did not expect...'

'Any expectations I had flew out of the window, Miss Darvill, when you walked into this Royal Receiving Room,' Rafiq said ruefully, taking her hand between his. 'Your arrival here in Bharym has been most *unexpected*. I hope it will also prove most effective.' A thick hank of hair had fallen over her forehead, partly obscuring one of her eyes. For some reason, it increased her sultry air. His fingers tightened on hers. 'Welcome to Bharym, Miss Darvill.'

He lifted her hand to his mouth, meaning to brush only a courteous kiss to her fingertips, but as his lips touched her skin, a bolt of desire shot through him, turning the gesture from one of polite courtesy to an overture he should not be making. She gave a little gasp. He had a glimpse of the heat he felt reflected in her eyes before she snatched her hand away, and he wondered if he had imagined it.

'I will have you escorted to the harem,' Rafiq said. 'Lest there be any misunderstandings,' he could not resist adding, 'my harem functions only as the quarters of the palace set aside for the female servants. I am sorry to disappoint you, but it contains not a single concubine. You will be the only other occupant.'

## Chapter Two

After following another servant through a different maze of corridors, Stephanie came to a halt outside a door guarded by a veritable giant of a man. A grille slid briefly open. The door swung inwards. The servant made his bow and ushered her in, where a genteel-looking older woman stood, obviously awaiting her arrival. 'I am reliably informed that you speak our language, madam?' she said after they had exchanged a formal greeting. 'My name is Aida, Mistress of the Harem. You will be so good as to follow me.'

She led the way into a huge terraced courtyard, the centre of which was open to the dusky desert sky. The floor was cool tiles studded with mosaic. A fountain tinkled, but Stephanie barely had time to register any of this before she was whisked off to the far corner. 'Your quarters, madam. I hope they meet with your approval.'

'Oh, my goodness.' Stephanie stared in wonder at the luxuriously appointed chamber. Somewhere between leaving the dhow this morning and the long, arduous trek through the desert, she seemed to have left reality behind and stepped into a dream world.

'There is a sitting room and dining salon across on the other side of the courtyard,' Aida informed her. 'I have taken the liberty of pouring you a refreshing cold drink. If madam would excuse me, I will ensure that the bath is made ready.'

'Thank you.' Stephanie picked up the tall frosted glass. The drink was both sharp and sweet, delicately scented with rosewater.

A high divan bed dominated the room, a homage to opulence. She had never seen anything so sumptuous. She trailed her fingers through the layers of voile hangings, stroking the silk covers, lifting a soft velvet cushion to her cheek. The tassels tickled her chin.

She was in a royal harem. In a royal palace. Belonging to a royal prince. Who happened to be the most handsome man she had ever met. Yet his harem was conspicuously bereft of concubines and wives. Had she misheard him or misunderstood him? Prince Rafiq must be around thirty, maybe a year or so older at most. Surely it was expected of him that he marry, if only for the sake of an heir? Royal families, whether Arabian or British, were not so very different in that respect.

Stephanie refilled her glass and perched on the edge of the divan. Prince Rafiq's marital status was not any of her concern, of course. Nor indeed, was the fact that when he had kissed her hand she had felt the most delicious *frisson*, had been so certain, for just a fleeting moment, that he felt it too. It was quite ridiculous to imagine that a man as attractive as the Prince could find her desirable. And even if he did, she wasn't going to be so stupid as to reciprocate his interest in her. She had sworn to learn from her mistake. This was the perfect opportunity to prove that she had!

Stephanie gave herself a shake. This room might look fit for a princess, but she was not here to lounge about dressed in silks and eating sweetmeats, she was here to try to cure the terrible sickness with ailed Prince Rafiq's Arabian thoroughbreds. A misfortune entirely of his own making, he had said, which was odd. How could he imagine that it was his fault? He did not strike her as a superstitious man. He had not summoned a soothsayer to his aid, but a man of science. 'And what landed on his doorstep instead was a mere woman of science,' Stephanie muttered to herself, 'who is likely going to have to work magic of some form, if she is to succeed in finding a cure.'

The butterflies in her tummy, which had never quite stopped fluttering since her arrival here, started up again in earnest. She so desperately wanted to succeed. So much depended upon it. She would no longer be a lost cause. She would have the means to support herself, and if she succeeded, the prestige of this appointment would surely outweigh the scandal which, despite a year spent in what amounted to hiding, still clung tenaciously to her like a noxious smell. Papa would never have urged her to come here had he thought her skills inadequate to the challenge, she reminded herself. He most certainly would not wish to do further damage to her already dented confidence by setting her up to fail. So she had better get on with it, starting with making sure she wasn't late for her dinner appointment with the Prince.

Opening the trunk which contained her clothes, and which had been deposited at the bottom of the divan, Stephanie groaned. There was absolutely nothing within in which to make a good impression. She had packed solely for her role as horse doctor, boxes of books and notes and instruments, expecting to live in the stable quarters and to spend her time with the horses. Her dismay was compounded as she turned away from her meagre attire to the long mirror which stood by the high lacquered cabinet.

She *must* have imagined the flicker of desire in Prince Rafiq's eyes when he kissed her hand. The man was sin incarnate, whereas she looked as if she had been rolled first in oil, then in the desert sand. Her hair managed to be both limp and wild at the same time and her face—now she could see why desert travellers used their *keffiyeh* for protection from the sun. With considerably less than an hour to make herself presentable, Stephanie tore off her clothes and rushed through to the bathing chamber clad only in a dressing robe. The room was decorated entirely in cool creamy-white marble. There was a washing fountain, and a long table which would presumably be used for massage, besides the huge bathing tub which was filled with warm water, the surface strewn with flower petals.

'Thank you,' she said to Aida, who discreetly—to Stephanie's relief—left the room. Though she longed to luxuriate in the delicately scented water, there was no time for anything other than a very swift but efficient *toilette*. Emerging much cleaner and considerably refreshed, she secured her newly washed hair in a chignon and was once again faced with the dilemma of what to wear. Aside from her spare riding habit and accompanying supply of shirts, she had only packed only nightwear, undergarments and one day gown. Fashioned from plain white cotton, with short puffed sleeves and a high waist, the *décolleté* gathered with a satin ribbon, the wide panel of white-work embroidery running down the centre of the gown from neckline to hem was the gown's only adornment. Clad now in her chemise, corsets and stockings, Stephanie held the dress up for Aida's inspection. 'I'm afraid I don't have anything else, do you think this will suffice?'

The Mistress of the Harem looked dubious. 'It is a pity I had not more notice of your arrival. I would very much appreciate the opportunity to dress a fine lady again.'

'Oh, I'm not a lady, I am an army officer's daughter and work with horses.'

Stephanie held the dress against her to study it in the mirror. It was a comfortable, cool garment, and it was her favourite. The trouble was, her affection for it showed all too plainly in its almost threadbare state. Perhaps she would ask Aida to make her a new gown. Nothing extravagant, but...

'You said that you would appreciate the opportunity to dress a fine lady *again*,' she exclaimed, turning back to face Aida. 'What did you mean by that? Do you refer to—to *concubines*?'

Aida flushed deeply, looking even more shocked than Stephanie felt. 'Indeed no, there have been no such women in the palace since the reign of Prince Bassaym, the grandfather of our revered and honourable prince. No, I refer to…' She paused, looking over both shoulders before continuing, speaking in a conspiratorial whisper. 'I refer to Prince Rafiq's wife, the Princess Elmira.'

So he was married. Why then had he implied that he was not, with his reference to an empty harem? And where was his wife, if she was no longer resident in the harem? 'I don't understand,' Stephanie said. 'Is the Princess Elmira elsewhere at present?'

'I'm afraid the Princess Elmira is no longer with us.'

'No longer—oh! I'm so sorry, do you mean she is dead?'

'Two years ago, the Princess Elmira died tragically in her sleep,' Aida said in hushed tones. 'Such a mortal blow for the Prince and for our people, for we long to see the Royal House of al-Antarah flourish once more.' The Mistress of the Harem shook her head sadly. 'But as it is for Bharym, so it is for Prince Rafiq. Until the Sabr is reclaimed, none of us can truly be happy.'

'The Sabr?'

'The Sabr,' Aida repeated reverentially. 'You said you work with horses. That explains your presence here, madam. The Prince has summoned you all the way from England in order to safeguard our chances, yes?' She lowered her voice to a whisper. 'At the stables they are sworn to secrecy, but I have heard rumours of a sickness.'

Prince Rafiq had not specifically forbidden her from discussing the nature of her business here, but then again, Prince Rafiq had not actually appointed her yet. Why would an outbreak of sickness be such a state secret? Curious as she was to know the answer to that question, Stephanie opted to change the subject instead. 'Now tell me honestly Aida,' she said, holding up her gown, 'do you think this quite unfit for dinner with Prince Rafiq?'

'It is not, in all truth, ideal. Unfortunately there is nothing to be done about the robe itself, madam, but if you will wait a moment, I may have a solution.'

Aida disappeared. Stephanie stepped into her gown and tied the ribbons at the neck and waist, the simplicity and ease of these only fastenings another reason for the gown's well-worn state. She had pulled on a pair of slippers, and was studying her reflection with resignation when Aida returned with a long length of fabric over her arm.

'May I?' It was finest crêpe de Chine, spangled with what looked like a galaxy of gold stars. Aida folded it in two and fixed it into the back of Stephanie's hair with a huge comb and a selection of pins, where it fell in filmy folds down her back, rather like the beautiful mantillas worn by the haughty Spanish ladies whom Stephanie had seen pay court to Wellington in Madrid. This mantilla though, was much longer. Taking up both ends, Aida draped it over Stephanie's arms so that it added a lustre to her gown, and covered the bare skin of her forearms which would have been rendered more decent by the addition of evening gloves, if she had any, which she did not.

'It's beautiful. My gown is quite transformed.' Delighted, Stephanie twirled around in front of the mirror. 'Now I feel suitably dressed to dine with a prince. How clever you are.'

Aida smiled shyly. The sound of a bell tinkling in the courtyard made them both jump. 'It is time,' she said, 'that is your summons, madam.'

A final glance in the mirror was reassuring. She barely recognised herself. Her eyes sparkled with anticipation. A new Stephanie. It truly was time for her to put her past behind her and embrace whatever the future might hold.

The dining room into which Stephanie was shown was even grander than she had expected. A perfectly square chamber, each of its walls was an exact replica of the other, with three tall arched windows topped by three half-size arches, the whole surrounded by another huge corniced arch stretched between two marble pillars. The walls between each of the windows were tempered a soft lemon, the simplicity a stark contrast to the geometric pattern of tiles in multiple shades of ochre, terracotta, umber, russet and mahogany, which decorated the floor, the pattern replicated in the ceiling. There were candles everywhere. Light flickered from the huge chandelier which hung on a long chain over the centre of the table, from the myriad candles which burned in the free-standing clusters of candlesticks which stood in each corner, and in the blazing sconces which adorned the walls.

The low circular table with scrolled and gilded legs took up most of the available floor space. It could, Stephanie reckoned, have seated at least thirty people, though there were only two places set with gold plates and crystal glasses. The servant who had escorted her from the harem waved her to the smaller collection of cushions, shaking his head when she would have seated herself. Two more servants stood by each of the four doors. Stephanie shuffled nervously from foot to foot. She was extremely hungry, but she wasn't at all sure she'd be able to eat anything. She was about to have dinner with a prince, for goodness sake.

The doors—different doors from the ones through which she had entered—were flung open. 'His Most Royal Highness, Prince Rafiq al-Antarah of Bharym.'

The servants did not bow, but stood sharply to attention. Stephanie dropped uncertainly into a curtsy. 'Your Highness.'

'Miss Darvill. There is no need to curtsy every time we meet.'

He had changed from his formal robes. Over the traditional white *dishdasha* robe buttoned high to a little round collar, Prince Rafiq was now dressed in a tunic of indigo-blue silk richly trimmed with gold braid. His hair was swept back in damp waves from his high forehead, his jaw freshly shaved. Once again, Stephanie's body reacted with an unmistakable shiver of desire. She resolutely ignored it.

'Please, sit.'

He took her hand to assist her on to the heap of cushions. His skin was so cool, it made her own feel uncomfortably hot. She dropped down with very little grace, almost as if her knees had given way under her. 'What a beautiful room,' Stephanie said inanely, in an effort not to stare at the beautiful man.

'My private dining room,' Prince Rafiq said, seating himself cross-legged on the large cushion at her right hand. 'I thought you would be more comfortable in a less formal setting.'

'A *less* formal setting?' Was he teasing her?

'The Royal Dining Salon can seat up to three hundred guests comfortably, the kitchens can spit-roast fifty goats simultaneously. I thought you would appreciate a more modest venue and less ostentatious menu. You may commence.'

Realising just in time that this last remark was addressed to the servant who had appeared, as if by magic, at the head of the table, Stephanie watched in astonishment as yet another of the room's four doors was flung open, and a positive cavalcade of servants, each bearing a covered gold platter, began to load the table with enough food to feed an army. The domed lid of each was removed with a flourish before being carefully placed on the table. Hot food was served in chafing dishes, the lid removed for the Prince's inspection and approval, before being replaced. The familiar, appetising aroma of grilled meat and warm bread mingled with other, less familiar but no less mouthwatering smells.

Stephanie tried to recall all her mother had told her of the eating customs of Egypt, but her mind was a complete blank. Was she to serve herself? The question was answered when the last dish was placed on the table, the doors closed, and two fresh servants joined them, each carrying a gold tray. Waiting for permission from the Prince—Stephanie made a mental note that the Prince's permission seemed to be required for everything—the servants knelt on the floor. A precursor to ritual hand washing, she realised, recalling some of her mother's stories hazily now, but she was not to be permitted to carry out that menial task for herself. Her fingers were dipped in the scented water. Her hand was rubbed with lemon, and then rinsed again. The linen which was used to dry her was pleasantly warmed.

Feeling slightly embarrassed, as the servant repeated the process on her other hand, Stephanie allowed her attention to drift to the man seated beside her. Prince Rafiq had very long legs. He was also very supple, for such a tall man. And very athletic looking, for a prince. It must be all the physical work with the horses. In the army, when they were not campaigning, the cavalry regiments spent endless hours training their horses, riding them over obstacles both wide and high. In the sunshine, the men often rode shirtless. Riding gave a man very strong shoulder muscles. The

flimsy silk and cotton robes he wore showed Prince
Rafiq's muscles off to fine effect.

'I can tell by your expression that you are ravenous, Miss Darvill.'

What on earth was wrong with her! Stephanie's
cheeks flamed. 'It all smells delicious, though I am
not sure that I recognise many of the dishes.'

'I will explain. We will converse in English,' he
said, switching to that language. 'By doing so we
can talk both freely and privately. As you can see,
the table has been laid with food of the same colours
grouped together. Green for prosperity. Yellow for
happiness. We begin with those. Then there are the
meats and the mixed salads. And finally there are the
sweets, dates and honey, which represent life.'

'Goodness, I had no idea.' She was vastly relieved
to see that her plate was being delicately filled by one
of the servants. Whether this was yet another new-
comer or not, she had no idea. 'Thank you,' she said to
him, relieved, when he returned her gesture, that she
had not broken protocol by doing so, and pleasantly
surprised when the Prince also thanked his servant,
calling him by name. In a palace whose staff must
run to hundreds, it was an impressive feat of memory.

'Please, begin,' he said. 'I have had them set out
silverware cutlery for you. We have no shortage of
European visitors here, and some are most averse to
our custom of eating with our hands.'

'Thank you, but I am happy to eat as you do,'
Stephanie replied, tearing a piece of flat bread and

preparing to scoop some tomato salad on to it, hoping fervently that she would not make a fool of herself.

'Your mother has retained the customs of her native land in your father's English household then?' Prince Rafiq asked.

'Some of them, though Papa prefers more plain fare, to be honest. And Mama's family are not particularly wealthy. I suspect she would be every bit as overwhelmed as I am, by this veritable feast.'

'It is a modest repast, believe me, compared to the state banquets I am required to endure. I am a man of simple tastes. Be careful,' Prince Rafiq added as she scooped what she thought was another piece of salad on to her bread, 'those dishes containing chilli are extremely spicy. Unless you are accustomed to them, they will destroy your palate. Let me explain the various dishes on your plate. The smooth purée topped with yoghurt is *moutabal*, which is made from roasted aubergine. The salad of tomatoes, mint and cucumber is called *fattoush*, and beside it is *tabbouleh*, which is made from steamed grains of bulgur wheat. Oh, and the little patties are *falafel*, made from chick peas.'

'My mother has talked fondly of *falafal*. She said that every family has a different, secret recipe that they claim to be the best and most authentic.'

Prince Rafiq smiled. 'My grandmother used to say the very same thing. What does your mother think of your coming to Arabia?'

The change of subject was smoothly done, but Stephanie was not fooled. This was not so much a private dinner as an interview. She was—unsurprisingly—being vetted. She studied the small fritter-like falafel, which tasted nutty, and nothing at all as Mama had described it. 'Once my father had persuaded her of the advantages,' she said carefully, 'my mother was most supportive. Though Egypt is some weeks' travel from Bharym, the presence of her family relatively nearby in Alexandria was of some comfort.'

Stephanie swallowed a mouthful of the wheat salad which she had scooped up on a piece of flatbread and absent-mindedly put her fingers to her mouth to lick a dribble of tomato juice. It was delicious, but she was suddenly conscious that the Prince was looking at her with the strangest expression. 'Oh, I do apologise,' she said guiltily. 'I've just remembered that my mother told me that it is considered rude to do such a thing before the end of a meal.'

He seemed to be fascinated by her mouth. Was there a smear of juice on her chin? She couldn't resist checking. She wished he wouldn't look at her like that, as if—as if he wanted to lick her fingers. And where on earth had that ridiculous thought come from! Stephanie took a sip of iced sherbet.

'If one licks one's fingers before the end of a meal it indicates to one's host that one has finished eating, though is not yet replete,' the Prince informed her. 'Which is deemed a negative reflection on the quality of the repast.'

'I assure you, I intended no such slight,' Stephanie replied hastily. 'On the contrary, the food is utterly delicious, but I am not quite accustomed to using my fingers and so when I licked them...'

'Please,' Prince Rafiq said, giving his head a little shake, 'there is no need to draw attention to your—I assure you, no offence was taken.' He seemed to be suddenly thirsty, taking a long draught from his glass. 'I am interested in the—advantages, I believe you called it—this appointment provides you with.'

Whatever had been distracting him a moment before, he was completely focused on her now. Stephanie stared down at her half-empty plate. 'The opportunity to gain experience working in such a prestigious stud farm is a prize beyond rubies. Success here, Your Highness, will go a long way to ensuring my success back in England, in a field of endeavour in which, as you have pointed out, my sex is a great disadvantage.'

Prince Rafiq raised his eyebrows. 'It did not prevent you from securing a position on a leading English stud farm, Miss Darvill. I believe you said you had been working there for the past year.'

Her plate was removed, and Stephanie was thus granted time to consider her answer while another was set out with a variety of meats. It went completely against her nature to prevaricate, though her naïve belief that everyone, especially army officers, valued honesty and integrity as highly as Papa, had taken a severe knock. But a partial truth was no lie. 'My father is not without influence, and facilitated matters. His reputation assisted me in establishing my own credibility,' she said.

'And association with my name—or more accurately, the name of my stud farm—will further enhance it?'

'If you will be so kind as to permit me to use it as a testimonial,' Stephanie said. 'Assuming, of course, that I am successful in effecting a cure for the mysterious sickness. There is also,' she added awkwardly, 'the matter of financial reward. Not having my father's experience, I would not expect you to compensate me quite so generously, but frankly, Your Highness, with apologies for raising such a vulgar topic, even half of the remuneration which you offered would give me the freedom to set up my own establishment and live independently. Something which I am very eager to do.'

Thinking about what it would mean to her, and to her parents, to have her future secured brought a lump to her throat. Aware of the Prince watching her carefully under those sleepy lids, Stephanie concentrated on making a little parcel of roasted goat meat and couscous studded with pomegranate.

'What induced you to leave your father's patronage to work on a stud farm? Did you tire of military work, Miss Darvill? It has been your life, you said so yourself.'

'Army horses, Your Highness, are heavy working breeds, either draught horses for pulling artillery or chargers, neither of which are used for breeding purposes. Working on a stud farm was, my father felt, an excellent way of filling this gap in my knowledge.'

She had not lied, her experience at the Newmarket stud had been invaluable, it was simply that she wouldn't have left her army life and gone there were it not for another, much more unpleasant experience.

Prince Rafiq's expression gave absolutely nothing away, yet somehow she was certain he had detected her unease. Flustered, Stephanie picked up her fork then set it down again. Her food was no more than half-eaten, but she had quite lost her appetite.

'You have had a sufficiency?'

'Yes, thank you.' Her plate was cleared. Another was prepared, of sweet pastries dribbled with honey, dates covered in chopped nuts. The foods representing life. Most appropriate since her presence here was driven by her desire to establish a new life for herself.

She hoped that the changing of dishes and the serving of the final course meant the topic was now closed. The Prince, however, had merely been biding his time. 'Your desire for independence is intriguing, Miss Darvill,' he said. 'A most unusual ambition for a woman. A more common aspiration is marriage, surely?'

Stephanie Darvill's glass slipped from her hand, spilling sherbet over the table. In the moments it took for one of his servants to clean the mess up, Rafiq watched her covertly, noting the effort it took her to regain her composure. The robe she wore was cut demurely enough at the neck, but it was still low enough to show the rise and fall of her breasts as she breathed. Her curves distracted him. He wondered if the ribbon tied at the neckline was the only fastening of the dress. He wondered what she wore beneath that gown. It looked flimsy enough, but it was most likely an illusion. In his limited experience, the complexity of the undergarments worn by European women seemed expressly designed to repel a man's advances.

Miss Darvill herself, on the other hand, seemed designed to encourage just such advances, yet she was not married, and nor was she, in her own words *that sort of woman*. What sort of woman was she? And why did she crave what she called independence? Would she live alone? Why would a woman wish for such a thing? Though admittedly, his experience of Western women was not extensive, he did not think they were so very different from women in the East. Didn't all women wish for a husband, children? But this woman—he had never met anyone quite like this woman.

'I have no interest in marriage, Your Highness,' Stephanie Darvill said, interrupting his thoughts, 'and I confess I fail to understand what my aspirations— or lack of them—in that direction have to do with my ability to cure your horses. Save of course,' she added tightly, 'that as a single woman without a husband to dictate my movements, I was free to travel to your aid.'

'My apologies,' Rafiq said, equally tightly, for he was quite unaccustomed to being placed in the wrong. 'You are in the right of it. What matters are your skills as a horse surgeon, and whether those skills will compensate for the disruption your presence in my stables will undoubtedly generate, for they are an exclusively male domain.'

'Then they are no different from any other stables in which I have worked.'

'The difference, Miss Darvill, is that here you have neither your father's presence nor his reputation to shield you from what can be a rough-and-tumble environment.'

'Not as rough and tumble an environment as a battlefield,' she countered, 'although Papa would never permit me anywhere near the actual fighting. I was left in sole charge behind the lines. My place will be taken by his new assistant, in this conflict with Napoleon that is to come. For all I know, battle may even have commenced by now.' For a moment she was lost to him, her gaze unfocused, her thoughts clearly with her family, but then she gave a little shrug, a tiny smile. 'He made me promise not to worry about him. It is a promise we who followed the drum—family, servants, wives, children—were always being obliged to make, though I doubt any of us ever managed to truly keep it. It was worse, in a way, being so far from the battle lines, imagining what was happening not just to one's family but one's friends, and of course the horses. Though I would never equate an animal with a human life, I do not subscribe to the view that they possess no feelings.'

'Nor I,' Rafiq said warmly. 'In fact I would go further, and say that there can be a true affinity between a horse and a rider.'

'Oh, I agree,' Miss Darvill said enthusiastically. 'If a man is afraid going into battle, he transmits that fear to his horse. I have seen it so many times. And though you may scoff, I have also seen a horse make a man braver with a display of—of eagerness. That sounds silly, but...'

Rafiq shook his head, smiling. 'Not at all. Arabians, mares especially, are highly valued for their fearlessness in a battle charge, which can give a rider the confidence he lacks, or enhance what fortitude already exists. But it is more than that. In the most hostile parts of the desert, I have seen a horse struggle on, carrying her master to the safety of an oasis when all hope seemed lost.'

'And in battle too,' Stephanie said eagerly, 'there have been many, many times when Papa has witnessed horses returning men almost dead in the saddle to the safety of our lines, often at great cost to themselves. And those same men, they will do almost anything to save their horses too. I have seen the most battle-hardened of soldiers weep for the loss of his steed. And weep too, when an animal which looked beyond recovery has been saved against the odds. That,' Stephanie Darvill said, clasping her hands together fervently, 'is one of the very best aspects of my vocation.'

He could not help but be endeared. 'Your love of horses shines through.'

She beamed at him. 'As does yours.'

'I quite literally grew up around horses,' Rafiq confided. 'When I was three months old, I was sent out to be raised by a Bedouin tribe. It is the custom here, for a prince's sons to live outside the palace confines for ten years in this way. Bedouins treat their horses as part of the extended family. They even bring them into their tents at night to shelter from the chill desert air.'

'Those early years then, sowed the seed of your ambition to establish the Bharym stud farm?'

'Bharym has a proud legacy of breeding the finest thoroughbreds. It is part of our heritage.'

She flinched at the edge in his voice. 'I'm sorry, I had no idea. I was under the impression that this stud was relatively new.'

'In a literal sense you are correct,' Rafiq said stiffly. 'The stables were rebuilt when I inherited the kingdom eight years ago, but I believe—and my people also—that they are a continuation of what has gone before. The seed of my ambition, as you put it, was planted fourteen years ago, on the day when Bharym lost the Sabr.'

'The Sabr? Aida—your Mistress of the Harem— mentioned this Sabr, what is it?'

'The Sabr is the most prestigious annual endurance race in all of Arabia.'

'Like the Derby in England?'

'There is no comparison,' Rafiq said. 'To win the Sabr brings prestige not only to the owner, but to the whole kingdom. The Sabr is a symbol of national pride.'

'So this race, it is to win it that you established— re-established—the stud?' Stephanie Darvill was frowning. 'Your Highness, this outbreak of sickness, why must it be kept secret? Aida—you must not think badly of her, she said nothing indiscreet, save only that it was not to be talked of.'

'This year, after fourteen years' absence, we finally have a string of horses with sufficient stamina and fleetness of foot to compete with the very best. All my people's hopes are pinned on winning. This sickness puts not only a horse race but Bharym's entire future at risk.' He smiled thinly. 'I am certain that to you that must sound preposterous. How can a mere horse race determine the fate of a kingdom? With respect, you are a stranger, you cannot understand the history of Bharym and the Sabr, but I assure you, its importance to my people cannot be overstated.'

To say nothing of how critical it was to him. Could this foreign woman save the race for them? Could she be the one who would help him defeat the fates and secure a future for his country, his people, himself? A preposterous notion, he'd thought when he first set eyes on her, but now—now, his instincts told him to trust her. And his head told him he had no better option. 'Tomorrow,' Rafiq said, 'I will tell you the story of the Sabr. Then you will understand how vital it is that you save my horses.'

Her eyes widened. 'Does that mean you will permit me to treat them? I cannot tell you how much this means to me, Your Highness.'

Her smile, the first real smile he had been granted, lit up her face. 'Rafiq,' he said, checking first that the servants had left the room. 'When we are alone, you may call me Rafiq.'

'Then I must be Stephanie. If it pleases Your Highness. Sorry, Rafiq.'

*She* pleased him rather too well. It was to be

hoped that her abilities matched her enthusiasm, for one thing was certain, Stephanie Darvill would not please his Master of the Horse. Once before, Jasim had violently objected to a woman's presence in the stables. Rafiq shuddered. The outcome had not been Jasim's fault, but his. Only he was to blame. But he refused to think about the past tonight. Tonight was about securing the future.

'Tomorrow,' he said, 'your work will commence. I will be frank, Miss—Stephanie. I am concerned about your reception in the stables. It is likely to be very hostile.'

'As I said, I am accustomed to that. Your Highness—Rafiq—it is my experience that those who work with horses do so because they love them. When they see that I share that love, that I can alleviate the suffering of sickness or injury, they don't see a woman, but a veterinarian.'

She spoke with an assurance that he admired, but which in one case was undoubtedly misplaced. 'That may be true for the majority of my grooms and stable hands, but my Master of the Horse is a different matter. Your role here does not depend upon Jasim's good opinion, but you will find your task a great deal easier if you can find a way to earn it. There is little he does not know about Arabian thoroughbreds.'

'Save how to cure this sickness,' Stephanie pointed out. 'When he understands that we are both working towards that goal then I am sure he will co-operate.'

'He will co-operate, because I will instruct him to do so.'

'I would prefer you did not.' She grimaced. 'I am sorry to contradict you, but I am not, as you have already pointed out, the type of person to tell you what you want to hear, rather than what you need to know. Respect cannot be imposed, it must be earned. Please do not make matters worse between myself and your illustrious Master of the Horse by forcing him into a pretence of co-operation, it will only make it more likely that he will resort to sabotage to discredit me. I prefer to fight my own battles.'

Admirable sentiments, though thoroughly misguided. Resolving to take matters into his own hands, but deciding it would be better for Stephanie if she remained oblivious to his manipulation of events, Rafiq bowed over her hand. 'You are a very surprising woman. I hope that you will prove to be equally gifted.'

His kiss was the merest whisper, the lightest touch of his lips to her fingers. He would have done no more, had she not shivered at his touch. But she did, and he reacted instinctively, his fingers tightening around hers, pulling her a fraction closer. The folds of her gown brushed against his leg. Her hair had fallen over her eye again. He could not resist pushing it back, and then he could not resist trailing his hand down the curve of her cheek, to rest on the slope of her shoulder. She shuddered again, and he responded to that shudder. When she tilted her head, her lips parted. He bent his head, drawn irresistibly to her. The sound of a door opening and then being hastily closed made them jump apart.

'Forgive me,' Rafiq said, taking another step backwards, away from further temptation.

'There is nothing to forgive,' Stephanie said, blushing furiously. 'It was as much my fault as yours. I should not have—but I am fatigued. The effects of a surfeit of sun too, no doubt. So there is nothing—'

'The hour grows late,' he said tersely, cutting short her embarrassment and his own. 'We will meet in the stables in the morning. As of this moment, you are formally appointed Royal Horse Surgeon.'

His words, spoken primarily to remind himself of her purpose here, made Stephanie gasp. 'The appointment will be for six months,' he continued in a brusque manner, 'by which time you will either have cured this plague which has descended on Bharym, or we will have established that you are incapable of curing it. Your remuneration will be on the terms I proposed to your father.'

She gazed speechlessly at him. He wished she would not look at him that way, as if she was having to work very hard to prevent herself from throwing her arms around him in gratitude. 'The appointment may be terminated by me at any time prior to the end of the six months,' Rafiq continued, more sternly than he intended, 'if I feel your presence has compromised the smooth running of the stables. You understand?'

'Perfectly.'

'Excellent. Then I will see you in the morning.'

'Rafiq.' He had turned to leave, but Stephanie caught his sleeve, yet another breach of protocol. 'Thank you,' she said, with a shy smile, 'for trusting me. For giving me this opportunity to prove myself. I am extremely grateful and very much aware of the honour you confer on me. I promise you I will do all I can not to let you down.' She surprised him once again, this time by bending over his hand, pressing a light kiss to his knuckles before opening the door herself, startling the waiting guard.

Watching her follow a servant along the corridor back to the harem, her sashaying walk drawing his eyes to her swaying rear, Rafiq sighed. His passions had been all but dormant since this plague descended. It was inconvenient to say the least, to have them re-awakened by the woman who had come to Bharym to cure that self-same plague. Though perhaps it was apt. A sign that he was coming back to life.

The end which would be a new beginning was so terrifyingly, tantalisingly close. The vision he had once carried so close to his heart, of the colours of Bharym tied to the Sabr trophy, of the victory flag flying proudly above the palace and above every city and village in the kingdom for the first time in two generations, was one he hardly dared conjure for fear the fates would deprive him of it.

But they would not. Stephanie Darvill would ensure that they could not. His stud would bring victory to Bharym, confidence to his kingdom, joy to his people, and quieten his troubled conscience. Payment for his crime. Reparation fully made, all debts repaid.

Departing the dining salon, Rafiq headed for his own chambers, and the meagre solace it provided.

## Chapter Three

⁕

Exhausted as she was, Stephanie was far too anxious to sleep. Tossing and turning on the huge divan, she spent the night alternating between feeling daunted by the enormity of the task which lay ahead and reliving her dinner conversation with Rafiq. Her excitement at her appointment was mitigated by embarrassment and no little confusion at the unexpected manner in which the encounter had concluded.

From the moment she had set eyes on the Prince in all his regal splendour, she had reacted to him on an almost visceral level. Her skin tingled when he touched her. She had wanted him to kiss her. No, the urge was stronger than that. She had longed for him to kiss her. When his fingers had trailed down her cheek, her throat, they had set off the most disconcertingly pleasurable fluttering low in her belly.

Stephanie pulled the lace-edged sheet over her face, her toes curling up in mortification. Had experience taught her nothing! Painful enough to have her exploits openly discussed in the officers' mess, but Rafiq was a royal prince and any scandal would be magnified a thousandfold. Even more importantly, he was her employer and her potential route to salvation. This time it was not simply her reputation but her entire future that was at stake.

Stephanie groaned. Casting back the sheets and abandoning the divan, she opened the door of her chamber and padded across the courtyard to the fountain. Above her, the stars were fading, the sky turning from indigo to grey as dawn approached. One of Papa's tenets was that a good veterinarian learned more from experience than they ever did from textbooks. It was a tenet that she ought to apply to all aspects of her life. Experience had taught her that she lacked judgement when it came to matters of the heart, and that she could not trust her feelings. Experience had also demonstrated graphically the unbridgeable gulf between her own lowly origins and those with lofty pedigrees to protect. More than anything, experience had taught her a very hard lesson in the differing social status afforded to men and women. While a gentleman could boast about his conquest with impunity, the conquest herself was branded a harlot. The iniquity of it could still make her clench her fists with fury.

But there was one field in which she could succeed on her own terms. One field in which, second only to Papa, she knew herself to be expert—more than the equal of any man, no matter how well born he might be. It was time for her to prove that. Returning to her chamber, Stephanie began to prepare for the long and taxing day ahead.

A little over an hour later, breakfasted, dressed and armed with her precious box of instruments, Stephanie emerged from the royal palace in the wake of a servant, into bright morning light and what was clearly the stable complex. She was dressed simply, in a cambric blouse teamed with her wide, plain skirt, belt, riding boots, and her broad-brimmed hat. Despite having decided to leave her jacket behind, she was already too hot, and despite the confidence-boosting talk she had given herself en route, she was already feeling nervous.

Rafiq, in contrast, looked cool, confident and regal as he strode across the cobbles to meet her. Today, he wore a plain white open-necked shirt tucked into riding breeches, worn with long boots. His hair was swept back from his brow, the natural curl forming a wild halo which, combined with the smattering of dark hair at his throat, gave his handsome looks a savage edge. Despite herself, Stephanie's stomach lurched as he approached, a combination of attraction and apprehension that did nothing for her composure.

'Good morning, Your Highness,' she said, making a curtsy, conscious that there would be many eyes watching them.

'I trust you slept well?'

'Oh, like a babe in arms,' she said, the silly lie making her colour. Panic threatened to render her ineffectual. There was a world of difference between her dream of treating the thoroughbred horses of a royal prince and the reality which now confronted her. These stables were overwhelmingly and entrancingly beautiful, and clearly more prestigious than anything she had ever before encountered. She wasn't just daunted, she was petrified.

'As you can see from the position of the sun, we are on the north side of the palace,' Rafiq said. 'It is cooler here, which makes it the ideal location for the stables.'

Stephanie felt far from cool. Perspiration trickled down her back. Her corsets, though she had laced them loosely, felt far too tight. The huge paddock to the front of her was shaded by clusters of tall palms and acacia trees with their feathery leaves and white flowers. At the furthest side a large pool of water gleamed, reflecting the tall spikes of papyrus grass in shades of sea-green, their fronds tipping down to the pool as if to sip from it. The dusty ground was covered in patches of scrub, burnt brown, acid-yellow and silvery-grey in colour, but nevertheless giving the paddock a veneer of lushness.

'Bharym's relative proximity to the sea, and those mountains over there,' the Prince said, pointing to the rugged violet-coloured hilltops in the distance, 'mean that we are blessed with unusually high rainfall and consequently produce a good quantity of succulent grazing. The pool over there is a *birket,* a cistern dug from one of the many underwater springs which Bharym is fortunate enough to possess. That is one of the reasons why our horses thrive. Though the Arabian breed is renowned for its stamina compared to other horseflesh, they are still horses and not camels.'

More stands of trees provided shade for the stable buildings themselves, which featured a long, low façade of mellow stone in the classical Greek style, with a large central arch which provided entry to the courtyard and which was topped by a pediment carved with the image of Pegasus, the legendary winged horse of ancient mythology. Terraces flanked the inner courtyard, mirrored by the balcony which ran all the way around the first floor.

The business of the day was just getting underway. A string of horses were being led out for their early morning exercise. Rafiq greeted the riders, a mixture of stable hands and grooms, casually by name. Formalities were dispensed with here, Stephanie noted. The men returned his salutations only with a small bow, their eyes shying away from direct contact with hers.

'Unfortunately, I've had to despatch Jasim on urgent business,' Rafiq informed her. 'We had promised two of our yearlings to a Bedouin sheikh, but the transaction simply cannot be completed while the stud is under the shadow of the plague. It is imperative that both the sickness and knowledge of its presence here be kept secret, so Jasim has gone armed with a plausible excuse as a delaying tactic. It therefore falls to me to act as your chaperon.'

Stephanie, having braced herself for a first encounter with the Master of the Horse, had mixed feelings at this surprise development. 'I was keen to meet Jasim as soon as possible. I believe I made it clear I prefer to fight my own battles, without assistance.'

Rafiq stiffened. 'Your tenure is dependent on your not ruffling too many feathers here at the stables. Talk of fighting battles is not conducive to that.'

He spoke coldly. He clearly was not accustomed to being challenged. Stephanie straightened her shoulders, wishing she did not have to look up quite so far to meet his eyes. 'Sometimes one has to battle in order to gain respect. I would not expect you to understand that, since you are automatically accorded it,' she said with far more confidence than she felt. There was a long, uncomfortable silence. She felt like a very small mouse looking up at a very large hawk.

'Your honesty is refreshing, your resolve admirable, but your judgement is flawed. I sent Jasim away because winning the trust and respect of the other stable hands and grooms should be your first priority. Jasim would be hostile to your presence even if you were a man. You must not forget, he has failed to cure the sickness himself. As my race trainer, he has every reason to want this sickness cured, but as a man nursing considerably bruised pride, he will grudge any success you have. I am trying to facilitate that success, not patronise you, as you seem to imagine.'

While he talked, Stephanie had the distinct impression that she was shrinking. Now, she felt as if she really was the size of a mouse. 'I see that now,' she said, in a voice to match.

'To that end,' Rafiq continued, as if she had not

spoken, 'I have fully briefed the men on the nature of your appointment, and emphasised the respect with which I wish you to be treated.'

Which explained the lowered eyes, the sidelong glances she had been receiving. 'Thank you,' Stephanie said, in a voice which singularly failed to sound grateful.

Rafiq laughed gruffly. 'If you had witnessed the outrage on their faces an hour ago, you would say that as if you meant it.'

'Rafiq, what I do know is that your belief in me means a great deal. Thank you.'

'An apology, but not a capitulation. You are a very stubborn woman, Stephanie Darvill.'

'I prefer to call it determined.'

He had the kind of face that was quite transformed by a genuine smile. It softened the austere perfection of his looks, but paradoxically added considerably to his allure. Her body responded with a jolt of pure lust that left Stephanie smiling idiotically back, quite transfixed for several seconds, oblivious of where they were and who was watching, until Rafiq broke the spell, turning abruptly on his heel.

'Come,' he said brusquely, 'let us proceed with your introductory tour. The stable layout is straightforward. There are horse stalls lining both walls. The tack rooms and the feed stores are at the back, and in the centre there is a training arena.'

She followed him inside, quickly shaken out of her daze as the dry, dusty scent of the desert gave way to the more familiar one of hay, leather and the unmistakable odour of horse, but instead of calming her, it stretched Stephanie's nerve endings still further. It was pleasantly cool in here, the slatted shutters across the high windows filtering out the worst of the harsh sunlight, the terracotta floor tiles and white-marble interior further mitigating the heat. The room was immense. A cloistered ceiling was supported at intervals by plain Doric columns, with at least thirty large stalls set on either side. As she gazed around her, her mouth was as dry as if she had swallowed half the desert. 'And you say this layout is replicated in the other wing?'

'We have at present a string of over one hundred horses. The majority are mares, obviously, for Arabian mares are most in demand for their gentle temperament, their stamina and their affinity with people, but we also have a number of stallions, mostly for breeding purposes. They are kept out in the desert in a separate paddock. There is another segregated area at the end of this wing for the mares currently in foal, and we have other paddocks for the camels, the mules, and for the horses who have been put out to pasture.' Her expression must have looked every bit as daunted as she felt, for Rafiq smiled reassuringly. 'Your duties will be restricted to the care of animals suffering from the infection. Everything else is Jasim's domain.'

Stephanie cleared her throat, striving to keep her voice steady. 'I had no idea, I confess, of the enormity of your equine empire. The value of the horses in this part of the stable alone is inestimable. How many of them race competitively?'

'None, at the moment. We have been keeping our powder dry with respect to the Sabr, until we felt we were competitive enough to win.' Rafiq frowned heavily. 'If this sickness persists, even if it does not strike down the horses which we have specifically trained for the race, I cannot in all conscience compete. I will not expose the livestock of others to this plague that ails us.'

Walking down the central isle, Stephanie noted that everything in the royal stables was immaculately clean, the equipment pristine. It was obvious that these horses were extremely well cared for, and she said so.

'Naturally,' was Rafiq's response as he stopped in front of a magnificent mare. 'Sherifa,' he said, opening the stall gate for her. 'She has blessed us with three top-class foals, haven't you, my beauty?' The mare was a grey, with the finely chiselled bone structure, arched neck and high-carried tail so typical of the breed. She tossed her head playfully as he patted her neck.

'Your affection is obviously mutual,' Stephanie said. 'She is a magnificent creature.'

'She is indeed,' Rafiq replied, rubbing the horse's nose. 'She has been with us for five years. Sherifa was my late wife's horse.'

'Aida mentioned the Princess Elmira. My condolences for your sad loss.'

'The marriage was arranged. My wife died two years ago.'

Stephanie was struggling to interpret his carefully neutral tone. An arranged marriage, but that didn't necessarily mean he hadn't loved her. Did he imply that two years was time enough to grieve and recover, or insufficient?

'You will wish to examine Sherifa?'

It was a command, not an invitation. 'Yes, yes, of course.' Flustered, Stephanie stepped into the stall. The mare, sensing her nervousness, backed away from her, her breath exhaling in short puffs, her nostrils flaring. She knew better than to attempt to touch such a highly strung horse when her own nerves were so taut. Closing her eyes momentarily, she took several deep breaths.

'Hello, Sherifa.' Stephanie held out her hand. The mare's mouth was soft. Her eyes were gentle. 'Lovely girl.' Her fingers were perfectly steady as she stroked the mare's nose. Calm suffused her. Beginning the meticulous process of examination, she utilised all of her senses just as her father had taught her, in the same way as the great Dr Hunter had tutored her father. By the time she had finished, her mind was completely focused on the task in hand and not the distracting prince standing behind her watching her every move.

Later that day, with a weary sigh, Rafiq closed the weighty leather-bound tome that was the official Bharym Stud Book, carefully fastening the lock with the heavy gold key. There were now six year-lings overdue to be delivered to their carefully vetted owners. Though Jasim assured him that no mention of the plague had passed his lips, Rafiq knew it was only a matter of time before word got out.

Only a matter of time too, until the sickness struck his stables again. Watching Stephanie at work this morning, any remaining doubts he had as to her claim to be Richard Darvill's assistant had dissipated. His Head Groom, Fadil, had also initially been highly sceptical of her abilities. It had not taken her long to prove her mettle though, with her plethora of probing questions, her refusal to accept anything other than extremely detailed answers, and her complete confidence when faced with examining Basilisk, a strapping specimen of a stallion with every bit as lowly an opinion of females as Jasim.

Rafiq smiled to himself. Naturally, he would remain cautious. Of course, it would be foolish to hope for too much. But there was hope. It had arrived in the delightful and distractingly desirable form of Stephanie Darvill. It was too early for her to have made any meaningful progress, he knew that, but he was anxious to hear her initial thoughts and, yes, there was no harm in admitting, he was eager to enjoy more of her company. These last months had been claustrophobic, exposure to company curtailed by necessity. What he needed was a fresh perspective and an escape, if only for a short interlude.

Pausing to instruct a servant as to his specific requirements, Rafiq headed for the stables. Stephanie was sitting on a bench in the inner courtyard, shaded by the balcony on the floor above, watching the constant stream of horses being led in and out for exercise in the relative cool of the late afternoon. Her hair had obviously escaped from its pins at some point in the day, and was now carelessly tied back, though the usual tress had escaped to fall over her brow. It was a lighter shade than the rest, almost golden. Her skin in the bright sunlight seemed more olive, though her cheeks were flushed. She wore the same skirt that she had arrived in. Practical perhaps, but it was far too heavy for these conditions, and though her white top looked to be cotton, it was tightly fitted from neck to wrist. No wonder she looked like a wilting flower in dire need of water.

'Your Highness.' She jumped to her feet when she saw him, dropping into a curtsy.

'Please, there is no need for such formality here at the stables,' Rafiq said. 'Tell me, what are your first impressions of my horses?'

She beamed. 'I have never seen such magnificent specimens. I've examined Sherifa, of course. And Kasida. Tamarisk. Mesaoud. Azrek. Nura. Riyala. Shieha. I am afraid I can't remember all their names.'

Her enthusiasm was endearing. Her smile was dazzling, drawing attention to the perfect whiteness of her teeth, the endearing little fan of faint lines that appeared at the corner of her eyes when she smiled. She had the kind of slightly husky voice that disconcertingly made Rafiq picture her wearing nothing but her underwear. 'The Bharym Stud Book records every horse, every bloodline, back into the mists of myth and legend,' he said, trying to banish the vision which had floated into his mind.

'Legend?'

'It is said that the Arabian horse was first formed from the south winds. That is why the Bedouins call them Drinkers of the Wind. It is said that a herd of these wild creatures was tamed, and then as a test of their obedience, first deprived of water, then sent racing towards an oasis. Only five returned immediately when called, and these mares are the founders of the five Arabian breeds: Keheilan, Seglawi, Abeyan, Hamdani, and Habdan. I can trace the bloodlines of every one of my horses through the sires, back to one of those original breeds.'

'It's a charming tale,' Stephanie said, looking more dubious than entranced. 'But I confess, I'm rather more interested in the story of this Sabr race. In the stables, your men can talk of little else.'

Rafiq smiled. 'It is something of a national obsession with my people. I thought you might like to take a ride out to the oasis where we graze our stallions. It is cooler out there, and it will allow you to see a little of the desert landscape, but if you are too fatigued...'

'No, I would love to do so.'

'Good. I will see that the horses are readied.'

Stephanie watched him go, enjoying the rear view of Rafiq in his long boots and riding breeches striding towards the stalls. When he returned, he was leading three horses. He had put on a white-silk *keffiyeh* held in place with a plain black scarf. It framed his face, drawing attention to the breathtaking perfection of his features.

'I had them put on an English saddle for you, but you will have to ride astride.'

'Luckily I learnt to do so at an early age.' Stephanie picked up her hat from the seat beside her. 'I was quite a tomboy when I was growing up.'

'Now that, I find easy to believe, since you are a walking paradox.' Rafiq produced another square of white silk, folding it to form a headdress. 'Put this on, it will protect you from the worst ravages of the sand much more effectively than your hat,' he said, placing it over her head.

He tied it in place with a bright red scarf, tucking her hair under it. Though his touch was impersonal, she was none the less acutely aware of it. Standing directly in front of him, her face was level with his throat. His shirt was white, with a high neck, fastened with a row of tiny pearl buttons. He smelled of the soap made with olive oil, reminiscent of the one she had used this morning.

'There.' Rafiq took a step back. 'You can tuck the ends in like this.'

'Yes. Thank you.' Flustered, Stephanie turned her attention to her horse. 'Kasida,' she said, her eyes wide. 'Rafiq, I cannot possibly ride such a prize horse.'

'Do you not consider yourself an accomplished enough horsewoman?'

'No, I—I mean obviously, I've ridden racehorses before at the Newmarket stud, but Kasida…'

'Stephanie, I know you well enough already to be convinced that if you thought you couldn't handle her, you would say so. Am I correct?' He waited until she smiled and nodded reluctantly. 'Then what are we waiting for?'

Her heavy wide skirts made her feel uncomfortably hot, but at least they gave her freedom of movement. Putting her boot in the stirrup, Stephanie managed to mount with relative decorum, and a great deal of excited anticipation.

'Kasida is one of our gentlest mares,' Rafiq said, mounting his own horse. 'Unlike Basilisk, here, who does not like to be mastered—as you know from examining him earlier. He is one of our best stud stallions, however. Now he has performed his duties, I will return him to the stallions' paddock and return on this other mare.'

Taking up the rope halter of the spare horse, he preceded Stephanie out of the stable yard. Just like all the stable hands, Rafiq rode Bedouin style, with no stirrups and only a rope halter instead of a bridle or bit, which required an adroitness which Stephanie could not imagine replicating. Basilisk, despite Rafiq's assertion, seemed to be very well aware which of them was in command. As they left the stable compound, passing the drinking pool and out on to a wide flat expanse of desert, Rafiq urged the stallion into a gallop and Stephanie gave herself over to the thrill of the ride.

The ground consisted of compacted umber-coloured earth rather than sand. Every now and then, a cluster of acacia trees, a patch of bright yellow and green indicated the unmistakable presence of water. The distant mountains which she had thought uniformly an unusual violet colour, now took on multiple hues, the highest peaks a pale silvery-blue, shading to amethyst and violet, lavender and lilac, while the foothills segued from plum to a peaty brown. She had imagined the desert to be flat, uniform sand and little else, much like the terrain she had traversed from the Red Sea port yesterday, but the Kingdom of Bharym was like nothing she had witnessed on any of her travels. Above her, the sky and the sparse puffy clouds seemed to reflect the mountains, a palette of blues that would have taxed the most talented of artists to capture. Stephanie was thinking that she had never seen anything so beautiful, when the oasis came into view, and took her breath away.

The water was deep blue, consisting of a lake with a palm-covered island in the middle. Around it, the ground was lush with verdant greenery making a meadow of the desert, sweetly scenting the air, and reflecting in the mirror-like surface of the water. But there was little time to admire it, for Rafiq had ridden on at a brisk canter.

She heard the whinny of the stallions before she saw them, Kasida's ears pricking up in response. The enclosure was high-walled. Dismounting, she waited while Rafiq unlocked the gate, pausing only for her to lead her horse in before closing it behind her. A collection of the finest stallions she had ever seen greeted her in the huge compound, in the midst of which was another smaller pool and a large cluster of shady palms. Stephanie gazed around her in astonishment. 'How many are there in the herd?'

'Thirty-two, including Basilisk,' Rafiq replied, removing the saddle from the stallion and setting him free to trot off and rejoin the milling herd. 'Now we have completed our business, we can enjoy what is left of the daylight. Come.'

He led her round to the far side of the oasis, where a charming little stone bridge led to the island. Enchanted, Stephanie picked her way across, through a gap in greenery to a clearing in the shady embrace of a circle of palm trees. The ground was covered in rugs and strewn with plump cushions. A large hamper sat in the middle. 'Oh, what a delightful surprise!'

'I was reliably informed that you were so engrossed in your work today that you did not stop to eat,' Rafiq said, opening the hamper and beginning to lay out the contents, 'and so I took the liberty of having some food sent ahead.'

His thoughtfulness, his generosity, but more than anything his willingness to trust her, to have faith in her, brought a lump to her throat. 'Thank you, you are very kind,' Stephanie said, sinking on to a large cushion.

The tremble in her voice made Rafiq look up from pouring them both a cool drink. 'What is wrong, was this a mistake? Are you fatigued?'

She shook her head, managing a weak smile. 'I'm just being silly. Everything is perfect.'

He pressed a tall, cool glass into her hands. 'Drink this, you may be a little dehydrated, especially if you have not eaten.'

Stephanie took a sip. 'Thank you.'

He set a plate of food in front of her. 'Eat.'

'Yes, Your Royal Highness. At once, Your Supreme Highness.'

Her teasing tone earned her one of Rafiq's rare and perfect smiles. 'Eat,' he commanded.

Suddenly ravenous, she did. The food, like last night, was a delicious mixture of fresh, citrusy salads, spicy meats, and light, flaky pastries. She sampled more adventurously than she had at dinner, though a pickled chilli made her gulp down an entire glass of sherbet in one mouthful. Finally, too replete to manage even a fig drizzled with honey, she pushed her plate to one side and washed her hands. 'That was delightful,' she murmured contentedly.

'Yes,' Rafiq said, 'it was.'

She had the distinct impression he was not talking about the food. His smile had a sinful quality about it—though what she meant by that, she had no idea.

'This precious race of yours,' she said, striving to focus her thoughts on the reason she was here, 'the Sabr. Tell me about it.'

'History, heritage, heart,' Rafiq intoned. 'That is how we think of the Sabr here in Bharym.' He sat up, crossing his legs with graceful ease. 'Sabr means fortitude or endurance. The race, like my Arabians, has its origins in legend. It is said that it was first mentioned in one of the tales of *One Thousand and One Nights*, though our records show that it was first raced a hundred years ago this year, its centenary. An earlier Prince of Bharym, a direct antecedent of mine, designed the victor's trophy, agreed the rules and set the course. There are four Sabr towers, spaced about twenty-five miles apart, to mark out the circuit, which is completed twice. Each section traverses very different terrain. In places flat and hard packed as you can see here, but one of the sections is across shifting dunes, and another meanders the foothills of the mountains.'

'Two hundred miles in total!' Stephanie exclaimed.

'It *is* the ultimate test of both horse and rider,' Rafiq said wryly, 'though there are eight of them, and only one of him.'

'Good grief! That means the race must take...' Stephanie screwed up her nose. 'How long does it take a horse to complete each stage?'

'It depends on the terrain, but usually between two and three hours. The race starts at first light and lasts all day and through the night. A true test of endurance, though as I said, it is about a lot more than the race itself.'

'History, heritage, heart,' Stephanie said.

'Precisely. From the very beginning, the Sabr belonged to Bharym. Not once did our horses fail to triumph. Every year as I grew up, I watched as our colours crossed the finishing line first. Like everyone in Bharym, I believed we were invincible, that our horses could never be vanquished, that they truly were descendants of the legendary Drinkers of the Wind. The Sabr is in our blood. Without the Sabr, my people believe we have lost something vital, our sense of national identity.'

She could believe it, looking at him now, his eyes alight with almost childlike enthusiasm as he described the race, so very different from the intimidating Prince she had met only yesterday. She could easily imagine Rafiq as the victorious rider, travelling like the wind across the searing desert sands towards certain triumph. She could hear the raucous cheers of his people, visualise their ecstatic faces, and Rafiq, proudly lifting the huge gold trophy. 'It sounds magical,' she said when he had stopped talking. 'All that is required is a princess as the prize for the winner, and it truly would be a tale from *One Thousand and One Nights*.'

The glow faded from Rafiq's eyes. His expression darkened. 'It is the tradition that all the losers forfeit their best horse to the winner. Fourteen years ago, my father's greatest rival, a Bedouin prince, Salim, entered the race with a team bred from new bloodstock acquired from the far reaches of Arabia. My father coveted that bloodstock. It induced him to enter into a secret side-wager with the Bedouin, where the loser would forfeit all of their stallions, the jewel of their breeding stock, to the other. You can guess the outcome.'

Stephanie covered her mouth in horror. 'How could he have been so foolish?' she whispered.

'Complacency? Greed? We had never lost, there was no reason to imagine that we ever could—but we did. Even now...' He winced, unfolding his long legs and getting to his feet. 'Even now, I find it incomprehensible, that he risked something so precious. I remember watching the stallions being led out before being taken away. It felt as if the very lifeblood was being drained from our nation. But that was not the end of it.'

He held out his hand to help her up, and they headed out of the clearing, back to the little bridge, where there was a view into the stallions' compound. 'I awoke in the night to see a great light blazing in the sky. It took me some moments to realise it was coming from the stables.'

'No!' Stephanie exclaimed, appalled. 'Oh, no, Rafiq.'

He pressed her hand fleetingly. Gave her a grim little smile. 'My father released all the mares and foals into the desert first. He could not bear to look at them, to be reminded of his folly, but he could not bear to harm them. We tried desperately, but it was too late to save anything. I will never forget standing among the burning embers, a blizzard of ash swirling around me. It was the end of my dreams to ride to victory in the Sabr. I vowed then that I would find a way to rebuild the stables, restore our bloodstock, breed a new Sabr team to win back the trophy for my people.'

Stephanie waited, her heart overflowing with pity, as Rafiq gazed sightlessly out over the oasis, his throat working, afraid to say anything lest she embarrass him by witnessing the strength of his emotions. Dark shadows flitted over his face, and slowly his countenance hardened, his eyes became bleak. When he spoke again, his tone was harsh. 'I was sixteen, too young to comprehend the true extent of our loss, the devastating impact it would have on our kingdom. Every year, we were forced to host the Sabr, to watch another nation win what was rightfully ours. My father went into a terminal decline and our kingdom languished. When he died, eight years ago, though I did not forget my oath, I had other priorities. There were so many things to attend to which my father had neglected. Our kingdom's wealth, health and morale had all suffered. I envisaged winning the Sabr as the culmination of our recovery, but all my people were interested in was the race. It was like a—a festering sore, a painful boil to be lanced. What could I do, but change my focus to winning the race? I gave my people my word that I would do what they desired, and bring the Sabr back to Bharym, breed a winning team which were descended from the very bloodstock my father forfeited.'

'Thus restoring your heritage in the true sense,' Stephanie said, awed. 'How on earth did you manage to achieve such a feat?'

Rafiq's countenance did not change dramatically, rather it froze. There was a bleakness in his eyes that reminded Stephanie of the soldiers she had witnessed returning from battlefield like lost souls. 'It cost me more than you can possibly imagine.'

She knew instinctively he did not refer to gold,

and she also knew instinctively not to ask him what he did mean. There were some questions better left unspoken. Some secrets better kept under lock and key. After all, she had her own.

'You have taken a terrible burden of responsibility on your shoulders. The weight of expectation of a whole nation lies with you.'

'As Prince, it is my duty to shoulder that responsibility,' Rafiq replied, 'although I confess it sometimes feels onerous. My people think me a hero. They have raised me so high that I am sometimes afraid to look down. But I will prevail, Stephanie, not only for my people's sake, but for my own.'

'It matters to you personally, then. Because of your father?'

'That is part of it.' He took hold of her hands. 'Now fate has brought you here to me and for the first time in many moons, I have reason to hope.'

His smile, the way he was looking at her, made her feel as if she was standing on the edge of a precipice. The responsibility terrified her, but the trust he had placed in her made her feel oddly powerful. 'Rafiq,' she said, meaning to caution him. It came out sounding like a caress.

'Stephanie.'

He made her name sound exotic. She shivered. Her heart began to pound. It was impossible not to close the gap between them, for her body was being drawn towards him as if pulled by invisible strings. She smiled up at him, and her smile made his eyes gleam. For a second, which felt like an hour, he hesitated. A second in which she thought she might expire if he did not kiss her, because she had been waiting for that kiss, longing for that kiss, since last night.

And then it happened. 'Stephanie,' he said, whispering her name, sliding his arms around her waist, drawing her to him, and the world went hazy as his lips touched hers. Softly at first. A butterfly kiss, his tongue sweeping the line of her lower lip. Then another kiss, gently teasing her mouth open, the tips of their tongues barely touching, yet it made her tingle. Wrapping her arms around his neck, she angled her head, hungry for more. His mouth slanted over hers, shaping hers, and he kissed her again. She had never been kissed in this way, with such gentleness generating such blazing heat inside her, with tongue and lips, lips and tongue, so she could not tell what was one kiss and what was another.

She felt as if she was melting, her entire body being brought to a slow simmer by his kisses. Her fingers tangled in the silkiness of his curls. Her body was pressed against his, her breasts brushing his chest, making her nipples tingle. And the unmistakable ridge of his arousal brushing—

The kissing stopped abruptly. Rafiq shifted, creating a gap between them, and let her go. His eyes glittered black, like anthracite. His breathing was very slightly irregular, though not as fast as her own. 'I have been wanting to do that since last night, but I should not have taken such a liberty. Forgive me.'

His words were like a dousing of cold water. 'There is nothing to forgive,' Stephanie said, horrified to discover that her voice sounded tearful. 'I wanted you to kiss me.' She turned away, snatching up the *keffiyeh* and silk scarf from the ground, throwing it over her head and most of her face. 'I can't think what came over me. It won't happen again.' The simple act of tying the scarf in place defeated her. She snatched the headdress off, scrunching the soft silk between her fingers. If she did not put an end to this highly distracting, highly dangerous attraction between them, it would fatally compromise her very reason for being here. 'Rafiq,' she said resolutely, 'I am your Royal Horse Surgeon. A Royal Horse Surgeon has no place kissing the Royal Prince who appointed her.'

His smile faded abruptly. 'You are not a servant, Stephanie, and even if you were, I would never take advantage of my position.'

She believed him. She did believe him, there was no comparison between Rafiq and—and it made no difference. Her face was scarlet now. She would have given a great deal for a freak wave from the oasis to envelop her, but nature resolutely refused to co-operate, forcing her to continue. 'Rafiq, I merely meant that as your Royal Horse Surgeon, your horses should be my primary—my only focus. We do not have time to indulge in—in kissing, even if we want to, even if it was not completely wrong for me to—you are not only a prince, Rafiq, you are my employer,' she said wretchedly.

'You are, of course, quite correct.' His tone was clipped. His expression was decidedly haughty. 'Your first and only concern must be for the welfare of my horses. I have state business which will take me out into the desert for a few days. You will be able to work without distraction. For now, it is time we returned to the palace before it gets dark.'

And that was Rafiq's final word on the subject. The journey back to the palace was a total contrast to the outward leg, conducted at a sedate trot and in virtual silence. Ample time for Stephanie to reflect, and to regret, and to aver that she would not be so foolish as to play with fire again.

## Chapter Four

The massive double doors of the cavernous Hall of Campaign closed behind the last of the Village Elders as they trooped out in single file. Quarterly Petition Day was usually one which Rafiq relished, for it allowed him to familiarise himself with the more general concerns and welfare of his people, as well as the specific requests their Elders made on their behalf. Today however, the major topic of conversation for all concerned was whether or not Bharym would finally be re-entering the Sabr this year. The same question had been the very first on the lips of the Bedouin Prince he had been to visit.

Ten days in the desert, away from the palace, had given Rafiq a great deal of time to reflect. Though he had not yet spoken to Stephanie since his return late last night, he had received a comprehensive report of her progress. There had been no new case of the sickness since her arrival nearly two weeks ago now, but there had been another new arrival in his

absence. A foal to Sarmadee, which he had been informed Stephanie expertly delivered. The foal had
appeared with one hoof bent back, a presentation that
could have proved fatal for both foal and mother were
it not for Stephanie's intervention, performing a birth-
ing manoeuvre which required a difficult balance between strength and delicacy. Fadil, who had assisted
her, was almost as impressed by Stephanie's achieve-
ment in coaxing the highly reluctant mare to her feet,
against all the animal's natural instincts, as he was
by her saving the foal. There was no doubting, from
the respect in his Head Groom's voice, that Stephanie was doing what she said she would do, and winning his men over. He had been right to send Jasim
away. When his Master of the Horse did return to the
stables, he would find it more difficult to undermine
the new Royal Horse Surgeon.

Rafiq sat down on the divan, removing his formal headdress and the belt which held his scimitar in
place, setting both down beside him. Ten days since
he had seen Stephanie. Ten days since he had returned
to the palace from the oasis in high dudgeon, furious
with her for compelling him to concede that he should
not be distracting her from her task. More than sufficient time for him to cool his both his ardour and
his temper. Stephanie Darvill appeared to be exactly
what she claimed, an excellent veterinarian, and an
excellent veterinarian was all he required, but still,
he had not been able to forget that kiss.

Did she think about it? Her response had made it
clear that she wanted him as much as he had wanted

her. Why was such a sensual woman determined to
sacrifice her life to animals, to what she called her
vocation? She had told him that very first day that
she preferred horses to men, but he had taken it for a
witticism. She had also told him that she 'wasn't that
sort of woman', but though her kisses had been neither practised nor artful, they were not the kisses of
an innocent. What kind of woman was she?

A woman whose kisses were sweet and heady.
Whose smile connected straight to his groin. Whose
smoky voice conjured up a vision of her voluptuous
body naked, tangled with silk sheets. Perfume, and
the distinctive scent of female arousal. That *frisson*
of anticipation like no other just before he entered
her and afterwards, sated, flesh clinging damply...

Rafiq shook his head ruefully. Stephanie Darvill
was here to minister to his horses, but he might as
well stop pretending that he didn't wish she might
minister to him. She reminded him of the decadent
delights of the flesh, the pleasure of a union which
was not a marital duty. Impossible that these fantasies
could be fulfilled, but there was no harm in indulg-
ing in them. And no point in denying that whatever
else she might be, Stephanie Darvill was a fascinating woman.

Stephanie discovered the array of outfits laid out
on her divan when she returned from the stables in
the heat of the afternoon. Aida had worked quickly.
And expertly. The garments were simple and practical as Stephanie had requested, but the Mistress of

the Harem's creations were also unmistakeably feminine, and quite exquisite. There were several tunics in the male *dishdasha* style which could respectably be worn for her work in the stables, loose muslin robes with long sleeves, high necks fastened with tiny buttons, in soft shades of cream, lemon, mint-green and sky-blue. There were two white muslin cloaks with matching headdresses which would protect her from the desert sands when riding, and a variety of silk scarves with which to tie them. Undergarments comprised of sheer silk were shockingly flimsy, pantaloons and camisoles trimmed with lace replacing her stiff petticoats and corsets.

Stephanie picked up a handful and let them fall in a soft cloud back on to the divan. Plain clothes, fit for the stables, she had requested, but these garments seemed redolent of the harem. And there were some things Stephanie had not requested. A vibrant gown of silk woven in a splash of pinks, cerise and fuchsia, violet and lavender, the long sleeves slashed to fall open at the shoulder, with a tasselled belt and a long length of voile to be draped mantilla-like into a veil, if required. There were pink slippers to match, the curled toes adorned with tiny silver bells. And a robe which might be for dressing, or which could be worn over a *dishdasha* to make it more formal, in bottle green, fitted at the waist, the sleeves and hem embroidered with a bold symmetrical pattern in the russet colours of English autumn leaves that reminded Stephanie of the tiled ceiling in Rafiq's private dining room.

Rafiq. She was aware that he had returned to the palace. She suspected that Fadil had fully briefed him. Perhaps that was how it was to be from now on, she was to be kept at arm's length. A good thing, she thought, for it would mean she had no further opportunity to make a fool of herself. No chance to prove she had grossly exaggerated the effect of that kiss. No excuse to kiss him again.

Stephanie quickly stripped and, donning her dressing wrapper, padded through to the bathing chamber where her bath was waiting. Stepping into the soothing water, she closed her eyes and tried to empty her mind, but it was no use, the image which lurked there was too enticing. There was Rafiq with his sinful smile. His arms around her waist. His mouth on hers. She could feel the touch of his tongue. She could taste his lips. His hair was silky-soft. And his body was hard.

Her own tightened in response. Not tension but anticipation. That feeling of standing on the edge of a cliff again. That warm, trickling heat again. That odd feeling. Yearning? Wanting? The frustrated urge to touch and to stroke, to discover for herself the ripple of Rafiq's muscles under his skin. And to have him touch her, stroke her, his hands on her naked body.

Stephanie sat up in the bath, picked up the fresh bar of olive-oil soap which Aida insisted on providing every evening, and began to wash. What was wrong with her! The memory of those kisses ought to fill her with shame, not fill her with longing for more. She was not a harlot, despite what they said, so why was her body trying to beguile her once again into acting like one? Respectable women did not crave kisses. They did not enjoy kisses. They were not disappointed when the promise of those kisses was unfulfilled.

But Rafiq's kisses were so very different. His ardour had been—not restrained exactly but kept tightly leashed. His kisses coaxed and teased, as if there was all the time in the world, as if those kisses were the whole point, not a prelude. Rafiq's kisses were very different indeed to Rupert's.

Rupert!

She stepped out of the bath and began to dry herself ruthlessly. She would not allow his name to contaminate her new life. She wrapped her arms tightly around herself, screwed her eyes tight. She was not a harlot, no matter what the whispered innuendoes had claimed. She was a silly fool who had thrown away her reputation on a man who had no respect for her, never mind any intentions, but she would not allow the mortification to follow her here. She would not!

Returning to her bedchamber, Stephanie found Aida awaiting in an agitated flutter. 'His Royal Highness requires your presence in the Hall of Campaign without delay, madam. Which of your new garments would you like to wear?'

Stephanie had donned the beautifully embroidered green robe over the mint-green tunic. On her feet were slippers of the softest leather, which slipped and slid on the polished marble floors she crossed.

Her body, freed from the confines of her corsets, felt strange. Bits of her moved of their own accord. Her unstockinged legs felt shockingly naked, even though they were clad in pantaloons under her tunic. The silky fabric of her undergarments was a constant and distracting caress.

The Hall of Campaign, Aida had informed her, was where Rafiq carried out state business. Today was one of four set aside each year during which each of Bharym's Village Elders were permitted to petition the Prince. The audiences had begun at daybreak and had only just finished. Stephanie was prepared for a formal state room similar to the Royal Receiving Room, but when the double doors were flung open, she gasped in astonishment.

The chamber was a massive space with a soaring vaulted ceiling supported by six—no, eight—ribbed columns on either side, splitting the space into three distinct aisles. The lower walls were covered in a frieze of dark wood carved into intricate scrollwork, while above rows of huge circular ceramics studded the plaster. Thin metal rails were fixed at half the ceiling height to the columns, and from these were suspended hundreds of glass-domed lanterns, at present unlit, for the sun had not yet gone down, and light blazed in through the enormous circular window facing her. Under which was a divan. Sitting on which was Rafiq.

He was dressed as he had been when first she met him, in his formal robes. White silk, gold, diamonds, though his headdress, belt and scimitar had been discarded and lay on the divan beside him.

'Your Highness.' Her stomach was a swirling cloud of butterflies, just as it had been that first time. She was glad of the excuse to curtsy and not have to meet his gaze.

'Stephanie, we are quite alone, there is no need to be so formal.'

He took her hand, helping her up. Just the touch of his fingers made her tremble and blush. She mustn't think of the last time she had seen him. She mustn't think of that kiss. 'I expect you wish to know how I am progressing,' she said, keeping her gaze on her feet.

'I do.'

Relieved to be on safe ground, Stephanie launched into the report she had been preparing, refining and rehearsing for the last ten days. It was extensive and comprehensive, and as she drew to a close, she was slightly breathless. 'I have taken the decision to isolate the horses which are being trained to run in the Sabr, and to keep them at the training grounds, well away from the stables.'

Rafiq's expression brightened. 'You think that will prevent them from becoming infected?'

'I honestly don't know, since we have not established the source of the sickness or indeed the method of infection, but as a precaution it can certainly do no harm. Since it seems to strike randomly it occurred to me that by compiling a diary of events of the circumstances surrounding each case of infection, we might identify some commonalities.'

'An excellent idea.'

'Thank you.' If she didn't look at him, she would be able to keep her mind focused. 'As a result I have been able to discount any link between the disease and the animal feed, or the water at the stables paddock.'

'Fadil is most impressed with you.'

She wished he wouldn't smile, it made him unbearably beguiling. She oughtn't to allow herself to become too pleased with herself, though it was very good to have it confirmed that she had made as good an impression as she had hoped, and that the Head Groom's respect was based on her skill, and not his Prince's authority. 'It is a start, but I haven't achieved anything of note yet.'

'You saved Sarmadee's foal, and possibly Sarmadee herself, if there had been further complications with the birth. That is both of note and most impressive.'

'It was nothing,' Stephanie said, but she couldn't help smiling. 'Nature is just so wonderful. It is like watching a miracle every time. 'They are both doing very well.'

'And so are you. When I said that I wished to know how you are progressing, I meant you, not my horses. In one aspect at least, I can see that you have made a significant advance. Our Eastern clothing flatters you most becomingly.'

'Oh.' And now she was blushing again! Thank you,

Aida is a gifted needlewoman.' She gazed around her, made awkward as ever by compliments. 'This is a very magnificent room. Do you receive your people here in order to overwhelm them?'

Rafiq looked quite taken aback. 'I receive them here in pomp and state because it is what is expected of me. It is where petitions have always been heard by Princes of Bharym. To receive the Village Elders in a more modest venue would be to insult them. The intention is not to overwhelm them, as you put it, but to pay them a compliment, to demonstrate how much I value their opinions.'

'I didn't think of it in that way,' Stephanie said contritely. 'I'm a farrier's daughter who has been raised following the drum, I'm afraid my experience of royalty is limited to my contact with you. And the Duke of Wellington, I suppose. Though he is not royalty, he believes himself to be, an opinion shared by most of his soldiers.'

'Though not by you?'

'His Grace does not concern himself with my opinion. With neither breeding nor beauty to recommend me, I am thankfully quite beneath his notice.'

'I had heard he was a discerning man. Obviously he is not,' Rafiq said. 'You have met the great Duke of Wellington then?'

'He has looked down his nose at me several times when consulting with Papa,' Stephanie said, 'but he has never spoken to me. I tended to his horse, Copenhagen, in Spain, when he was Sir Charles Vane's mount. Where are we going?'

Rafiq had led her out of the Hall of Campaign, through a door concealed in the wooden panelling. 'To a less overwhelming part of the palace,' he replied, as Stephanie followed him through a narrow corridor notable for its lack of guards.

'Oh!'

They had emerged into a courtyard surrounded by very high walls. The evening sun turned the stone mellow, casting soft shadows. There was a terrace on one wall, where a selection of cushions and low divans were set out, but the majority of the space was given over to a huge bathing pool. A wide set of shallow steps led down into the green-blue water, dappled gold by the sun.

'The pool is fed from an underground stream,' Rafiq said, urging her forward into the courtyard. 'You can see in the corner there, the bubbles where it comes to the surface.'

Stephanie couldn't resist stooping down to let the ice-cold water trickle through her hands. 'It is lovely. Quite utterly lovely.'

Rafiq, watching the curve of her *derrière*, clearly revealed through the soft fabric of her new attire, agreed wholeheartedly, but refrained from saying so. Instead, he retired to the shade, seating himself on his favourite cushion and taking a glass of mint tea in order to distract himself from the beguiling vision. Her clothes were modest, loose, and actually revealed a great deal less of her figure than the gown she had worn the first night to dine with him, yet the filmy fabric clung to her like a caress, drawing attention to the soft flesh beneath. Realising that he had, despite his best intentions, been staring, Rafiq hurriedly looked away.

What was it about her that made her so difficult to resist? He had known far more beautiful women, far more experienced women, women who were accomplished in the arts of love, but none of them challenged him the way Stephanie did, and certainly none of them questioned him. They smiled at him, they fawned over him, they were pleased by him, with however little he offered, or however much. He was a prince, it was how it should be, but the reality was, now he came to think of it, not tedious exactly, but rather predictable.

Stephanie didn't bore him. She was like no other woman he had ever met, which most likely explained her appeal. That, and the fact that she had given him hope. Now he no longer despaired, he was coming alive again. It was not surprising that he should desire the woman responsible. It was a pity that he could not act on those desires, but he could at least indulge his curiosity about her.

He poured Stephanie a glass of tea, calling to her to join him. Smiling her thanks, she sank on to the cushion opposite him. 'This pool reminds me a little of one I saw in Italy, though the waters there were warm, fed from a hot spring.'

'You have travelled a great deal, then? Won't you miss that when you set up your own permanent establishment?' Rafiq asked.

'I doubt it. I have been fortunate enough to visit a great many countries, but travelling in the wake of the British army leaves one precious little time to enjoy the scenery. So much of the day is spent setting up bivouacs, obtaining supplies or chasing lost equipment, and maintaining what meagre household possessions one has. You would not believe the amount of hours devoted to mending uniforms and clothing and sheets and all manner of things.'

'No, I would not,' he answered, smiling. 'Have you never had a permanent home?'

'There were times—when we were encamped near Madrid, for example—when we remained in our digs long enough for them to begin to feel like home. We had a little farmhouse there which Mama was very sad to leave, but more often than not our accommodation consisted of tents.'

'It is no wonder then, that after such an itinerant life, you desire to settle in one place,' Rafiq said. 'Have you a location in mind? Near Newmarket, where your skills will be in high demand? Or near relatives, perhaps? Though you did say you wished for independence. Does that mean you prefer to live in solitude?'

'I meant financial independence,' Stephanie replied. 'I don't suppose you will understand it, having been born to all this, but to a woman in my position, an income is a necessity if one is not to live beholden to others.'

'A woman in your position,' Rafiq mused. 'I confess, I don't profess to understand your position at all. You are what—twenty-five years old?'

'Twenty-six, though I don't see...'

'For twenty-five years you have been beholden to your parents, as you put it. Why the sudden desire to change that? Did you quarrel with them?'

'No, of course not. I have never—not even when— I have never quarrelled with them.'

She was shifting around on her cushion, crossing her legs, uncrossing them. Clearly, the conversation was agitating her. He ought to change the subject, but he was far too intrigued. 'Then why the desire for change? Why make life so much harder for yourself by swapping your parents' protection and the work that you so obviously love, for an uncertain future?'

'I am—it is simply that I can no longer live with them,' Stephanie replied, colouring. 'And since I don't wish to be married, what other option is open to me, save support myself?' she demanded. 'Why do you think this appointment means so much to me, Rafiq? The money is not for pretty dresses and fripperies, it's about putting a roof over my head, food on my table, while I establish myself. Do you think that's going to be easy?'

Before he could formulate any sort of reply, she jumped to her feet. 'Well it's not. It's going to be *bloody* difficult! I'm going to have to be twice, three times better than any man, and I'm going to have to accept half the recompense or less. Does that sound fair to you? No, of course it's not, but that's how it's going to be.' Stephanie crossed her arms, staring at him belligerently. 'That is why your commendation will mean so much. That is why the remuneration which you have promised me is—it is...'

Rafiq held his hands up. 'I did not intend to upset you.'

'You haven't,' she said, glowering at him, clearly determined not to cry. When she spoke again, it was in a softer tone. 'You have been fairness personified. Not only are you paying me what you would a man, once you recovered from the shock of my gender, you did not try to devalue my skills on the grounds of it. You have given me an opportunity that few other men would have granted me. I am truly very grateful for it, and I should not be burdening you with my personal travails. It is most unprofessional.'

'If you tell me one more time that you are here to tend to my horses...'

He was rewarded with a faint smile. 'Do I say that often?'

'I suspect you recite it in your sleep.'

Her smile broadened. 'I suspect I'm trying to ensure I know my place. When I came here I did not expect to be living in a royal harem, to be conversing with a prince. I assumed I would be given quarters in the stables.'

'Now that would be guaranteed to make Jasim resign his post forthwith. My Master of the Horse has already made his views on the presence of women in his stables crystal clear.'

'You have had a woman working in your stables before me?'

'No.' *Interfering*, was the word Jasim had used. And *undermining*. Then ultimately, and most damning of all, he had described it as *contaminating*. 'He was alluding to my wife,' Rafiq admitted unwillingly, realising that he had to say something. 'She was a Bedouin princess. She had a great affinity with horses, which Jasim did not appreciate.'

'A nomad?' Stephanie said in surprise. 'I suppose in some ways, my life has been akin to that of the Bedouin, which you experienced when you were a child. Though we never permitted our horses to enter the tent.'

It was an uncomfortable analogy. Rafiq did not want to think of Stephanie as a nomad. He did not wish to make the link between the ghost that haunted him and the woman sitting opposite, who would help him close the door on the past for ever.

'Despite their itinerant lifestyle, some of the Bedouin tribes can trace their regal heritage back as far as I can,' he said, happily reminding himself that Stephanie, without a single drop of royal blood in her veins, was really nothing like Elmira at all.

'Well, I have no heritage to speak of, regal or otherwise,' she agreed blithely. 'It seems to me that if your Master of the Horse would not even tolerate a royal princess, he is likely to make the life of a mere army farrier's daughter unbearable, even if we do share an itinerant lifestyle and an affinity with horses.'

'You are nothing like Elmira,' Rafiq exclaimed, infuriated by what seemed to him her persistent desire to force him to compare the two.

She mistook his tone. 'I am sorry, of course I'm not. The subject is painful to you. I beg your pardon.'

'The past is not a place I care to visit.'

'We have that much in common then.'

Her words were tinged with sadness. This independence she was so set on was costing her very dear. Not a choice, but a painful necessity. Whatever the reason, he was not inclined to pain her by further questions, but he had to admire her spirit. 'When the Sabr trophy is restored to Bharym, my kingdom will be free to embrace its future. You will be free to embrace yours. And I, too, will be free to embrace mine.'

Her dazzling smile made him forget everything save her nearness and the strength of his desire for her. 'I confess I find myself thinking of a different kind of embrace at this moment,' Rafiq said.

The pink tip of her tongue flicked over her lower lip. 'We said we would forget what happened between us,' Stephanie said, making it clear that she was equally aware of him.

'Have you forgotten?' he asked.

'No.' Another flick of her tongue that made his blood stir. 'I wish I could,' she said.

If only she had forgotten. If only she did not desire him, or he her. Was there really so much harm in a kiss? He pulled her into his arms, and her lips touched his, and his resistance crumbled.

It was an illusion, Stephanie tried to tell herself, as she pressed her lips to Rafiq's. It would not last, this sweet, hot desire which had her in its heady grip.

This tingling she felt as he kissed her did not herald something more profound, only a prelude to ultimate disappointment. Yet when he feathered those delightful kisses over her bottom lip, she shivered. Slowly, surely, his kisses coaxed her into wanting more, into believing that more would be even more satisfying. It was different this time. Was it? She didn't want to compare. It didn't compare. Did it?

Rafiq stroked her hair, fluttered kisses over her eyes, nibbled on the lobe of her ear, kissed the sensitive skin behind it, making her shudder with delight. Then he began his assault on her mouth again and she forgot to think, surrendering to the slow dragging, drugging pleasure of his kisses, his tongue, his hands on her hair, caressing her back, her hair, her back again, showing no inclination to explore further. Only stroking her in the least provocative and intimate of places served to be provoking all the same.

She didn't want it to end. Could it be that Stephanie was, after all, the kind of woman she had been branded? The thought shocked her into dragging her mouth from his. 'No.'

Rafiq set her free immediately.

'I can't. I mean I must not,' she added hurriedly. 'You are my employer, and…'

'And as such, I have already assured you that I would not take advantage of the situation. I may have your future in my hands Stephanie, but does it not occur to you that you have *my* future in yours?'

It had not. Ashamed and embarrassed, she gazed at him mutely.

'What do you imagine I would do if you rejected my advances?' he asked, his tone softening. 'Forgetting for the moment that all I have done is kiss you, nothing more. Do you think I would risk everything, my kingdom's hopes and aspirations, my family's reputation, my own solemn pledge, by summarily dismissing you?'

'I thought that you would think—that you would say—you respect me, Rafiq. I don't want to endanger that.'

'Why would my desire for you as a woman endanger my respect for you as a veterinarian?'

'You don't understand.''

'Then enlighten me.'

She could feel the flush of mortification burning its way across her chest, up her throat to sear her cheeks. Unable to trust herself to speak, she shook her head, keeping her eyes lowered, her fingers clasped tightly together. Her toes were curled up tight inside her slippers. Her throat felt clogged. She knew she owed him some sort of explanation, but the very thought of telling him the shameful truth was too much to bear. 'I'm sorry,' Stephanie said, ignoring the hot tears which were trailing down her even hotter cheeks. 'I can't.'

'I respect you as my Royal Horse Surgeon. I kissed you because despite the fact you are my Royal Horse Surgeon, I don't seem to be able to resist you, and because I thought that you too—but I should not have.' Rafiq sighed, tugging at the high collar of his formal tunic. 'When you kiss me I forget that you cannot be experienced.'

'I'm not experienced, but I'm not an innocent either, and I seem to be just as unable to resist you as you—' Stephanie broke off embarrassed, for she had taken herself as well as Rafiq completely by surprise. It appeared she was not as proficient at learning from experience as she had imagined herself.

She gave herself a little shake. 'However we feel, it doesn't alter the fact that we have far too much to lose, to allow ourselves to be distracted, no matter how tempting. Now if you will excuse me, I will return to the duties which I have been appointed to carry out.' It was cowardly of her, but Stephanie gave Rafiq no time to reply, heading for the sanctuary of the stables with necessary but most undignified speed.

## Chapter Five

Stephanie was struggling to continue reading in the gathering gloom. With a sigh, she untied the scarf which held her hair back and closed the covers of *The Compleat Horse Doctor,* which she had been perusing in the hope that she might have missed something of import. She had not, and her battered copy of *Instructions for the Use of Farriers Attached to the British Cavalry and to the Royal Board of Ordnance* proved as irksome as ever, with its outdated remedies and procedures more likely to kill than cure. Checking her copious notes, she was forced to accept that she had done all she could for now. The sensible thing would be to go to bed.

Lighting a lantern, she quit the little office space she had purloined, and headed into the main stable block, making her way down the row of boxes until she came to Sherifa's stall. The mare snorted, taking the dates Stephanie offered with a haughty toss of her head. Two years ago, her mistress, Princess

Elmira had died. 'Do you still miss her?' Stephanie whispered. Did Rafiq?

*'The past is not a place I care to visit,'* he had said yesterday. In that respect they were of like mind, though their motivations were very different. Rafiq's past was tragic, whereas hers was simply sordid, her shame exacerbated by the knowledge that her downfall was entirely of her own making. She had allowed herself to be dazzled by the attentions of a handsome man. She had allowed herself to believe he meant his charming declarations of love. She had not allowed herself to reflect on the disparities in their situations. She had effectively let her heart rule her head, to disastrous effect. And now here she was again, dazzled by the attentions of an even more handsome man, whose station in life was so far above her own as to be risible.

She fed Sherifa another date. She had imagined herself in love with Rupert. She was under no such illusions when it came to Rafiq. It was as unthinkable as it was impossible. Rafiq was a man of honour and integrity. Despite the apparent similarities, the two men, the two situations could not be more different.

She smiled to herself. For the first time since she had fallen so catastrophically from grace, her loss of reputation struck her as strangely liberating. What's more, looking at things from this fresh perspective, the fact that Rafiq was a prince was also a liberating factor, since he was so far beyond her reach as to inhabit another planet. She would never, ever be so foolish as to imagine that she could be anything to him other than his Royal Horse Surgeon. And that should, provided she always remembered it, make things both simpler and safer.

It was a comforting thought. Not that she had any intentions of acting on it. Quitting the stables, Stephanie was taking the long way back to the palace, enjoying the cool night air under the glittering discs of the desert stars, when a painful hacking cough emanating from the mules' enclosure stopped her in her tracks.

When he was roused by his personal servant in the middle of the night, Rafiq knew it could mean only one thing. Another outbreak of the sickness.

'I was reluctant to have you disturbed, sire,' his man said, 'for the case in question is not one of your thoroughbreds but a mere mule. However, your Royal Horse Surgeon was most insistent you be alerted.'

Were it not for his anxiety at this worrying new development, Rafiq would have smiled at that. Stephanie would not have insisted, she would have demanded. Quickly donning his riding clothes, he made his way through the silent and sleeping palace out through the courtyard to the stables, sick at heart at this new proof of the plague's persistence. It would be wrong to expect too much from Stephanie's first case. He could only hope she did not fail completely.

Flambeaux had been lit in the stable yard. Stephanie had had the distressed beast brought in to one of the enclosed stalls primarily set aside for mares in foal. As he approached the hushed huddle of his stable hands gathered outside the door, he could hear the ominously familiar sound of the animal's laboured breathing punctuated with a hacking cough. Until now, the sickness had confined itself to the horses, but even before he entered the stall, Rafiq knew with heart-sinking certainty that it had spread to the pack animals.

Stephanie was at the mule's head, trying to calm the animal. She looked up when he closed the door softly behind him. 'Thank goodness. They said I should not disturb you because it was only a mule, but I knew you would want to be here, and besides, I need you to verify that the symptoms are the same.'

She wore a plain white tunic similar to his own, an *abba* of the same cotton. Her hair was down. It was shorter than he had imagined, falling just past her shoulders.

'Rafiq? Can you see the swelling and redness around the eyes? The discharge from the nostrils and the fever? Though it is not so severe as you described it...'

'The cough is the same. And the laboured breathing. There is no doubt that it is a case of the sickness. What course of action do you recommend?'

'Do nothing,' Stephanie said after a long, tense moment's thought.

'Nothing!' Rafiq stared at her in consternation. 'You don't think bleeding, or a poultice or...'

'Nothing,' she said firmly. 'Jasim has tried these treatments before, has he not?'

'Yes, but you can't mean to sit back and do nothing,' Rafiq said incredulously. 'What about an emetic, cautery—there must be something you can do, some course of treatment you can attempt?'

'All the standard remedies have been tried by Jasim to no avail. He has been very thorough, but we are obviously dealing with something new here,' she replied gently. 'So we need to do something different. It strikes me the one thing that hasn't been attempted is to let nature take its course without interference. Poor Batal here will need all his strength to fight the fever. In my experience all the remedies which you suggest will only serve to weaken him further.'

'But to do nothing—!'

'Is sometimes the very best course of action, when one has no certain knowledge of the cause. We can calm him. We can keep him cool, and we can keep him on his feet walking, fighting. Trust me.' She turned her attention briefly from her patient to face him. 'Rafiq. I will not dose him with powders or drain away his lifeblood just to demonstrate to you that I am well versed in traditional treatments. Perhaps Batal will live up to his name, prove himself a hero and survive. Perhaps he will not, but at the very least we will have ruled out this approach as a treatment option without having added to his suffering.'

She would not defer to him, nor would she lie to him. She gave him no false promises, but that in itself raised his hopes. Rafiq nodded his agreement. Stephanie's satisfied smile was cut short when the mule gave a distressing hack and tried to escape her hold, bucking feebly and tossing his head.

'Here, let me,' Rafiq said, taking the rope. 'Trust

me,' he added when she looked as if she would refuse, 'I too know what I am doing.'

Stephanie watched, fascinated, as Rafiq murmured to the terrified mule in a language she could not understand. In less than a minute the animal had calmed, his breathing eased marginally, and he had ceased straining at the halter. It was almost as if Rafiq had managed to put Batal into a trance.

'Are you a horse mystic?' she asked, only half-joking. She had heard tell of such things, but she had always been sceptical.

'I learned some of the ways of the Bedouin as a child,' he answered in a whisper. 'If you wish to cool him down now, he won't resist.'

She did as he suggested. The mule's flanks were worryingly swollen, his fur already damp, though the water she doused over him seemed to give him some relief. They worked together, calming and cooling, listening, their own breathing suspended, their own hearts pounding, while Batal grew worse, every breath a tremendous effort.

'Is there truly nothing you can do, at least to ease his suffering?' Rafiq said, breathless with the effort of keeping the mule on his feet during the last, grim bout of coughing.

Stephanie shook her head. Her own feeling of helplessness was reflected in his expression. 'We must not despair,' she said, far more reassuringly than she felt. 'Hope is the most mysterious of all healers. Batal will sense it if we give up on him.'

'Then we won't give up,' Rafiq said grimly.

\* \* \*

They did not, though it was a long, exhausting night. The lanterns were extinguished, the first grey morning light filtering through the high window of the closed box when Stephanie carried out her half-hourly check of the mule's heartbeat. Rafiq had no need to calm him this time. She thought at first that desperation had misled her, but a second listen was reassuring. 'I think he has turned a corner. He is not out of danger yet, but his breathing has eased marginally, and his fever is slowly abating. I think he has a fighting chance of a full recovery.'

'You can have no idea how much this means to me.'

'Rafiq, we must not get ahead of ourselves. This proves nothing as yet. Batal's infection was a less severe case, I think. It may affect mules differently from horses. You must not think I have necessarily found a cure. I simply let nature take its course.'

'Which achieved more than all of Jasim's remedies put together.' He pushed her hair back from her face. 'Thank you.'

Rafiq's touch was gentle, he smelled of sweet sweat and fresh straw and olive-oil soap. It was a very different kiss from that one yesterday by the pool. A gentle kiss, their lips clinging, almost tender in the dawn's light, after the long night's vigil. Her fingers in his hair, his in hers, threading themselves through her tangles, so gently, the warmth of his palm on her nape, the soft flutter of his breath. She was acutely aware of his body, though there was still a tiny gap between them which neither moved to close, because this lingering kiss was enough, more than enough.

They broke apart slowly. Their eyes met, slightly dazed. Stephanie did not speak. She had no words, and no desire to spoil the tenderness of the moment. Rafiq's mouth curled into a half-smile that twisted her insides, reminding her that desire was not entirely a foreign country after all, and so she busied herself with the now exhausted Batal. 'I think we can let him lie down and rest now.'

'I think all three of us would benefit from a rest,' Rafiq said. 'I will ask Fadil to look after Batal. No,' he said, when she made to speak, 'there is no need for you to stay here with him.'

'But, Rafiq…'

'You will be no use to Batal if you don't rest yourself. You have been up all night. That is a command, Stephanie, from a prince. Do not pull a face as stubborn as your plucky patient here.'

She was forced to laugh. 'Very well. Only let me see him settled—and, no, I won't leave that to anyone else, no matter what you command.'

'Very well.' Rafiq kissed her cheek. 'Thank you. I will see you and your hopefully restored patient later.'

She watched him go, listened to him issuing orders in that commanding way he had, wondering what it was in his tone that made it clear he took instant obedience for granted, for she had never heard him raise his voice. She put her fingers to her mouth, reliving the gentle touch of his lips on hers.

Batal brayed, a plaintive little sound, but a valiant one. Stephanie ruffled his ears. 'You really were named well, my hero,' she said softly. 'You are going to get well, little man, I promise you.'

A noise in the doorway made her turn. Fadil stood there, a gaggle of stable hands gathered behind him. 'It was an auspicious day when fate brought you to us,' he said. 'His Royal Highness was a wise man to appoint you his Royal Horse Surgeon, Miss Darvill. Now we dare hope that the Sabr will return to Bharym as our Prince has promised.'

Rafiq, who had returned to the loose box to check on Batal, was not surprised to see Stephanie walk in. 'You managed to obey my command for two whole hours,' he said blandly, 'I suppose I should consider that progress.'

Stephanie had bathed and changed, her hair tied back with a fuchsia-pink silk scarf, a colourful contrast to the muted pink-and-cream stripes of her tunic and cloak.

Though it had been a very different kiss, that kiss this morning, a kiss fuelled by relief on both their parts, by gratitude on his, it had been there all the same, that tiny thread of awareness that linked them, no matter what the circumstances. It was present now. He could no longer pretend that it was abstinence which fired his desire. It was Stephanie. This particular woman, most likely because of these peculiar circumstances. Circumstances which made him hesitate to act, for though his desire for her was fierce, his desire to rid himself of the past was even stronger, and

Stephanie held the key to that. He could not afford to lose her. That much, he sincerely hoped, he had made clear to her, though she could never understand the true significance of the Sabr to him.

Batal's survival was a portent, another step towards the future, when Bharym's people would recover their spirit, when Bharym's Prince would rid himself of his guilt. He had a foretaste of how that would be when he was with Stephanie. He was a different man, with her. He caught himself sometimes, talking to her, teasing her, laughing with her, in a way that was quite alien to him. He didn't recognise that man, but he enjoyed the change, no longer a man haunted by his past, but a man who relished the present. Stephanie gave him a glimpse of how it would be in the future. He wished fervently that there was a way to glimpse more of it, to indulge their mutual passion, without endangering the future itself.

Was there a way? Watching her rise from checking Batal, Rafiq wondered. It could mean nothing to either of them, they had already established that. If Stephanie wanted to—and he was pretty certain she did, as much as he—then surely they could come to some sort of tacit understanding, within strict boundaries?

Meeting her eyes as she dried her hands, Rafiq smiled.

'I think Batal here has made a quite remarkable recovery,' she said, 'though how he became infected in the first place is a question which I can't answer at the moment, for he shares neither food, water nor bedding with the horses in the stables.'

'Batal is what we call a companion,' Rafiq told her, ruffling the mule's ears. 'Despite his behaviour last night, he is a placid beast, and has a very calming influence on our more highly strung thoroughbreds. He has seen some of our most nervous mares through difficult foalings, some of our friskiest yearlings through their early training.'

'So he may have become infected here?' Stephanie said. 'I will check when he last performed his companion duties. We will need to keep an eye on the other mules now too, lest Batal here has infected them, though proximity to an infected animal does not seem to result in contagion.' Stephanie pursed her lips. 'I have eliminated a good many causes, but I am still no closer to finding the source.'

'You have only been here two weeks, and this is your first case.'

'Yes, but...'

'Enough, for now. I have a prescription for you, veterinarian. You will take a break for the rest of the day from horses and from the stables and from the palace,' Rafiq said. 'It is time you saw a little more of my kingdom.'

The city was far more extensive than Stephanie could have imagined from the glimpses she'd had when she first arrived in Bharym. Viewing it now from the vantage point which the approach from the palace afforded her, she could see that the red-brick buildings extended right into the foothills of the mountain, climbing in terraces up the sheer rock face. Though all the tightly packed buildings were square and flat-roofed, some were narrow, some broad, some had only two storeys while others soared six, seven, or more storeys high.

She and Rafiq rode unescorted. 'I believe I informed you on your first night here, that I have not my father's fondness for pomp and ceremony,' he told her, when she commented on this. 'In his day, a journey to the city would have involved a caravan of at least thirty camels, and any number of standard bearers. My father had the most cumbersome saddle too, more like a mobile throne, which took a considerable toll on the camel which had to bear it.'

But as they passed through the soaring stone arch of the city gates, it became apparent that Rafiq had no need of camels or bearers or throne-like saddles to proclaim his majesty. He wore a simple white tunic and cloak, his *keffiyeh* held in place with a red-silk scarf, the only gold the glittering hilt of the sabre hanging from the belt at his waist. She was reminded of her first glimpse of him in the Royal Receiving Room, her urge to kneel before him, distinctly different from the most disrespectful urge she had had the last time the Duke of Wellington had inspected Papa's regiment. The Commander-in-Chief's arrogant assumption of superiority had raised Stephanie's hackles. Glancing over at Rafiq, smiling and gesturing his kneeling subjects to their feet, her blood heated for a very different reason.

They entered an open space bordered by market stalls. Rafiq brought his camel to a halt, summoning one of the cluster of small boys who had gathered around to take the reins as he dismounted, gesturing to another small boy to tend to Stephanie's animal as Rafiq helped her to dismount. 'The streets are extremely narrow. It is easier if we progress on foot,' he continued in English quietly. 'It is my custom to hear informal petitions on such occasions, so we may be somewhat besieged at times but fear not, you will be perfectly safe.'

She had no time to respond, for they were at that moment swept away into the recesses of the city. A noisy, cheerful, excited rabble of people of all ages surged in a wave around them, making their progress into a procession. Though she was separated from him, Rafiq made a point of halting every now and then, the crowd parting automatically to usher her through to join him, and then they continued.

She was content to observe, and there was a great deal to absorb her attention. The city itself, with its myriad of idiosyncratic buildings, decorated with pale stone swirls which, when seen close up, formed themselves into elaborate geometric patterns. So closely packed were the houses that the cobbled streets were cool, even in the blaze of the afternoon sun. Fountains trickled at every junction, some mere stone pedestals, others in the shape of scallop shells, fishes, serpents. The air here smelt sweeter, with no trace of the dusty, gritty desert which lay beyond the gates.

The women of Bharym wore no veils, though they

protected their heads from the heat of the sun in a variety of ways. Some wore huge squares of fabric, big enough to act as both headdress and cloak, others cleverly draped long strips, like evening stoles, to form a hood and a scarf. A few sported turbans decorated with beads. And some, like Stephanie, wore a *keffiyeh*. The Sabr seemed to be their only topic of conversation when she chatted with them in their own language while Rafiq was otherwise engaged.

*'When the Sabr returns to Bharym, we can once again hold our heads high.'*

*'When the Sabr returns, the rain will fall in torrents.'*

*'When the Sabr returns, our Prince will be blessed with an heir.'*

*'When the Sabr returns, my goat will produce milk again.'*

*'When the Sabr returns, the market traders will stop trying to short-change us.'*

*'And my mother-in-law will compliment my cooking!'*

These last two sallies provoked an outburst of laughter, but no matter how preposterous Stephane might think some of the claims being made for the Sabr—for there was a part of her that still couldn't credit a race with such power—she was left in no doubt of his people's feelings for Rafiq. He was not only a prince but a hero to them.

They had reached a surprisingly large open square, right in the middle of the city. Rafiq held up his hands, said some words Stephanie could not catch, and the crowd began to disperse. 'What is happening?' she asked, when he beckoned her over.

'It is the hottest part of the day. Everyone retires inside,' he answered, ushering her towards the tallest building on the square and producing a key. 'Including us.'

'Goodness, surely not another palace?'

Rafiq laughed. 'No, it is merely the royal viewing gallery.'

'To view what, your subjects going about their daily business?'

For answer, he led her up three steep flights of stone stairs and through a door into a high-ceilinged room, the principal feature of which was the window. Or row of windows, to be more precise, six tall arches divided only by the thinnest layer of supporting brickwork, facing out on to the piazza they had just left.

'It is breathtaking,' Stephanie said, 'and it makes me a little giddy. 'I can see why you call it a viewing gallery, but what do you view? Oh, goodness, surely not...'

He laughed, for the horror of what had just crossed her mind must have been clearly reflected on her face. 'No, we do not carry out either public executions or floggings, nor have there been either in Bharym for a great many years.'

Stephanie shuddered. 'In the military, regrettably, flogging is all too common.'

'How so?'

She stared out at the piazza, deserted now, for the sun was at its zenith. 'We have been at war for a

very long time. Some of the men have been away
from their families for years, since only a very small
minority of them are permitted to have their wives
travel with them—and to be honest, many chose not
to, for the conditions are very harsh. It is not surprising that they reach a point where homesickness
overrides loyalty to the crown. Or where the constant
risk of death erodes their willingness to fight. As if a
whipping would make any difference,' she said bit-
terly. 'We treat our soldiers a great deal worse than
our horses, in the army. No officer would dream of
beating his horse, but most officers believe it their
duty to beat their men. Save my father. Just one of
the many things which sets him apart.'

'What do you mean?'

Stephanie shrugged. 'He has served for most of
his career with the Seventh Hussars, but it is only
recently that he was promoted from army farrier to
Veterinary Surgeon, an appointment which in theory
carries with it an officer's rank.'

'In theory?'

'Papa is the son of a Scottish farmer, Rafiq. The officers of the Seventh like to think they are more blue-
blooded than their horses—and they pride themselves
on their horses' lineage. They dare not shun Papa
outright, but none would ever invite him to spend his
leave on their family estates. Not that my father would
accept such an invitation, unless it was to spend time
in their stables. Papa has never been the least bit interested in pedigree, human or equine.'

If only he had been, if only he had taught his

daughter to make the distinction, she might not have made such a catastrophic mistake. 'What *do* the Princes of Bharym witness from this viewing gallery then,' Stephanie asked, in a determined effort to lighten the mood, 'if not ritual punishment?'

Rafiq duly obliged. 'The Dash of the Camels,' he said with a grin.

She was so surprised she burst out laughing. 'The Dash of the Camels. It sounds like an Arabian version of a Scottish Reel. I take it that it's not a dance?'

He shook his head, smiling. 'It is a race, three times around the circumference of the piazza, riding camels bareback. They have a similar event, I am told, in Sienna, Italy, known as the Palio. Though they take it much more seriously, and they race horses.'

She gazed down on the square which was not actually a square, but an out-of-shape rectangle, with what looked like some hair-raisingly tight corners, and said so.

'You are right,' Rafiq said. 'We lay down wet sand, but it is still very, very tricky. Though of course that is part of the challenge for the riders.'

'And a source of amusement for the spectators, presumably? Where do the crowds stand?'

'In the middle of the piazza of course.'

'There are certainly advantages to being a prince. You have a prime view, and you're not likely to be stampeded.'

'It is true, a number of the camels do finish riderless, but we put up barriers to prevent them from endangering the crowds. It is a fun event, a spectacle for the populace,' Rafiq said. 'Every village enters their best jockey and camel, they parade it around the piazza ahead of the race, and there are prizes for the best-looking one, and the ugliest.'

'Do you refer to the jockey or the camel?' Stephanie said, laughing. 'I would imagine the ugliest camel prize to be hotly contested. To my eye they seem to have been constructed from a jumble of disparate parts selected from a number of different animals. And as to their smell...' She made a face. 'Whether it is produced from the front end or the rear, both are noxious. When is this Dash? I would love to witness it.'

'I'm afraid you've missed it. It took place six months ago. I don't put any of the royal camels forward since the Dash is a race belonging to the people. Besides, though it seems to have escaped your notice, my camels are white thoroughbreds and extremely rare, though I admit that a pedigree does not preclude the particular camel perfumes you allude to,' Rafiq said, with a smile. 'I took the liberty of ordering refreshments for us, I hope you don't mind.'

Stephanie, thinking that she would be unlikely to mind any liberty Rafiq chose to take, followed him to the back of the room, where a set of screens concealed an alcove containing a table laden with covered dishes, and a mountain of multi-coloured cushions.

'Everywhere we go, sumptuous banquets appear as if by magic. I do not mean to sound ungrateful— it is simply that your world and mine, they are so very different.'

'I was thinking only this morning, that very same thing,' Rafiq said, waiting until she had settled at the table before seating himself with his usual fluid grace. 'I have never met anyone like you before. And now you are blushing. Are you truly so unaccustomed to receiving compliments? I find that very difficult to believe.'

'I am perfectly happy to be complimented on my skills as a veterinarian.'

'Being a veterinarian, Stephanie, no matter what you may think to the contrary, does not preclude you from being an attractive woman.'

He smiled that smile again, and it did exactly what it did every time. Every particle of her was alerted to his presence. Every bit of her focused entirely and only on him. On his mouth. On his eyes. On the hard muscled body seated tantalisingly close to her. Her mouth went dry. 'We agreed we could not afford to be distracted.'

'Last night, this morning, caring for Batal together, proved where our priorities lie, don't you think?'

'I—I suppose it did, although we still—afterwards, we did kiss.' Her heart was pounding. Her voice sounded odd.

'A tender and heartfelt thank you, born of relief. Am I wrong to suggest that we might indulge ourselves, now that we have proved we won't compromise our relationship as prince and veterinarian?'

She wasn't sure what he was proposing, but she was curious to know. She bit her lip, laughed shakily. 'I was thinking the other day how liberating it is to realise that one can only lose one's reputation once, but the situation—our situation—it is not the same, but...'

'Will you tell me what happened,' he asked gently, 'help me to understand why it is so difficult for you to trust me?'

She grimaced. 'I do trust you. I'm simply not sure that I can trust myself. It is a sordid tale, which does not cast me in a good light. I fear your good opinion of me will be destroyed if I tell it.'

'My good opinion of you is based on my knowledge of you as I have come to know you, Stephanie. Your past cannot change that.'

'Do you really believe that? My past has shaped me. I thought I had left it behind, but it followed me here. I want to be rid of it, but my mistakes continue to haunt me. The best I can do is ensure I don't repeat them.'

Her words made Rafiq shiver. They could have been his. Would he be similarly haunted for ever by his past? It was unthinkable. He was sure that the mule's survival was a portent. The fates were no longer colluding against him. Stephanie had turned them in his favour.

He turned on the cushions to face her. 'I think you are quite mistaken,' he said firmly. 'The door can be closed on the past. When we have atoned for our mistakes, then their shadow no longer stalks us.'

'You think so?'

'I am certain of it,' he said in a tone that brooked

no argument. 'Now, tell me about the ghost that haunts you.'

She took a deep breath, clearly bracing herself. 'His name was—is Captain Rupert Thornhill of the Seventh Hussars. My father's regiment.' Stephanie rolled her eyes. 'My first error of judgement. He joined the Seventh two years ago. The Thornhills are a very old, established English aristocratic family. Rupert was—is rich, very well connected. My second error of judgement. He is also very dashing and charming, hugely popular, and exceedingly good looking.' Stephanie's smile was twisted. 'My worst error of judgement was to believe that such a man would choose me. I was dazzled and I was very flattered. I allowed my heart to rule my head—something I never do. I believed myself in love.'

Rafiq fought his rising anger. He could imagine the man, paying well-practised court to her, wooing her. And Stephanie, naïve despite her years following the drum, falling for it. With difficulty, he kept silent.

She continued, her tone making it clear that she blamed herself, making him even more furious. 'I know I'm not a catch. I have no pedigree, I have no dowry, and I am not a beauty, so when Rupert said he loved me, I believed him. I thought that he—he loved *me,* because there could be no other reason. I was such a gullible little fool.'

She pushed her hair back from her brow, tucking it behind her ear. 'He told me we would be married, that there would be no harm in anticipating our vows.'

'He seduced you.'

Stephanie hesitated. 'I wish I could say that was so, but the truth is he did not. I thought I was in love. I wanted to please the man I thought I was to marry, but I also wanted—' She broke off, shrugging awkwardly. 'I wanted what no respectable woman should want. But it seems I am not at all respectable, because you make me feel exactly that way.'

'Stephanie, there is nothing shameful in desire.'

'Oh, Rafiq, perhaps not for men. Or hussies. I knew it was wrong, but that didn't stop me. If only I had known—I thought it would be magical,' she said sardonically. 'Rupert did not seem at all disappointed, but I was. Fortunately it was over very quickly. Or so I thought.'

She took a long drink of pomegranate juice, steeling herself. Rafiq had a horrible premonition of what was to come. No wonder Stephanie found it difficult to trust him. She set the glass down. 'I knew Rupert had a reputation for never refusing a challenge, that he must always succeed where others failed. I never thought he would see me as a prize, but it seems I was. By simple dint of my having failed to respond to any overtures from any officer in the past, by refusing to accept the improper proposals made to every single female who followed the drum as a matter of course, by protecting my reputation, I was challenging their manhood,' she said disgustedly. 'Rupert succeeded because he didn't make me an improper proposal. Rupert pretended to fall in love with me.'

Rafiq was too angry to speak. Stephanie was too engrossed in her sorry tale to notice. 'You see now, just how much of a fool I was?' she continued, her voice bitter. 'Such a man would never marry me, and I was the only person in the regiment to think he would. When he boasted openly of his conquest, the gulf which separated our families made it easy for them all to conclude that I was a woman of easy virtue.'

Her eyes were bright, not with tears but with anger and with defiance. Her fists were clenched. 'It is so unfair. My reputation was ruined, while Rupert was slapped on the back. I was a fallen woman, whereas he was…'

'…an accomplished seducer without honour or scruples,' Rafiq exclaimed, unable to hold his tongue any longer.

'That makes it worse! I pride myself on my logic, my powers of deduction, the soundness of my judgement, yet I abandoned all three.'

'The man lied and cheated to steal your innocence. He deserves to be whipped. There can be no excuses for what he did, Stephanie. You are not at fault.' Rafiq cursed under his breath. 'Your parents must have— Your father…'

'Papa was…' Her anger fled. Her lip trembled. Her eyes filled with tears. 'What it did to Papa…that was the worst of it.'

'Stephanie…'

She held up her hand, shaking her head. 'Please.' She took a shaky breath, dabbed at her eyes, and continued, her voice tremulous, her words tumbling over each other, for she was anxious to be done. 'Afterwards, when I asked Rupert when we were to be married, he laughed in my face. Surely I could not possibly have believed that a blue-blooded Thornhill would wed a farrier's daughter? Well, I had, though I see now that it was preposterous. As a prince, you would probably agree with Rupert on that score.'

Rafiq could not deny it, so ingrained was the notion of bloodlines, of pure ancestry to him, though the knowledge made him deeply uncomfortable. 'Nevertheless,' he said through gritted teeth, 'he made you false promises, and in doing so he dishonoured the very heritage he claims to have been trying to protect.'

Stephanie pushed her hair away from her brow once again. There were no traces of tears in her eyes now. 'When I threatened to tell the truth regarding his bogus marriage proposal, in order to protect what little was left of my soiled reputation, he warned me that if I dared to do so, he would see to it that my father lost his position. Rupert was not Papa's direct superior officer, but he wielded significant influence within the regiment. Like many of his ilk and, unlike Papa, he had purchased his commission, achieved his rank through a combination of wealth and privilege. They all attended school together, their families socialised together, they were all related to each other in some way—what chance would Papa have, Rafiq, no matter how brilliant he is, if they closed ranks against him?'

Stephanie scrunched her eyes closed, bunched her fists tighter. 'Papa's life has been serving the army.

He is so proud of his position, I could not risk him losing everything he has worked for.'

'So instead, you exiled yourself from the life that had been yours too, and from your family? That is why you have spent the last year at a stud farm?'

'I had to. The shame, the scandal, the dishonour, it was mine, not theirs. I had no choice but to leave. Papa was not easily persuaded, he was so very angry, but Mama—oh, Mama could see clearly enough that any attempt to avenge me would simply result in more scandal, more gossip, that it was best for all of us that I get as far away from the scene of my crime as possible. And so eventually, Papa agreed.'

'You committed no crime, Stephanie.'

'Oh, but I did. My lack of judgement was a heinous crime. If it were only myself who bore the shame, it would not be quite so bad, but my parents—when I think of what they have suffered on my account— that is what has kept me awake at night this last year. That, and a determination to find a way to stop them from worrying about me.'

'Independence,' Rafiq said, smiling, for finally he understood it.

'Precisely,' Stephanie said, smiling tentatively back. 'You see now, how valuable a gift you have given me with this appointment? It is my way of making good the harm I have done. My own form of reparation.'

Her words struck a chord. Though she could never know, though he would never explain—yes, he and this strange, exotic Englishwoman had a great deal in common. 'I do understand, Stephanie. After such an experience, it is little wonder that you are reluctant to trust anyone, least of all someone in my position.'

'Oh, thank you.' Her hand fluttered to her breast. 'I know there is no comparison between you and Rupert. I know you are a man of honour, that you would never lie to me, and that you truly do value me for what I am, that you mean it when you say that you respect me. You don't flatter me by telling me I'm pretty...'

'Pretty is much too insipid a word to describe you. Clever, unusual, brave, bold, witty, sultry, seductive, captivating, enticing, entrancing—you are all of those and much more. You are quite extraordinary. It makes me very angry to hear that you gave your innocence to a man so undeserving of you.'

'I don't want you to be angry, I want you to understand. The fact that there can never be anything between us, Rafiq, is one of the things about this situation I find reassuring,' Stephanie said. 'It draws, if you will forgive the pun, a very clear line in the sand. You are a prince, I am a farrier's daughter, and in six months' time—less if I find a cure for the sickness sooner—I return to England.'

'Once again, your way of looking at a situation is—unique,' Rafiq said, laughing. 'Does that mean I should not have suggested...?'

'No, it means that I am glad you did,' she said, blushing. 'I know it's a very shocking thing to admit, but...'

'Stephanie, it's not shocking. It is a very natural thing, and it can be a very pleasurable thing.'

'Really?'

'Really. Passion is not only the province of fallen women. Even respectable women experience desire.'

'I'm not sure that I want to be respectable. If you're right, and we proved last night that our overriding priority will always be curing the sickness, then I would like to—what exactly *are* you suggesting, Rafiq?'

'That we indulge our passion in whatever way we choose,' he said, taking her hand and kissing the tip of her little finger. 'When we can safely do so without fear of compromising our other duties.' He kissed the next finger. 'That you can choose just how much or how little you wish to give.' Another kiss, on her middle finger. 'That you can put an end to it at any time, without fear of the consequences.' He sucked on the tip of her index finger. 'And above all that we take pleasure in what we do. Whatever we do.' He drew her thumb into his mouth, smiling wickedly. 'Is that a proposal you can agree to, do you think?'

She shivered. 'Yes.'

'Are you sure?' he asked seriously.

'Yes,' she said, smiling again. 'Now that I have agreed Rafiq, do you think we should...?'

'Yes.' He pulled her into his arms. 'I think we should begin immediately.'

# *Chapter Six*

Stephanie was nervous, he could sense it in the slightly brittle tone of her voice. 'One word from you and we will go no further,' Rafiq said.

'I know.'

He thought fleetingly, vengefully, of the bungling, selfish, dishonourable man who had betrayed her, before dismissing him as beneath contempt. He would make sure this experience was as different from her last in every possible way. He pushed back her hair to kiss the fluttering pulse at her temple. 'Try to stop that impressively large brain of yours from thinking and concentrate on your body instead.'

She chuckled weakly. 'I am not sure if I can.'

'Then let me assist you.' He kissed her carefully, soothing kisses, focusing his attention completely on her, wanting only her pleasure. He kissed her eyes, her temples, her mouth, fluttering kisses that sought nothing in return, and gradually she relaxed, her lids closing, her mouth softening under his, then returning the pressure, her tongue touching his, her body melting.

He laid her down on the cushions, easing his body away from hers, reining in his own sudden jolt of passion. Her eyes flickered open. 'Nothing,' he said, reading the question contained there, 'you need do nothing.'

'But I want to. Don't you want me to...?'

'Yes.' His body rather graphically agreed, but he ignored it. 'I do want you to, very much, but not yet. Before we discover each other, you must first discover yourself.'

He decided, for once, to follow his instincts. He knew how to please a woman, but this was Stephanie. Such a very different woman. He kissed his way down her throat. He smoothed his hand down her side, brushing the outside of her breast, watching her nipple burgeon under her tunic. He watched her as he cupped her breast, teasing her nipple, when she shifted very slightly to encourage him. He knew himself to be an accomplished lover, but never before had he made love like this, so careful of her, every move only for her, in response to her.

She reached for him, seeking his mouth, and he kissed her. Her tongue, her lips, made it difficult to think. He unfastened the buttons on the front of her tunic. He kissed her breast, sucking through the silk of her camisole, making her shift restlessly on the cushions, making her want something, something more. His mouth on her other nipple? Yes, and his hands, stroking her flanks, pushing her tunic higher, stroking the inside of her thighs through her pantaloons.

She tensed. *What next?* she seemed to be asking him. He kissed her in answer to her silent question. She kept her eyes closed. Her breathing was shallow and fast. Her body beside him on the cushions was burning hot, the brush of her hair silky on his skin. Gently, he eased her legs apart. She did not resist, though she tensed again. What now?

'Stephanie, should I stop?'

She opened her eyes. They were heavy with desire. 'No,' she said. And then when he hesitated, 'Please, don't stop.'

He unfastened the sash at her waist. His fingers on the bare skin of her belly made her shiver. He slid his hand down, covering her, cupping her in that most intimate place, kissing her slowly on the mouth. 'There is no hurry, no need to rush,' he whispered.

'No,' she murmured.

Another kiss, and his tongue slid inside her mouth, and his fingers slid between her legs, and she cried out, a hoarse, harsh sound that he mistook at first for pain, until she clenched around him. She was slick, wet, tight. His shaft swelled, his groin tightened in response. Still his focus remained only on Stephanie. Her needs were his. His fingers slid over her and around her, teasing her and stroking her, making her body arch under him. Little whimpering noises encouraged him and aroused him. He kissed her, stroked her, coaxing her to a climax with his mouth and his tongue and his fingers. She was close, she was closer, and then with a wild cry her climax took her, shook her, so violently that she clung to him as if he would save her from drowning in pleasure.

When it was over, she opened her eyes and she loosened her grip and she smiled languorously at him, a smile that made him catch his breath. 'I had no idea,' she said.

And that was his satisfaction. It was better than release. Who would have thought it! He laughed then, with sheer delight, holding her closely, feeling his laughter reverberate against her chest. 'And now you do,' he said.

'Yes,' she replied, with a sated smile. 'Now I do. Thank you.'

'Stephanie,' Rafiq said, kissing her, 'believe me, the pleasure was entirely mutual.' And he meant it.

Rafiq retied the sash at the waist of her pantaloons. He buttoned up the front of her tunic. He kissed her lightly on the lips. 'Now we will eat, and satisfy a different appetite. There is an ante-room through that curtain where you may first refresh yourself.'

There were rose petals scenting the water in the urn. There was a fresh cake of soap in a dish. There was a stack of soft towels. And a mirror. Stephanie stared at her reflection, wondering that she did not look more different. Her complexion had a rosy blush to it and her hair had escaped from her scarf, and her lips—yes, it was obvious that her lips had been satisfyingly kissed. She wrapped her arms around her waist. Those kisses had not been the only satisfying thing. She still couldn't quite believe it. That Rafiq had—and then she had…

And the result had been earth-shattering. So much, much more than she could have imagined. As if her body had broken into a million little shards of indescribably intense light. When it ended, when she sank slowly back from the sparkling sky where she had been flying, she felt as if she was reassembled in a different manner. Her smile had a touch of smugness to it now. She was just a little bit pleased with herself.

'Harlot,' she told her reflection. 'Brazen hussy.' The words that had stung, made her hang her head in shame for the wrong she had done, had a very different effect on her now that they were not being whispered behind her back, publicly branding her. Here in Bharym, she was not Stephanie Darvill, fallen woman, she was the Royal Horse Surgeon, and in public she would make *damned* sure that was how it would stay. But in private she rather liked the idea of living up to the names that had condemned her. She would like to be a great deal more wicked, provided she took great care there were no *unfortunate consequences*.

Her face fell. Mama's words, and Mama's biggest concern, when the vicious rumours of her daughter's ruin reached her. The resultant scene had been mortifying for mother and daughter—Stephanie resorting to medical terminology in order to try to reassure Mama that she knew enough of the workings of the body to have managed that risk, at least, seemed to appal Mama even more. If Mama could see her now, proving every insult hurled at her to be true, she would be shocked to the core. As far as Mama was concerned, her daughter's fall from grace could only be mitigated by a lifetime of chastity. It's what Stephanie had believed too, and thought she had come to terms with in that last long, lonely year at Newmarket.

But she was on the other side of the world now, and Mama would never know what her daughter was getting up to here. When she returned to England, Stephanie Darvill's fall from grace would be history, and Stephanie Darvill, veterinarian to a royal prince, would make her fresh start. She would make her own way, and she would ensure that people judged her only on her medical skills. She would prove herself the equal of any man.

But England was months away. She was in Arabia now, and she intended to make the most of it.

Rafiq poured Stephanie another glass of iced pomegranate juice and helped her to some honey-drenched pastries. 'You are very subdued. Are you regretting what happened?' he asked.

'Oh, no. Quite the contrary.' Her smile sent the blood rushing back to his groin. 'You know Rafiq, that an enquiring mind, and a willingness to experiment are fundamental to my success as a veterinarian.'

It took him a moment to understand her meaning, but when he did, his shaft, not yet fully subsided, stirred into life. 'Are you suggesting that we experiment with pleasure?'

She chuckled. 'I'm suggesting that I would like to experiment. I doubt very much that I can teach you anything.'

He touched her cheek. 'You underestimate yourself. Today was as new an experience for me as it was for you. Everything with you feels like the first time.'

'Well, it is pretty much *all* new to me.' Stephanie set her empty plate aside and licked her fingers. 'I will rely on your experience to guide me. As a veterinarian, I can consult any number of instruction manuals and handbooks, but there are no textbooks for fallen women to follow.'

'You would be surprised,' Rafiq said.

Her eyes widened, not with shock but with curiosity. She was a bold innocent, another in her litany of paradoxes. It was a heady combination. 'There are many such books. My grandfather, I am sorry to say, was an avid connoisseur of such matters, and has an extensive collection. Though I must say, I prefer your suggestion, of experimentation.'

Her expression clouded. 'I have almost everything to learn, while you—I am afraid you will be disappointed.'

'Stephanie, you are incapable of disappointing me.' He kissed her hand tenderly. 'Every day you surprise me.'

'By being insubordinate and disrespectful and...'

'With your refreshing honesty. And your novel slant on the world.' He kissed her hand again. 'You make me see things differently.'

'Now that is a compliment which I am happy to accept.'

His laughter obscured the pounding at the door at first. Rafiq jumped up, adjusting his clothing. When he returned, his face was grim. 'Another case of the sickness has struck. One of my brood mares this time. We must make haste and return to the stables.'

Stephanie got a taste of what it would feel like to race in the Dash of the Camels on the manic journey back to the palace. Clinging on grimly, she let her beast take its lead from Rafiq's, feeling as if she were being tossed about in a storm at sea, though the sick feeling in her stomach had as much to do with the anticipation of what lay ahead of them. Rafiq had no details, save that Batal was continuing to make an extraordinary recovery. He had sent his man back ahead, with word that they were on their way.

'Two cases in twenty-four hours,' she said to Rafiq, panting breathlessly as they slowed in front of the imposing façade of the palace. 'That has not happened before, has it?'

Grimly, he shook his head. The huge door in the wall which connected to the stable complex swung open. 'I should have stayed,' Stephanie said. 'I should have been here.'

'It is not your fault. Whatever happens, it is not your fault.'

Rafiq dismounted quickly before helping Stephanie down. In the archway of the stable buildings, a man was waiting, silently watching their approach.

He was tall with a slight stoop, and very thin, dressed in the traditional robes, a striped tunic under a loose cloak. His headdress of muslin fell almost to the ground, and was held in place by a thick double band made of silk rope. The face framed by his long pleated and oiled locks, was of a man who could have been any age from forty to sixty, with a strong aquiline profile, and a narrow chin made prominent by a pointed beard. Though his stance conveyed an air of sanguine world-weariness, his hands belied this, working incessantly at a set of worry beads. Stephanie felt a horrible, almost palpable, sense of foreboding.

Stepping towards them from the shadows he made his formal greeting, not to her, but to Rafiq. 'Your Highness. I regret to inform you that you are too late. The mare, Anadil, is dead.'

'No! Oh, Rafiq—Your Highness…'

'Miss Darvill, may I present to you Jasim, my Master of the Horse? Jasim, as you are aware, Miss Darvill is my recently appointed Royal Horse Surgeon.'

She received the very smallest of bows in answer to her own formal greeting. Jasim's eyes did not deign to meet hers, though whether he had noticed her slip in addressing Rafiq informally, or simply because she was a woman, Stephanie had no idea, and at this moment could not have cared less.

'Where is Anadil? I'd like to see her, please.'

She spoke brusquely in Arabic, directly to Jasim, but he ignored her, looking to his master for direction. 'Do as she asks,' Rafiq said curtly.

'But, Highness, the animal is dead.'

The Master of the Horse knew as soon as the words were out that he had made a mistake. Rafiq's expression froze. He seemed, to Stephanie, to grow at least six inches. Jasim's knees bent, stopping just short of obeisance. 'Do you recall,' Rafiq said, in a soft, icy voice that made the hairs on Stephanie's arms stand on end, 'the conversation we had before you left the palace on business?'

'Yes, Highness,' Jasim replied, his voice no more than a whisper.

'I informed you that Miss Darvill had complete authority in all matters pertaining to the sickness, did I not?'

'Yes, Highness.'

'And that as my Royal Horse Surgeon, she has the right, in such matters, to expect your full and unquestioning co-operation?' Rafiq said, his tone as sharp now as the glittering blade of the scimitar he wore at his waist, making Jasim flinch, as if he had been stabbed. 'If I hear that you have questioned her instructions again, you will face the consequences. Do you understand me, Jasim?'

'Highness.'

'Then what are you waiting for? Take us to see the mare.'

'Highness.' Stephanie's voice startled them both. 'I think it would be best if I—there is no need for you to be present, Your Highness.'

She had spoken in Arabic, having no desire to set Jasim further against her by imagining her plotting with his master, but she begged him with her eyes. Rafiq hesitated for a long moment. 'I sincerely hope you know what you are doing,' he said in English, before heading out of the courtyard and into the palace.

Turning, Stephanie caught Jasim unawares. His expression was venomous, which was no surprise, but it was the fact that he made no attempt to disguise it that made her heart sink. No point in countering his animosity with flattery, a technique she had used effectively in the past. This man, whom she had never even met before, was already her sworn enemy, and she had better not forget it.

'What are you waiting for?' she demanded curtly, deliberately using Rafiq's words. 'I want to see Anadil, and I want to know exactly what happened. To have developed the symptoms and deteriorated so badly in the few hours of my absence is contrary to all previous patterns of this sickness.'

The reason for Anadil's premature demise was clear the moment Stephanie walked into the loose box, though she could see that Fadil was doing his best to clear up the evidence. 'On whose orders was this horse bled?' she demanded.

'Mine.' Jasim stared at her boldly, with not a trace of repentance. 'I returned to find the mare gravely ill. You were not here, and so I acted. In all conscience, I could not stand by and do nothing.'

'By doing nothing, we saved Batal. Had I been consulted, doing nothing would have been what I would have instructed.' Stephanie glanced at Fadil, but the Head Groom merely shrugged apologetically and continued with his work. Fadil, and every other man in the stables, knew that Batal had survived because he had neither been bled nor subjected to any other treatment. He must have told Jasim so, and yet Jasim had gone his own way regardless.

'What else did you submit this poor animal to?' Stephanie demanded.

'Since we have not yet found an effective combination of treatments, I tried a new variation,' Jasim replied.

He addressed this remark, as he had addressed his previous ones, to a point over her shoulder. Stephanie was torn. Anadil was beyond suffering, what was the point in torturing herself with the knowledge of what she had endured, especially when her examination would serve to antagonise the man responsible? But even as she hesitated, she heard Papa's voice. She must see for herself the effects of this sickness, and try to find something, anything, which would help her with the next case.

She asked Fadil to provide her with a bucket of warm water and a bar of strong soap. Having done so, the Head Groom left, looking visibly relieved to make his escape from the tension in the stall.

Stephanie rolled up the sleeves of her tunic, and prepared to discover for herself what had transpired. She took her time, conscious of Jasim's malevolent presence attending her every move, and the flitting, curious stares of various of the other stable hands passing the open doorway. When she was done, she made a point of closing the door to the loose box.

'You were made aware that Batal survived the sickness?' she asked, leaning against the door, feeling distinctly like a boxer preparing to enter the ring.

'A mule. Hardly of any consequence, or indeed relevance. It may not even have been the same illness.'

Stephanie's hackles rose, but she spoke carefully. Jasim was one of those men who habitually riled in order to gain an advantage. 'There was no doubt. Prince Rafiq will confirm that.'

'Prince Rafiq is a man at the end of his tether. That is why he has been forced to resort to appointing...'

He did not finish his sentence, but the gesture he made left her in no doubt. Stephanie slowly unrolled her sleeves. She took her time gathering up her instruments from the bucket of water in which they had been steeping. Only when Jasim turned his back, making for the door, did she speak. 'I have some questions I would like answered, before you go.' He ignored her, his hand reaching for the latch. 'Very well. I will ask Fadil instead,' she said.

'Fadil takes his orders from me.'

'And Prince Rafiq has made it plain that regarding the sickness, you take your orders from me.' Stephanie pulled herself up to her full height, which still, infuriatingly, required her to look up. 'Let me speak plainly, Jasim, while there is no one else present. I will not step on your toes if you do not step on mine. I will not interfere with your running of the stables unnecessarily, but I will not tolerate you interfering with my tending to the Prince's sick animals. Ultimately, we are working to the same goal. If I cannot cure this sickness, your horses will not race in the Sabr.'

She refrained from pointing out that she was here because Jasim himself had been unable to effect a cure, but she could see he was thinking it, and that it pained him greatly. 'I understand how difficult this must be for you, but this sickness, it is something quite new. You must not blame yourself.'

She had made a tactical error by letting her compassion show. It had also been a mistake to assume that he was merely pained by his failure. Jasim spat on to the straw at her feet. 'How dare you presume to know anything of me? You, a woman, whose very presence in these stables is an insult. How dare you tell me how to treat a horse when you, the Royal Horse Surgeon, were not even present when the sickness first struck Anadil?'

Stephanie caught herself as her head almost dropped at this barb. 'No, I wasn't,' she said so vehemently that Jasim took an automatic step backwards. 'But it takes many hours for the sickness to kill. My instructions were very clear. If there was any sign, I was to be summoned immediately.'

'Those orders were followed.'

'To the letter? I don't think so. How long did you wait, Jasim? I have a good idea, for I can see how many remedies you tried on that poor creature. I did not neglect my duties, you did. If I had been here then at the very least I would have prevented Anadil from suffering. If you had summoned me straight away, she may still be alive.'

But Jasim was not so easily cowed. He moved in, pointing his finger, his breath hot on her face. 'Can you be certain of that? Are you claiming to have found a guaranteed cure? Of course not, you are floundering around in the dark just like the rest of us. That is the truth of it. Do you know how much this mare was worth? And only a week ago, put to stud too. That counts as two we have lost, Miss Royal Horse Surgeon Darvill. I pray that we find a cure, though I doubt it will be thanks to you. The sooner the better, for it is an ill omen to have a woman on these premises.'

'Do not be ridiculous,' Stephanie said firmly, 'that is mere mischief making.'

'Ridiculous?' Jasim shook his head, his smile contemptuous. 'Once before, he allowed a woman here, and look what came of it.'

'You are referring to Princess Elmira, I presume?'

'She despoiled the place. She upset the harmony. She contaminated our male domain with her presence. And she paid the price for it, Miss Darvill. He took my side, in the end. You would do well to remember that,' Jasim added, before turning on his heels and striding from the stables.

Batal was still being kept in isolation in a loose box. The mule, it seemed to Stephanie, was the only male in the entire stables who was pleased to see her. She sat down beside him in the straw thinking to close her eyes for a few moments and order her thoughts. She was certain that somewhere in the uncomfortable exchange she had just had with Jasim lurked a clue to this wretched, horrible sickness. A vital piece of information, but for the moment she could not put her finger on it. Rafiq would be expecting a report from her. She didn't want to go to him without something positive to say. Truth be told, she wasn't sure if she wanted to face him at all.

Today had begun on such a high note, she thought, ruffling Batal's ears. She had been so full of hope. And then this afternoon—oh, this afternoon! It had been astonishing. Astounding. Ecstatic.

Batal gave a wheezing little bray. He was still very congested. The sickness seemed to particularly affect the lungs and the heart. She settled him as best she could, then went to fetch him some fresh water. The stables were quite dark. Outside, the night sky was littered with stars. Returning to the loose box and setting down the wooden pail, Stephanie shivered. Someone walking over her grave, Papa would say. A shadow in the corridor moved. She knew, though she could not see him, that it was Jasim.

*She despoiled the place. She upset the harmony. She contaminated our male domain with her presence. And she paid the price for it. He took my side, in the end.*

Whispering goodnight to Batal, Stephanie closed the door of the loose box and crossed the courtyard of the stables. Rafiq had taken her side today. Rafiq had told her, right from the start, that Jasim would resent her, that Jasim would think her an interloper. And he'd told her too, that Princess Elmira had had an affinity with horses, which Jasim had not appreciated. Jasim was simply trying to frighten her. He was trying to intimidate her, put her in her place. Rafiq was on her side. They were all on the same side, if only Jasim could see that.

She tapped lightly on the door of the harem. Time and again, she had tried to persuade Aida not to wait up for her, to no avail. Luxurious as her surroundings were, delightful as it was to have her warm bath run, a cool drink poured, there were occasions like this when the harem felt claustrophobic. She didn't like being locked in behind that huge door with its observation grille and Aida as its gatekeeper. She didn't like feeling watched. She didn't like the sense that she was never, ever alone.

She was exhausted. Whatever price the Princess Elmira had paid for whatever perceived crime she had committed by being in the stables, it could be nothing compared to the price Anadil had paid tonight. The loss of the mare hit her anew, as Aida ushered her into the steaming bathroom. Stephanie climbed into the bath, immersed herself in the water, and wept.

Stephanie had requested that Rafiq stay away from the stables for a week in the wake of Anadil's death and Jasim's return, and that week was now up. Rafiq had spent the morning in Council.

Apart from the Sabr, only one topic roused the

Council from their apathy. It was not the new trade deal which Rafiq had struck with the neighbouring kingdom of Nessarah, but the fact that beautiful Princess Tahira of that kingdom was betrothed to the Prince of Qaryma, for the Council believed she would have made Rafiq a most suitable bride. This last had been stated at the end of the meeting with an air of expectation. The twelve men of his Council had failed to disguise their disappointment when Rafiq had made no comment, but he knew it would not be long before the subject of his lack of a wife was raised formally, especially if victory in the Sabr was secured.

But the Sabr was very far from won. Though Jasim continued to put the potential runners, now housed permanently at the training grounds, through their paces, Rafiq had not had the heart to watch.

One step at a time. One week, and no more cases. He changed out of his formal robes and made his way to the stables. Stephanie was sitting on her favourite seat. Though they had made no arrangement to meet, she had obviously been waiting for him, jumping to her feet and crossing the courtyard to greet him. She was wearing a tunic he had not seen before, alternating blue stripes the colour of the morning sky and the Arabian Sea, with her usual plain white *abba* over it. Her hair had lightened considerably, the golden streaks like new-minted gold now predominant, her skin also burnished by the sun, making her lips look pinker. Her smile lifted his mood. He had missed her company. He had not noticed, until she came to Bharym, how much of his time was spent alone.

'I hoped you would come,' she said. 'I heard that you had a Council meeting, but I hoped…'

'A week, you asked me to stay away,' Rafiq said, returning her smile. 'It has been a long week.'

'Did I ask too much? I wanted to prove…'

'That you did not need my protection,' Rafiq said.

'Yes.' Stephanie glanced back at the stables.

'Jasim is at the training grounds.'

'It's not only—it's all of them. Even Fadil. I feel that they are all looking over my shoulder, waiting for me to make another mistake.'

'Stephanie, Anadil's death was not your fault.'

'No, but if I had been summoned earlier, then perhaps I could have stopped…' She coloured.

Rafiq stiffened. 'Stopped what, precisely? Did Jasim have the nerve, against my express orders, to try to treat the mare in your absence? Do not answer me, I can see from your expression that he did. Why have I heard nothing of this?'

His tone made her flinch, but she straightened her shoulders and glared up at him, just exactly the way she had squared up to him that first day. 'I did not tell you, because I did not want you to intervene again. I know your intentions were noble, but I recall quite clearly telling—asking you *not* to command Jasim to co-operate with me the very first night, when we dined together, I told you—suggested—that it would only make him more defensive. I thought you agreed with me, Rafiq, but obviously you simply thought that it would be easier not to argue with me, and to do what you thought was best regardless.'

'With your best interests in mind.'

'But you still went behind my back.'

'So you repaid me in kind by omitting to tell me that Jasim had interfered with Anadil's treatment?'

'I did not…' She stopped, running her hand through her hair, heaving a sigh. 'You had already berated the man in front of everyone, Rafiq, and as far as I know he has not disobeyed you since.'

'He should not have disobeyed me in the first place. I will make it clear to him that I will not tolerate another incidence.'

Stephanie sighed again. 'He is your Master of the Horse and vital to your aspirations regarding the Sabr. I did underestimate the extent of his—his resistance to women. So it was unfair of me to berate you when all you were doing was trying to protect me.'

He *had* been protecting her, but he had also gone against her wishes. And although he had been right to do so, he had been wrong not to tell her, as Stephanie had been quick to point out. Having his actions questioned was a novel and slightly unsettling experience. 'Stephanie, it is done and dusted. Let us forget it.'

'No, you're right to be angry. You are, after all, my employer and a prince and on both counts are entitled to know exactly what is going on.' She screwed up her face apologetically, tried to smile. 'Sorry.'

'Stephanie,' Rafiq said, utterly beguiled, 'I am not angry, I am discomfited. Something you can evoke

in me with frightening ease. That is a compliment.
I think!'

'Truly?'

'Truly,' he said with a smile.

## *Chapter Seven*

Two days later, Rafiq was waiting for Stephanie in the Hall of Campaign. 'You wanted to see me?'

'More often than I ought to,' he answered, kissing her hand. 'I was thinking that my Royal Horse Surgeon had earned a well-deserved break from her duties. Does she agree?'

'I think she may, if the Prince intends to join her.'

'He would be delighted to.' Rafiq led her through a door located at the back of the Hall of Campaign. 'My grandfather, Bassaym, was known as the Smiling One,' he said, heading towards the far corner of the covered terrace, where he reached into a niche built into the wall, and emerged with a key for a door she had not noticed. The lock turned with some difficulty, and he ushered her through. 'This was his private sanctuary. It is not a place which I am in the habit of visiting.'

'It's a library,' Stephanie said in surprise, looking

at the elaborate glass-fronted book cases that lined the room.

'Dedicated to books on one very specific subject,' he informed her.

Her eyes widened. 'All of them?'

Rafiq smiled his wicked smile. 'I believe so, though I have not actually browsed more than a few, and then only when I was much younger.'

She eyed the bookcases dubiously. 'I find it difficult to believe that the subject merits quite so many tomes.' These shelves of books made her uncomfortably aware of the extent of her ignorance. Last week, in the tower, she had been so sure she wanted to *experiment,* but now, in the cold light of day, while she *did* still want to, she desperately didn't want him to think her utterly clueless.

'Stephanie, was I wrong to bring you here?'

'I had no idea—it's all a bit overwhelming.'

'I am not expecting you to peruse them all.' He smiled. 'You bemoaned, in jest, the lack of a text book for fallen women. I simply wanted to demonstrate that such things do exist.' Rafiq opened one of the cases and selected a large folio which he set out on a low table, indicating that she should sit beside him.

It took her a moment to realise what she was looking at, and when she did, colour flooded her cheeks. Each illustration was a drawing of a man and a woman, naked and entwined, but not in any way she recognised. Who would have guessed that behind those elaborately scrolled and embossed covers lay such shocking images? And who would have imagined that a man and a woman could enjoy carnal relations in quite so many different ways? 'I don't believe that one is physically possible,' Stephanie said.

Rafiq shook his head. 'The risk of potential injury to both parties would be a fatal distraction. I much prefer this one.'

They had names, the illustrations, she noticed now. The one Rafiq indicated was called *Bend in the Rainbow*. There was *Tail of the Ostrich,* something about Archimedes, and *Love's Fusion,* which name, at least, seemed to bear some relation to the illustration. Her curiosity began to override her embarrassment. Stephanie scrutinised the man and woman portrayed in *Love's Fusion.* 'That one, have you...? Oh, no, don't answer that. I shouldn't have asked.'

'As it happens I haven't, no,' Rafiq said, 'but I admit it looks—tempting.'

'Have you tried—these drawings—have you, with other...?'

Rafiq closed the book over and turned on the cushions to face her. 'Stephanie, I do not measure you against any other woman. You are literally incomparable,' he said, taking her hand. 'I want the time we have together to reflect that.'

'I'm not sure I'm ready to try anything quite so exotic.'

He pulled her towards him, kissing her softly. 'I showed you that book only to demonstrate that love-making is an art which takes many forms, but those illustrations, they represent the—the summit of the ascent of pleasure. We are barely in the foothills.'

'Speaking for myself, I have barely climbed one step. So you really do expect me to study the theory first?'

'Not on your own. We agreed to experiment together, remember?' He pulled her down on the cushions beside him.

'I cannot imagine any library in England containing books such as these.'

'I suspect there will be some, though kept firmly under lock and key. In England, I think lovemaking is not a subject much discussed, is it?'

'Not among the female gender, certainly.' Rafiq was stroking her hair. Her head was nestled on his shoulder. Her leg rested against his. 'That is, perhaps among married women, it is talked of in whispers, but…' She relaxed against him, placing her hand on his chest. She could feel his heart beating. 'Is it so very different here?'

'Here in the East, it is not a taboo subject. We understand that ignorance is not bliss, that knowledge is the key to pleasure.'

'The kind of knowledge contained in these books?'

'Books are only one way to learn. Most people don't have access to books.'

She lifted her head. 'Then how…?'

'By talking,' Rafiq said. 'By understanding that pleasure is always enhanced when it is mutual. By practice, and…'

'…by experimentation.' Stephanie kissed him. The butterfly kisses she had learnt from him, fluttering over his lips, licking, teasing. Resting her hands on his shoulders, she kissed his brow, his nose, then his mouth again. 'What is the next step on our climb to dizzying heights, Rafiq?' she whispered, nipping at his earlobe.

He ran his fingers through her hair, pulling it free from the scarf which tied it back. 'I have no idea— that is the beauty of it. It doesn't matter where we go, save that we go somewhere,' he said, with one of his sinful smiles.

She laughed, kissing his mouth again, touching the tip of her tongue to his. The kiss deepened, making her heart beat faster, setting up that familiar fluttering low in her belly. 'What *have* you in mind?' she asked, dragging her mouth away.

Rafiq's eyes darkened with simmering passion. 'Absolutely nothing, save to know what you want, what you have in mind.'

'I can't possibly—I don't even know the correct terminology.'

'Then describe it to me in your own words.'

He ran his hand down her spine to rest on her bottom. She looked at him, dark eyed, impossibly handsome, and she knew exactly what she wanted from him, this man who could surely have any woman, yet who wanted her. This man with so much experience, who knew so many ways to please, yet who wanted only to please her. It was intimidating, but it was also very arousing.

'I want to do to you, what you did to me,' Stephanie said. 'I want to touch you as you touched me, to make you feel what I did. I want to explore your body, as you did mine.'

He laughed, a low growl that she felt in his chest. 'You never fail to surprise me.'

'I hope to continue to do so.' She pushed him back on the cushions, refusing to allow her lack of experience to dent her confidence. Lying on top of him, her breasts pressed into his chest, her legs curled on either side of him, it was impossible not to notice that he was already aroused.

She leant into him and kissed him, her kisses soft and fluttering. He sighed, his hands stroking her bottom, encouraging her to meld herself into him, and she opened her mouth, deepening the kiss further.

More kisses, and still more. Mindless kisses, hot kisses, sweet, rousing kisses.

'Take your top off, Rafiq. Since we are not prince and veterinarian at the moment but a man and a woman, I may ask what I will.'

'I cannot imagine a command I am more happy to obey.' He pulled his tunic over his head and sat back on the cushions. 'I am completely yours to do with as you wish.'

His skin was the golden colour of desert sand. His musculature was every bit as defined as she had imagined. His chest was covered in a smattering of soft hair, arrowing down the dip of his abdomen, disappearing below the belt of his trousers.

The temptation to feel his skin against hers was too great to resist. Stephanie pulled off her own tunic. Rafiq's eyes widened at the sight of her in her camisole. Colour slashed his cheeks. Emboldened, she slipped the garment over her head. He drew his breath in sharply. His chest lifted. The taut muscles of his belly rippled. She pulled him towards her, so that they were sitting facing each other, though twined together. Their kiss had a new, exciting intimacy. Mouth on mouth. Her breasts against his chest, the rough hair making her nipples tingle, teasing them into hard buds.

What now? She remembered the way he had cupped her breasts, making her nipples tauten. Would it be the same for him? She touched him, tentatively flattening her hands over his chest. She could feel his heart thumping. His skin was damp, hot. His nipples were dark brown. When she covered them, they peaked just as hers did, and Rafiq breathed faster, just as she did. She used her thumbs to stroke, to circle, and when his breath became even more shallow, she leaned over, took his nipple in her mouth and sucked. He shuddered, and she felt an answering twist inside her. 'You like that,' she said. A statement, not a question.

'Very much.'

She licked the other one, but then she began to panic. What next?

Rafiq must have sensed her hesitation. 'You do not have to do anything you don't want to,' he said. 'One word is all it takes, remember? There is no rush.'

'I know, but I don't want—it's just that I don't know what to do,' she confessed.

'I can show you, if you would like me to.'

'I would.' She wrapped her arms around him. 'I would like that very much.'

He eased her on to her back, one hand on one breast, his mouth on the other, sucking, licking, circling, setting up a fiery, tingling path of sensation from her breasts to her belly, between her legs. He lifted his head from her breasts and kissed her mouth. 'An element of control heightens the pleasure, Stephanie. Let us test ourselves,' he whispered, rolling her on to her stomach.

'Rafiq, what…?'

His body covered hers. His chest to her back. His mouth on the nape of her neck. His hands tracing the swell of her breasts at her sides, the dip of her waist. She could feel his arousal pressing against her bottom. His hands slid under her, untying the sash, and then he slid her pantaloons away. She could not see him. She could only feel him. And hear him. Rustling. The sound of clothes being discarded. And then he was on top of her again, quite naked.

He did not move. She could feel him breathing, his chest rising and falling against her back, the shallow whisper of his breath on her neck. And then his mouth again, on her shoulder, and he eased her carefully on to her side, one leg over hers. His hand on her breast, his arm around her waist to steady her, and the thick, hard length of him between her legs.

She shuddered. Instinctively, she arched her lower body against him, and felt him shudder too. 'Rafiq?'

She thought he was ignoring her, but when he spoke, his voice hoarse, she realised he was simply fighting for control. 'Feel what you do to me,' he said, taking her hand, wrapping it around his girth. Her fingers brushed her own sex. She was hot, wet. In contrast Rafiq felt silky, hard. He pulled her leg on top of his, angling himself away from her. 'Slowly,' he said, showing her how to stroke him. 'When you do that to me, this is how it feels.'

He slid his fingers inside her. Her muscles contracted instantly in response. His other hand still covered her breast, stroking her nipple into an aching bud. His breath was fast, shallow on her neck. And he pushed into her, his fingers sliding slowly in, her muscles clenching around them, holding them, turning the *frisson* when he removed them into a shudder. Encircled by her hand, his arousal throbbed with every slow stroke, as her muscles tightened with every thrust he made. She couldn't hold out much longer. She could feel it, that exquisite tightening, that prelude, and she clenched tight. 'Rafiq, I can't...'

His fingers thrust harder. Faster. Higher. And she stroked him, more urgently now. She felt him thickening. She felt herself losing control, and as she did, spiralling, shattering, into her climax, she felt him come too with a harsh groan, and he pulled himself free of her, though she felt him, his chest shuddering against her back, his hand still cupping her breast, as his climax gripped him.

A few hours later, it had grown quite dark while Rafiq sat alone, the Bharym Stud Book lying open before him. He turned the pages, looking despondently at the empty gaps waiting to be filled with the names of the new owners of Arabians which should have left the Bharym stables many weeks ago. Tomorrow, Stephanie had asked him to ride out to the stallions' oasis. A potential breakthrough, she had called it. With only two months to the Sabr, he fervently hoped that she was right.

He closed his eyes, lying back on the stack of cushions, and distracted himself by remembering their encounter earlier. The taste of her and the feel of her. The scent of her arousal. And his own. He didn't remember ever being so hard. When he came…

Groaning, Rafiq got to his feet, rolling out the kinks in his shoulders. Enforced abstinence—that would account for it. And he had never encountered anyone like Stephanie. There was that too. So bold and yet so innocent, so very alluring and yet so oblivious of that allure. So determined, tonight, to understand his needs, to make love with him, not to allow him simply to make love to her. Before tonight, he would never have believed that such lovemaking, without a true consummation, could be as satisfying. When he felt her pulsing around him, it had been every bit as arousing as if his shaft was inside her.

The intensity of his climax unnerved him. Lovemaking was so very different with Stephanie from any other previous experience. The way she watched him while she touched him, the way their bodies communed, the way they talked, there was an intimacy between them which made him realise how oddly lacking in intimacy his lovemaking had been before. A physical connection, a joining of bodies, but not of minds. He had always remained a prince while play-ing the lover. A prince while playing the husband. Duty had drained the pleasure from lovemaking.

His mind shied away from the memory. He would not permit that to happen again. Stephanie had re-minded him of how it could be, and she had proved to him how much more it could be. A foretaste of his future, though of course, it would be a future with-out Stephanie in it.

His mind rebelled at this thought too. Rafiq shook his head at himself in exasperation. Why couldn't he simply enjoy what he had while he had it! A woman who spoke to *him,* as if she saw straight through his princely façade. No one had ever dared do that before. She forced him to look at the world afresh. His plans for Bharym and his people were no longer hazy, but shifting sharply into focus. The weight of his guilt was as heavy as ever, but it was no longer an intrin-sic part of him. He carried it still, but it was a sepa-rate burden, one which he was preparing to discard for ever.

*When* the sickness was cured. *When* the Sabr was won. He had faith in Stephanie. What he lacked was faith in himself. Gazing out the high window, Rafiq saw that the stars had made their appearance. The sky was inky blue. It was very late. Like Stephanie, he would learn from his mistakes. Like Stephanie, he would be become a different person.

Waiting for Rafiq at the stables the next afternoon, Stephanie was finding it difficult to remind herself that she was the Royal Horse Surgeon awaiting the

Prince. Studying herself in the mirror last night, back in the harem, she had seen a wanton woman. A sensual woman, who was beginning to understand just exactly what the word sensual meant. When she touched him. When he touched her. There was a mutual delight in it. Last night, their bodies had communed. Their physical differences were fascinating, but their identical responses even more so. Pleasure echoing pleasure.

Last night had not satisfied her curiosity, merely whetted her appetite. She had learned that lovemaking was about looking and touching and talking and listening, it was the taste of his skin and scent of him, and the shivering sensations they triggered and shared. She smiled to herself. Pleasure. Mutual pleasure. Those illustrations were no longer shocking, they were intriguing. She still wasn't convinced by *Tail of the Ostrich*, but *Love's Fusion*—yes, she could imagine that, and the other one, where his body was nestled into her back—*that* was a very delightful image indeed. Her body delighted Rafiq, and Rafiq's delight delighted her. It was a heady feeling, knowing the effect she could have on him, it made her want to experiment further. It made her feel oddly powerful.

Though it also meant that now, watching him cross the courtyard towards her, she was struggling to suppress all these feelings, and to remember that she was a Royal Horse Surgeon with a difficult task to perform. She felt so different, yet he looked exactly the same. Ridiculously handsome. Sinfully attractive.

Stephanie got to her feet, pulling her *keffiyeh*

over her face before he could read her thoughts. 'The horses are ready, Your Highness. Let us make haste.'

After an hour examining the stallions' enclosure, Stephanie could find no evidence to back up her theory, but was reluctant to admit defeat. 'We must be missing something. Every case of the sickness has occurred seven or eight days after one of the stallions has been brought into the stables to cover a mare. Batal was infected because he was with Anadil when she was covered.'

'But we have lost only one stallion. And there has not been a case of sickness every time,' Rafiq said. 'If it is the water, as you suggest...'

'I know, they would all be infected. It doesn't make sense, yet there is a logic to it, Rafiq. It is the only discernible pattern. We *must* be missing something obvious.'

'Well, whatever it is, we are not going to find it today. It is too hot to ride back at the moment, let's rest in the shade for a time.'

On the other side of the enclosure, away from the horses, the oasis was beautifully tranquil. The air was sweetly scented, the palm-covered island in the centre of the pool a lush haven. Perched on the low stone wall of the little bridge, Stephanie could see her reflection in the still blue waters, with Rafiq standing beside her, frowning over at the high wall. He wore English-style leather riding breeches today, and long boots. His shirt was white, with wide sleeves, open at the neck. He had discarded his headdress as soon as they had arrived. His hair was dishevelled, clinging damply to his brow, just as it had yesterday in the library, when he was naked and aroused. And then naked and sated. She had brought that about. Just thinking about it made her feel giddy. So she'd better stop thinking about it.

A breeze flitted through the palm trees, making them rustle. In the paddock, one of the stallions whinnied. Rafiq sat on the wall beside her. Beneath them, the water was crystal clear, like a mirror.

Exactly like a mirror. There was her face and Rafiq's side by side. He smiled at her. She smiled back. Their heads drew closer until their temples touched.

'I have been giving what you confided in me last week regarding your past a great deal of thought,' he said. 'I cannot accept that you were in any way to blame. Surely there must be some way of bringing this man who seduced you to book.'

'Rafiq, I made love to him because I wanted to, and it was, frankly, now that I know better, a disappointing and frankly dreadful experience, but that is beside the point. It was my choice, and until lately I have deeply regretted it.'

'What has made you think differently?'

Stephanie chose her words carefully. 'I too have thought about it a great deal since last week, more clearly than I have been able to since it happened. Distance gives perspective, and hindsight is a marvellous thing. You know, I wasn't unhappy working with Papa, but I was beginning to question whether I wanted to spend my entire life doing so. I was looking for something more, something different, although I couldn't articulate what it was. Perhaps that's one of the reasons I thought myself in love, I don't know. But I do know that if I had not taken the path to ruin, I would not have been granted this opportunity, for Papa would never have permitted me to come to Arabia otherwise. What I'm trying to say, in a very roundabout way, is not that I would gladly make the same mistake again, but having already made it, I need have no more regrets.'

'But that man…'

'Rupert is weak, and he is dishonourable, and he is a liar The world did not extract a punishment from him for those sins, while I was forced to pay beyond price by my shame, but it's that same shame which has obliged me to take responsibility for my own life. My total lack of judgement still takes my breath away. I will never, ever be so stupid again. But I'm done with looking over my shoulder, I want only to look forward, to the future. So I'm not in the least bit interested in revenge. Do you see?'

'To be done with regrets, to be done with looking back—yes, that I do understand.'

Though his eyes were hooded, his tone was bleak. 'Fear not, I will help you cure this sickness,' Stephanie said, touching his knee. 'You will win the Sabr as you promised you would.'

Her words, to her relief, had the desired effect. He smiled. 'I cannot help but wish that blackguard could be punished for what he did to you, but I cannot bring myself to regret the fact that it has led to your presence here in my kingdom.'

Their shoulders were touching. And their arms. And their thighs. Her heart began to race. He turned to her and stroked her hair. 'Last night was utterly delightful.'

'Yes,' Stephanie said with a sigh, 'it was. Will we ascend another step some time soon?'

He kissed her tenderly. 'Soon enough, but we both have business to attend to, and I will not rush *this* business. You are a woman who deserves to be savoured.'

'I am not a banquet.'

He laughed. 'A feast. It is a very interesting idea.'

'What do you mean?'

He kissed her deeply. Then he helped her to her feet. 'Patience is a virtue, don't they say?'

'I'm not feeling at all virtuous.'

He laughed again. 'No more am I, but we really must go. I have a banquet of a very different nature to attend. Besides, it will be dark soon, and the biting insects which infest this water will make their appearance. It is high time we returned to the palace.'

'What is going on, Stephanie?'

She had not seen Rafiq for five days when he strode into the stables wearing his state robes, though he had discarded his headdress. He had been on a tour of the outlying villages. He looked tired and harassed and she was going to ignore that silly little lurch of her heart, because unless she had a tropical disease, she knew perfectly well that hearts did not lurch.

'I take it Jasim has been to complain about me.'

'With good reason, on the face of it. This is a stud, Stephanie. We breed horses. In order to breed horses, we need to bring the stallions in to cover the mares.'

'But we have established that the source of the sickness is located at the stallions' oasis, Rafiq.'

'We don't know that for certain. We searched the paddock thoroughly and found nothing to justify halting the main function of these stables, never mind the sweeping changes you are proposing. It can't be done.'

Jasim had done his work well, Stephanie thought. 'If I had known you had returned, I would have discussed the matter with you personally as a matter of priority.'

'In all fairness, the smooth running of the stables is Jasim's responsibility.'

'Curing the sickness and preventing its spread are what you appointed me to do. If that requires me to make temporary changes to the regime here, then that is my decision, not Jasim's. And unless you wish to terminate my employment, it's not your decision either.'

Stephanie did not raise her voice. She mimicked the soft, deliberate tone Rafiq used when he was playing the Prince. She did not let the fury she was feeling show on her face, though she kept her balled fists hidden in the folds of her tunic. She held his gaze determinedly. His expression was always difficult to read, but she understood the nuances now. The way his sleepy lids flickered when he was challenged. The slight downturn of his mouth, when he was holding his feelings in check. And the lift of his brows, when he was forced into an unpalatable decision.

'Explain to me, the rationale for these measures, if you please.'

Tempted as she was, Stephanie refrained from pointing out that she would have been more than happy to, had he asked her. Though she didn't doubt that Rafiq valued her honesty, he still found any questioning of his authority a challenge, to say the least. 'Complete isolation,' she said. 'Now that we know that the source of the problem lies somewhere in the oasis, even though we do not know exactly what, we can prevent the disease from spreading. It is the same method I have seen used effectively in containing the spread of yellow fever or typhus among sailors in port. Your stallions at the oasis will still be at risk until we find the source, but there is no other secure place to move them. If we keep them isolated, we can protect the stables, and if we keep the Sabr horses isolated too, then there is no reason why you can't race them.'

Rafiq frowned, tapping his fingers against the gold buckle of his belt. 'The work of the stud will be suspended.'

*Bloody Jasim!* 'But you won't lose any more stock,' Stephanie said through gritted teeth, 'unless another stallion is infected.' She sighed, pushing her hair back from her face. 'It *is* a lot to ask. To suspend your breeding programme, to have different storage for foods, to keep so many different paddocks operating in isolation, but it means you can enter the Sabr, Rafiq, which is surely more important than anything else, including Jasim's wounded pride.'

'But there is no evidence. If I had proof…'

'Oh, for heaven's sake!' she exclaimed, finally giving way to her frustration. 'Even if I could give you incontrovertible proof, Jasim would still not co-operate. It will be just exactly as it was before. You will take his side again, in the end.'

'What exactly do you mean by that?'

That soft whisper. That icy tone. Stephanie took an involuntary step back, but then she collected herself, crossed her arms, and held her ground. 'He told me that you sided with him over Princess Elmira. He meant it as a warning. I thought you trusted me, but it seems he was right and I was wrong.'

She turned away, but Rafiq caught her. 'Wait.' The blaze of anger in his face took her aback, but it quickly dissipated. 'My Master of the Horse will not have his way this time. Implement your measures. I will speak to Jasim, tell him to hand over the stables temporarily to Fadil, while he remains at the training grounds. That way he will not interfere with your work. You understand the risk I am taking by placing my trust in you? I can ill afford to lose Jasim before the Sabr.'

Stephanie threw her shoulders back, standing ramrod straight, as if she were on parade. 'I understand perfectly, Your Highness.'

Rafiq gave a curt nod, and turned on his heel.

Stephanie remained where she was until she was sure her emotions were under control. *He took my side, in the end,* Jasim had said. And he very nearly had, again. Jasim must have had one of his many spies alert him to Rafiq's return. She could imagine, all too easily, how he would have slanted his case against her.

Why hadn't Rafiq sought her out? Why hadn't he listened to *her* side? But he had. Stephanie uncurled her fists and her toes. He had sought her out, he had listened. He had taken her side. In the end. It might feel like a defeat, but it was a victory. And a very real reminder too, that Rafiq was a prince first, foremost and last. She rolled back her shoulders and made her way back into the stables, because she was a veterinarian first, foremost and last, with a job to do.

## Chapter Eight

$A$lone in her private dining room the next evening, Stephanie picked half-heartedly at the fragrant array of dishes set out in front of her and wished she could escape the somewhat oppressive atmosphere of the harem for a while. But unless she wished to pay another visit to the stables, she had nowhere to go. The huge palace was effectively out of bounds to her, without Rafiq's express permission, and she wasn't foolish enough to imagine that she could go for a walk alone in the desert after dark. Though that, she thought, wandering listlessly into the courtyard and gazing up at the stars, is what she would like to do.

Though she had not seen Rafiq since yesterday, he had obviously had words with Jasim. The Master of the Horse had taken himself off to the training grounds, and his absence had considerably eased the tension in the stables. Fadil had been apologetically co-operative, asking her quietly if she believed the measures would allow the Bharym horses to compete in the Sabr. Her answer in the affirmative had certainly expedited the implementation of her orders.

She was sitting on the edge of the fountain, gazing distractedly down into the darkened basin when Aida arrived, bringing with her the summons. Assuming that Rafiq wished her to report on progress, Stephanie picked up her notebook and was about to head for the door when the Mistress of the Harem stopped her. 'Madam, you will surely wish to change first, prior to an audience with the Prince,' she said, looking shocked.

Stephanie had changed, after a swift bath, into a clean tunic of mint-green, her hair tied back in a matching silk scarf. She had brown slippers on her feet. Aida was holding up the silk robe, the one in shades of pink that Stephanie had never worn, though she had tried it on privately one sleepless night, wandering around the courtyard, enjoying the caress of fine silk against her skin. It was a beautiful robe, and it was a very flattering one, but it was not a gown to be worn by a Royal Horse Surgeon, and she presumed it was in that capacity which Rafiq wished to speak to her. So she shook her head, told Aida not to wait up for her, knowing that her wishes would have no effect on the Mistress of the Harem, and followed obediently in the wake of the waiting guard.

She was not surprised to be taken to the Hall of Campaign, but she was very surprised to find it empty, and to be ushered through the door at the back of the chamber which led to the bathing pool. 'Are you sure this was where you were to bring me?'

The guard nodded silently, and the door closed behind her. Alone, she made her way through the connecting corridor. Flambeaux had been lit around the pool in tall scones, the reflection of the flames dancing on the still waters. Rafiq had been sitting in his favourite spot, but he got to his feet when she arrived. He was dressed simply, in a white tunic. His hair was sleeked back, still damp from his bath.

Stephanie stopped just short of the covered terrace, opened her notebook and cleared her throat. 'I am pleased to be able to report…'

'I summoned you here in order to apologise.'

She stared at him blankly, her mind still on her report. 'Whatever you said to Jasim has certainly paid dividends, he…'

'…is a man one step from being summarily dismissed. While some of my sentiments were entirely justified,' Rafiq said, 'I should not have vented my anger and frustration on you.'

'No, but it was a pertinent reminder—not that I needed one—that you are the Prince of Bharym, and that ultimately your word is law.'

'You make me sound like a despot.'

'You once told me you found my honesty refreshing.'

'Refreshing, in the sense of a dowsing with ice-cold water from a mountain stream, on occasion,' Rafiq said ruefully. 'It is rather dishearteningly difficult for me to confess that I was wrong.'

'You were not,' Stephanie said, touching his arm. 'As I said, you...'

'No!' He caught her hand, clasping it tightly. 'No, I am sorry. And amidst all the fuss and commotion which Jasim created, amidst my quite unjustified fury at your putting an end to the daily business of the stud, I overlooked the single, most important point. Do you truly think that we can risk the race without infecting any of the other runners, Stephanie?'

She longed to promise him, but she could not bring herself to lie. 'I cannot guarantee it, Rafiq.'

He laughed softly. 'Of course you can't. There is no accounting for the vagaries of nature.'

'Exactly. But I do think there is hope. I think that the measures we have implemented stand a good chance of keeping the Sabr horses free from infection and therefore free to run in the race.'

He nodded several times, his lack of words making the depth of his feelings very clear. 'Thank you.'

'It's what you brought me here to do.'

He kissed her hand. 'It is no excuse, but I find it difficult, at times, to distinguish between Stephanie and my Royal Horse Surgeon. When you quite rightly pointed out that I should have consulted you, rather than pay heed to Jasim, I was...' He shrugged, shaking his head. 'I could see I had hurt you, and I wouldn't wish to harm a hair on your head.'

'The important thing is that you showed faith in me.' He was still holding her hand. 'Rafiq, you are not the only one who has trouble distinguishing—may I ask if I am still talking to the Prince?'

'The Prince has apologised to his Royal Horse Surgeon. The man wishes—hopes—to make it up to Stephanie. If she will allow him.'

Her mouth went dry. 'What do you have in mind?'

'I'll show you,' Rafiq said, kissing her hand again, and this time smiling at her wickedly. 'This terrace, you know, was once known as the Pool of Nymphs. When the palace was first built, it was part of the original harem. The library was formerly the changing room for the *hamam*.'

He turned the key in the lock and ushered her in. 'You may think it is luxurious now, but it was once fabulously ostentatious. Rich wall hangings, carpets from Persia, gold and silver embroidery on every cushion and covering, bone-china coffee cups and pots set with jewels. Would you like to see the next room?'

Stephanie nodded, intrigued and excited and just a little bit nervous. Rafiq opened the door into a small ante-room made entirely of white marble. 'This is where one would disrobe before entering the *tepidarium*. Would you like to recreate that experience, Stephanie?'

Was he really suggesting they take a bath together? Naked. Rafiq naked. Now that was a very different proposition. She picked up the robe he handed her and retreated behind a screen.

When she emerged, clutching her robe to her body, Rafiq had also changed. His robe stopped just short of his calves. He had very elegant feet. Slim ankles. When he kissed her lightly, she was acutely conscious of their flesh, separated only by two thin layers of silk. He raised his eyebrows questioningly.

She nodded, allowing him to lead her into the next room. The *tepidarium* was not, as she had assumed, an actual bath house. It was a white marble room set out with more divans, the marble cool underfoot.

When he kissed her again, she closed the gap between them. Their tongues touched. He cupped her bottom, pulling her closer. Her hands slipped and slid on the silk of his robe as she flattened her palms on his back. When they broke the kiss, his robe was gaping, giving her a glimpse of the swell of his pectoral muscles, the rough smattering of hair which covered his chest.

'Another step further?' he asked.

'Onwards and upwards,' Stephanie agreed readily.

Steam billowed out of the next room as Rafiq opened the door, obscuring her view at first. She stumbled forward. He caught her arm. The door closed. The steam cleared.

'The Great Bathing Chamber,' he announced.

They were in a room with a high cupola lit by what looked like stars, though they must be lanterns of some sort, covering the whole dome, like a night sky. There were more lights set into the outer walls. No windows. The steam hissed gently from gaps between the marble tiles underfoot. The marble here was not white, but veined with grey and black. Around the walls were basins. Slim marble pillars supported the cupola's arches, forming a circle in the centre of the chamber. And here stood the bath, a massive star-shaped construction edged with marble so wide it formed ledges, the bath itself a much smaller pool in the centre. There were other marble tables too, beside each of the fountains, and around the walls, benches had been inset.

She was very hot. Rafiq's robe was clinging to him. She could see the dark circles of his nipples. Looking down, she saw that her robe too was clinging, that her nipples were not only visible but quite obviously pert. And Rafiq had noticed too. His cheeks were flushed too. 'Onwards,' Stephanie said, pulling him to her.

They kissed slowly, lingeringly. He led her to the back of the room, to a large, low table draped with a sheet. Another kiss, this time as steamy, as languorous as the atmosphere in the bathing chamber, before he lifted her on to the table.

'What are you doing?'

Rafiq untied the sash of her robe. 'I am making it up to you. Apologising. Actions,' he said, sliding her robe from her shoulders, 'I have found, speak much louder than words.'

He cupped her breast, his thumbs caressing the hard peaks of her nipples. Stephanie was a mass of fluttering, tingling nerves, wild with anticipation and at the same time drugged by the heat.

She tugged the sash of his robe open, eyeing him blatantly as the garment slithered to his feet and he stood naked before her. His skin was damp, glistening with sweat. His muscles rippled as he breathed. He was already fully aroused. She ran her finger along his length. Satin smooth.

He kissed her, easing her down on to the table. And then, when she thought he would join her, he rolled her on to her stomach. 'My turn to act,' Rafiq whispered. 'Your only requirement is to enjoy the results.'

She looked so luscious spread before him on the table that Rafiq struggled to control himself. The lovely curve of her spine, the indent of her waist, the delightful swell of her buttocks, the intriguing shadow between her legs, he wanted to kiss every inch of her, to lose himself in her.

He picked up the glass vial of precious oil, gently eased her legs apart, and knelt between them. The oil fell, drop by delicate drop, along the ridge of her spine. He applied it in sweeping motions, working along her shoulders first, where the muscles were tensest and strongest. Her breath came in little whispering gasps. He leant over her, his chest brushing against her back, the oil sleek between them. He kissed her nape. He nipped the lobe of her ear. She whimpered.

More oil was applied, and he worked his fingers down the knots of her spine. A strong back. She was not soft, though she was becoming delightfully pliant under his kneading, stroking, sweeping, touch. And down, to the twin mounds of her buttocks, the flesh yielding, her shape so perfectly feminine. Up, sliding his hands up her sides, his fingers brushing her breasts, then down again. When he leaned over, his shaft nestled against that perfect rear. The sweetest torture. Up, slid his hands, his palms flat, and then down. He sat back. He dripped more oil on the base of her spine, working it into the little creases at the tops of her legs, easing her further apart, to slide down the soft flesh of her inner thighs, making her moan, her moan making his member throb, the responsive arching of her body giving him a tantalising glimpse of her sex.

Down, his hands slid, from her thighs to her knees, to her slim ankles, then up again. The flesh at the backs of her knees was tender. He kissed it. Slid his hands back up again, his mouth resting on the base of her spine, a soft kiss there, the distinctive perfume of her arousal almost too much to bear, her little moans and whimpers constant now, her hands curled into the sheet. His fingers slid so easily into her. She tightened around him. She said his name, pleading with him in that smoky tone that was like nothing he had ever heard, pushing against his fingers, forcing them deeper inside her.

But he wanted to give her more. He slid his hand out, down her thighs again, then back up her bottom, before easing her on to her back. It was almost too much. Her eyes glazed with passion. Her nipples dark peaks. Those auburn curls between her legs. And her sex, inviting him, tempting him.

She said his name again. He used the sheet to pull her body towards him, standing between her legs. He leaned over to kiss her. Her breasts on his chest, nothing muscled here about her, she was all soft, lush woman. Another taste of her lips, and then another kiss, of a very different sort, between her legs, that made her cry out.

He stilled her, his oiled hands on her hips, his mouth on her sex, willing her to hold on, wanting to taste her, to savour her. Slowly, he licked her, teasing, coaxing, taking her to the brink and then stopping, holding her, stilling her, before starting again, sliding his fingers into her equally slowly, allowing her to hold him before easing back out, until he knew she could not hold on any longer, and he licked into her purposefully, feeling her swell and harden under his tongue, tighten around his fingers, until her climax rocketed through her; her wild cries, the deep pulsing inside her, almost setting him over the edge.

One last deep kiss, and he let her go, picking up his sodden robe and draping it around himself, before he helped her up, draping her robe around her shoulders, kissing her softly on the lips.

'I will leave you now, for I believe I have reached the limits of my self-control,' he said. 'Enjoy the *hamam* bath.'

'But what are you going to do?'

'I am going to jump into the ice-cold water of the Pool of Nymphs.'

The *hamam* bath was deep, the waters hot, burbling from little jets. Stephanie lay back, closing her eyes and enjoying the sensation of the water pummelling her body. She let her mind drift, reliving the sensations of Rafiq's hands on her, his mouth, his tongue. And that most intimate of kisses. She could never ever have imagined such a thing.

Opening her eyes, she gazed up at the twinkling lights in the cupola. She could admit now that she had lain awake last night, fretting. She could admit now that she was vastly relieved to have relations restored between them, and in such a delightful way. She could admit now that Rafiq's opinion of her mattered a great deal.

More than it ought. Her insides did a strange somersault. Stephanie sat up. She had better be careful. She had better be very, very careful. Forcing herself out of the soporific warmth of the bath, she decided that a harsh dose of reality was required. Wrapping one of the huge drying sheets from a shelf in the *tepidarium* around her, she made her way back outside to the Pool of Nymphs. It was almost pitch dark, for the flambeaux had burned out, and the only light came from a hazy moon. The greeny-blue waters were perfectly still. Casting off the drying sheet, she plunged in.

The water was icy compared to the heat of the bath. The pool was much deeper than she expected. She emerged from it coughing, splashing, her hair plastered over her face, and with difficulty managed to reach the safety of the steps, where her scrambling was assisted by a strong pair of arms.

The scream died in her throat when she realised it was Rafiq. 'What are you doing here? I assumed I was alone.'

He wrapped her in the drying sheet, guiding her to the cushions in the gloom of the terrace. 'I was lying under the stars enjoying the sense of solitude. Does that sound strange to you, a prince who wants occasionally to escape his responsibilities?'

She shook her head, then realised that Rafiq wouldn't be able to see her. 'If you mean can I understand that you must sometimes feel both your duty to rule and this palace suffocating, then, yes, I can. There are so many rooms, and every one of them with a different defined purpose. The Hall of Campaign. The Royal Receiving Room. The Banqueting Chamber. The guards' quarters. The menservants' quarters. The harem. A place for everyone, and a guard to ensure that everyone is kept firmly in their place.'

She sensed from his stillness that she had upset him. 'Including you?' he asked.

'I am not at all ungrateful Rafiq. I am living in the lap of luxury in this palace. I am eating the most wonderful food. My clothes are laundered for me, my bath is run for me—it is wonderful, but—oh, I don't know. It's that horrid locked harem door, more than anything. That little grille which Aida peers through. And the armed guard outside.'

'The harem is locked and guarded in order to protect the privacy and virtue of those within it.'

'I know. And it's a tradition that is thousands of years old, and I truly am not meaning to sound like one of those awful people who visit foreign countries only to deride the customs. It is just that I am not *accustomed* to it, and I never could be, no matter how luxurious. I can't help thinking that it must have seemed like a gilded cage to a nomadic Bedouin like the Princess Elmira.'

The moment the words were out, she wished them unsaid. The air between them seemed to freeze. 'What have you heard?'

'Nothing.' Stephanie shifted on her cushion, but it was so dark now, she could make out only his silhouette. 'I only meant that as a Bedouin, accustomed to roaming the desert, it must have been an enormous change for her.'

'Too much of one.'

His voice cracked. Horrified Stephanie fumbled for his hand. 'Rafiq, I didn't mean to upset you. I'm so sorry.'

He shook himself free and got to his feet. 'I recall telling you, here on this very terrace, that I do not care to talk about the past.'

Stephanie scrambled up, tripping over the drying sheet. 'I've talked about my past with you. It was painful, and I was terrified that you would judge me harshly, but—but you helped me see it in a different light. You helped me put it behind me. So don't you think…?'

'No.' Unlike Stephanie, Rafiq seemed to have the night vision of a predator. He steadied her with his hands on her shoulders. 'There is only one thing which will allow me to put my past behind me.'

'The Sabr,' she said, not because she understood, but because it seemed to be the answer to everything.

'The Sabr,' Rafiq said heavily. 'My only route to atonement.' His grip on her tightened. His lips were cool on her forehead and then he was gone, his shadow merging with the night.

Stephanie shivered. Inside the library, the lanterns still burned. She dressed hurriedly in the changing room, and brought one of the lanterns back out to the terrace. Was there a group of servants responsible solely for the palace lighting? There must be a great many of them. It must be a very tedious occupation.

She sat down on Rafiq's cushion, shaking her head to clear it. Rafiq wanted to win the Sabr for his people. He wanted to win it to restore his family name. She understood both of those things, but what had he meant when he said it would allow him to put his past behind him, to *atone?* It made no sense.

She furrowed her brow, trying to recall exactly what had been said before this strange declaration. Elmira. He had once again been refusing to talk about Elmira, but what could Elmira have to do with the Sabr? Poor Elmira, who had died in her sleep two years ago. Elmira who, according to Jasim, *paid the price* for contaminating the stables with her presence. What heinous crime had she committed to force Rafiq to take Jasim's side against his own wife?

It was cold. The sky was dark, a layer of black cloud blanketing the stars and the moon. Rafiq couldn't have made it clearer that whatever atonement the Sabr represented, he would not confide in her. It hurt a little, but it was another apposite reminder. There were boundaries she must not cross, had no right to cross. She must not confuse the physical intimacy between them with anything more profound.

Picking up the lantern, with a silent apology to the servant who would discover it missing in the morning, Stephanie left the Pool of Nymphs and headed reluctantly back to her own luxurious prison quarters in the harem.

Rafiq sat alone at the second of the four Sabr marker towers. He could hear Nura, the chestnut mare he had ridden out, snickering softly to herself, though the night was too dark to see her. Black cloud covered the moon and the stars, but he did not need his eyes to sense the desert that surrounded him. The vastness of it never failed to fill him with awe. He leant back against the cool stone of the Sabr post, rubbing his eyes. He had intended to come out here to think only of Stephanie, to relive those charged moments in the *hamam*, but Stephanie had unwittingly conjured Elmira's ghost. The two women were so very different. When he was with Stephanie, he had a taste of his future, free of guilt. He didn't want to think of Elmira when he was with her. He didn't want to make any sort of connection between them.

But Stephanie had made it all the same. A gilded cage, she had called the harem. Rafiq dropped his head into his hands, groaning with despair. Guilt descended on him like a carrion crow, doubts, like the predator's vicious talons, picking at his conscience. So consumed he had been by his dream of restoring the Sabr, he had not listened, had not attempted to understand the consequences of his inaction and subsequent overreaction, until it was too late.

The clouds were beginning to clear. A single star appeared, and then another, and another, and the silver scimitar-like half-moon lit the desert, casting a shadow over the Sabr marker. It was too late for recriminations. Too late for regrets. Too late to wish it all undone. Too late for anything, save atonement.

Getting to his feet, he reverently kissed the stone of the Sabr post. The time had come to seize the day, be bold and act. Stephanie had shown him the way. Rafiq leaned against the marker, closing his eyes. Tonight had once again been like no other he could remember. It made him wonder how it would be when finally their bodies were truly united.

He hadn't liked being at odds with her, though it had taken him a good many hours to accept that it was this, and not Jasim's behaviour which troubled him. Stephanie's opinions had come to matter a good deal to him. She had forced him to accept he was human, capable of misjudgements. She was not his conscience, but she was rapidly becoming his touchstone. Who would fulfil that function when she was gone?

He did not need to think about that yet, because Stephanie would be here for a good few months more. Calling to his horse, Rafiq rode out into the dark desert night.

Stephanie shifted uncomfortably on the high saddle of her camel. The promise of a visit to a Bedouin horse fair had been too exciting to resist, though she had resisted, until Fadil had promised he would summon her immediately if any new case of infection arose. It was now more than a week since her precautions had been fully implemented, almost three weeks since the last case, so there were grounds for optimism. There was also the fact that since the *hamam* ten days ago, she had not had the opportunity to be alone with Rafiq.

Not that they were alone now. For the last hour, the desert trail they had been following had been crowded with camels, horses, mules and even men trudging along on foot. The surface consisted of hard-packed mud studded with jagged boulders and pockets of soft, sinking sand, which forced her camel to perform an occasional disconcerting ungainly curtsy, casting Stephanie forward in the saddle, a motion which the camel took great exception to, throwing his head back and expelling a cloud of his foul breath. She had never been so glad of the *keffiyeh* protecting her face.

'Is it much further?' she asked, manoeuvring her grumpy ship of the desert closer to Rafiq's own mount.

He shook his head. 'I promise you, it is worth it.'

She could tell by the way his eyes crinkled that he was laughing at her. 'It had better be.'

A few moments later, they crested a hill, and she forgot all her aches and pains at the sight which greeted her in the valley below. There were hundreds of tents, rows and rows of them, every one seemingly identical, black and conical in shape. Smoke from the many cooking pots cast a pall over the encampment. The noise of children's laughter echoed, mingling with the brays of mules and camels, the whinnies of horses. There were horses everywhere, some tethered by the tents, but the majority on long ropes attached to huge poles in the clearing in front of the tented village.

'Those are the horses to be sold at the fair,' Rafiq told her, edging them both to one side, away from the crowd.

'An auction?'

'It's a little more complicated than that. Fortunately, I will have time to explain. The Bedouin have very strict rules of etiquette. If I were acting as host today, I would be required to attend a number of audiences, which must be held in strict order of importance, with the various Sheikhs—bearing gifts, naturally. But we are outside Bharym's boundaries here, we crossed into the kingdom of Nessarah an hour ago, and my time is my own.'

'I had no idea that there would be so many tents.'

'There will be several tribes here today. The horse fair happens only twice a year in this part of Arabia, rarely in the same location. We are fortunate that it is so close to home this year.'

'Are we likely to meet…?' Stephanie hesitated. She did not want to spoil the mood, but it was an obvious question, wasn't it? 'Princess Elmira's family… will they be here?'

'I believe not.'

Did that mean he had checked? Because he wanted to meet them, or because he wanted to avoid them? His tone was carefully neutral. His expression was the one she thought of as princely, his lids languidly heavy, not a trace of emotion to be detected, not because it was lacking, but because Rafiq was being careful to disguise it.

'What about the tribe who raised you as a boy?'

'They travelled very far north from here some years ago, though I have heard word of them through the other tribes many times over the years. They did not raise me, Stephanie. I lived with them for periods of time in order to learn the ways of the desert.'

'Oh, I thought when you said—I thought it was all of the time.'

'You misunderstood. It was no different from the practice of the English aristocracy, to hand the care of their children to a governess or tutor who is expert in certain subjects, or to send their sons to school.'

'If I had a child, I would not wish to hand him into anyone else's care. Not that the occasion will ever arise.'

'You have no desire for children?'

She could tell him it was none of his business, but his determination to disguise his own emotions riled her. She would not pretend. 'I have always wanted children, lots of them, but now that is not to be. I wish I had had brothers and sisters. Though there were always lots of other children in the camp to play with, it wasn't the same.'

'I am sorry, I did not mean to upset you. I should not have asked.'

'Rafiq, of course I find the subject upsetting, but

I am not like you. I don't want you to change the subject.'

'Then what do you want?'

'I want to know if you would like children. I want to know if you would have liked to have sisters and brothers.' She was in danger of spoiling the day, and she had looked forward to it so much, but she couldn't stop herself. 'I'm tired of all the taboos you place on our conversation, Rafiq.'

'What, by all the stars, are you talking about? I thought we had a very clear understanding between us.'

He was right. As far as he was concerned, he was sticking to the rules. It was unfair of her to expect him to comply when she tried to bend them a little. And it was wrong of her to try, because it was those very rules which protected them both. 'We do,' Stephanie said dejectedly. 'I just wish occasionally you would trust me enough to let me glimpse behind the impenetrable cloak you use to shield your emotions. I would like to understand and, I suppose, be understood. But I am being illogical. Please let us forget it, and enjoy the day.'

'You are contrary, often contradictory but never illogical.'

She was forced to laugh. 'Thank you.'

'Only you would take such a remark as a compliment. You are quite unique, Stephanie, and that is what makes you so special.'

'Oh.' The tears rose too suddenly for her to catch the first one as it trickled down her cheek.

'Are you upset because I did not mention your skills as a veterinarian?'

His smile made her feel like the sun had come out, which was preposterous, because the sun was ever present here in Arabia. 'I'm crying because that is the nicest thing that anyone has ever said to me.'

'I wish very much that I could kiss those tears away.'

'I very much wish that you could, Rafiq, but we are in the full gaze of half of Arabia.'

'Then later tonight,' he said.

'It will be more like morning, by the time we ride back after the fair.'

'The sentiment, not the hour, is what matters,' Rafiq said. 'Now, let us join the fair. It would be sensible to keep your face covered, as it will be very dusty. Also, although English visitors are not unknown here, for the quality of the bloodstock attracts buyers from across the world, you will attract a good deal less attention if you are veiled.'

# Chapter Nine

Some of the women were veiled, many were not. Stephanie was at first quite overwhelmed by the crush of jostling bodies and the constant noise. Everyone seemed to speak at a shout and to walk at a snail's pace save for children and dogs who raced about madly, screaming wildly with excitement, dashing between the tall poles to which the horses were tethered. Men and women bearing trays of hot food and cold drinks called out to advertise their wares as they wandered aimlessly, meandering back and forward through the crowds. The air was heady with the scent of food and animals and people.

Content simply to absorb the atmosphere, unwilling to draw attention to herself, Stephanie kept in Rafiq's shadow. Despite the fact that he was not here in any official capacity, he was recognised by everyone, and the question on everyone's lips was the Sabr. Knowing how much it set him on edge, she watched with trepidation, and was consequently surprised to hear him not only joining in the speculation, but relishing it.

'This will undoubtedly be Bharym's year,' he said. 'This will be the year the Sabr returns to its rightful home.' With each assertion, his eyes met Stephanie's. His fingers gripped hers for a fleeting moment, under cover of the folds of her *abba*. 'For the first time, I truly do believe it,' he whispered.

They joined the milling crowds examining the horses. 'Though the trick is, as you will see if you observe closely, to pretend *not* to examine the best ones,' Rafiq explained to Stephanie. 'This is not an auction, but operates as a private bartering system. If a great deal of fuss is made over a horse then it attracts the attention of other buyers, thus raising the price. So a buyer feigns great interest in the horses he doesn't want, while offering a lower price for the ones he does, hoping that by ignoring them, no one else will compete with him. Do you follow?'

'No,' Stephanie replied. He could tell she was smiling. 'It is a preposterous system, since everyone knows the game and plays along accordingly. And, since almost every man and women here is an expert assessor of horseflesh, it must be obvious which are the best horses.'

'Yes, the ones standing neglected,' Rafiq answered, laughing. 'It is the custom never to discuss the price paid, and one can never be sure if the seller is bluffing when he tells you that he has been offered a higher price so bargains are difficult to find. The horses I have purchased at these fairs have all been outrageously expensive, though admittedly of excellent quality.'

'So you bought the stallions which formed your new stables at a horse fair?' Stephanie asked. 'I remember when you told me the story of the Sabr, you said that the stallions had cost you more than I could possibly imagine. At the time, I must say, I didn't think you meant gold, but it seems you did.'

She could have no idea, Rafiq thought. He felt a momentary urge to confide in her before ruthlessly quelling it. Was this what Stephanie meant when she accused him of hiding behind an impenetrable cloak? After the *hamam*, he recalled now, she had suggested he be more candid about his past, less guarded. They had been talking of Elmira. She could have no notion that they were talking of Elmira again. He didn't like this habit Stephanie was developing, of reminding him of his dead wife, no matter how unwittingly. Finding her gaze still fixed on him, Rafiq wished that he had kept his face covered too. He shrugged, turning away. 'I obtained the Bharym stallions from another source.'

An answer that was not an answer, they both knew full well, but Stephanie had obviously decided not to spoil their unspoken truce, and merely nodded. He should have been relieved. Instead, he felt guilty. He watched her playing the game with the horse traders, amused to see that she was, typically, challenging the system by making a fuss over the finest of the horses, to the glee of their owners, and undoubtedly incurring the ire of potential purchasers, though naturally none betrayed themselves.

Despite her veil, despite her perfect command of the language, she had been spotted as a foreigner, but she did not seem to be at all unnerved by the attention. He stood on the fringes watching her, ready to intervene if required, but could detect no sign of disrespect. It had been the same in the city, he recalled now. Her natural curiosity overcame any shyness, her modesty, her complete unawareness of her appeal, meant men, women and children alike were drawn to her.

Stephanie wanted children. Lots of them, she had said. Stephanie's independence was coming at an enormous cost. The unfairness of it struck him afresh. Why should she be punished so harshly! As a prince, *he* must marry a virgin, but Stephanie didn't have any title at all. Was purity really so much more important than all her other qualities? She did not have to declare her loss of innocence to the world.

His thoughts were making him very uncomfortable. Stephanie would be horrified if she were privy to them. She prized her precious independence beyond anything. She certainly had no intentions of getting married. Once bitten, twice shy, wasn't that the English phrase? Hypocrite that he was, he was glad. He didn't want to contemplate Stephanie with another man. He didn't have any right to feel proprietorial about her, and she would be outraged if she knew, but that didn't change the fact that he couldn't bear the thought of it. Which would only be an issue when she left Arabia and returned to England. And then it would be absolutely none of his business what Stephanie did, so he needn't concern himself with it at all.

The tall man talking to her distracted Rafiq from this moral maze. Though his dress was not distinguished, consisting of practical desert clothes bearing the hallmarks of a long journey across the sands, the man himself had an unmistakable air of authority about him. And an edge of danger. The scimitar which hung from his belt looked well used. The man himself had the perfect build to wield it.

Rafiq strode across the arena, pushing his way through the crowds. 'May I be of service?' he demanded.

The tall man's skin was deeply tanned, but his bleached brows and brilliant blue eyes betrayed him for a foreigner, albeit one who spoke perfect Arabic. 'Not at all,' he said blithely. 'I was complimenting Miss Darvill here on her taste in horses—understandable now that I know she is your Royal Horse Surgeon. You must be Prince Rafiq.' He held out his hand. 'I have heard a great deal about your stud, and the Sabr race. It is a pleasure to meet you. I am Christopher Fordyce.'

'How do you do,' Rafiq replied in English. The stranger might be dressed like a common man, but he had a most uncommon assurance. 'You are a very long way from home, Mr Fordyce.'

'Indeed. As is the delightful Miss Darvill here,' he replied blandly. 'You know, she is the third Englishwoman I have encountered here in Arabia in as many months. The region is awash with them! In Qaryma there was a botanist—though she's likely back in England by now. And then, in Murimon, the Court Astronomer, would you believe?'

'I am acquainted with Prince Kadar of Murimon. He owns one of my thoroughbreds.'

'Lucky chap. I would very much like to own one of your highly prized horses, but I keep my ear to the ground and I know better than to ask whether you brought any along to sell today.'

Rafiq stiffened. 'Why is that? What have you heard?'

'Only that it's well known in these parts that you sell only to those and such as those, and not on the open market,' Christopher Fordyce said, a slight frown pulling his bleached brows together. 'No need to take offence.'

'No offence was taken, I assure you. I take it that you are here to purchase some horseflesh, Mr Fordyce.'

'Oh, I'm just passing through.'

'First Qaryma, then Murimon, and now Nessarah. A rather circuitous itinerary. I am sure you have a good reason for it.'

The Englishman laughed. 'As good as reason as you do, for bringing Richard Darvill's daughter all the way from England to tend to your Sabr runners, Prince Rafiq. You see, I told you I keep my ear to the ground. But don't worry, secrets are my business and yours is perfectly safe with me, I promise. Now, if you'll excuse me. Miss Darvill, it was a pleasure. Your Highness.'

'One moment, Mr Fordyce. You understand, I am sure, that the desert is a very hostile place. You must also know, since you are so very well informed, that I have alliances with almost every Bedouin tribe. Any gossip regarding my stables, and in particular the health of my horses would soon reach me. I would take a dim view of that.'

All trace of insouciance left him. Christopher Fordyce's eyes hardened, and so did his voice. 'I understand your natural desire to keep your problems within the camp, so to speak, but do not deign to threaten me, however obliquely. I am a man of my word and that should be sufficient, even for a prince.'

'Indeed. I can see that you are. You will forgive me if I have offended you.'

The Englishman smiled, but it did not reach his eyes. 'I'm not sure if that is a request or a command, but either way it is granted.'

With the sketchiest of bows, he turned on his heel and was lost in the crowd. 'What a very singular man,' Stephanie said. 'Though rather charming. Why do you think he is here in Arabia?'

'Putting his ear to the ground,' Rafiq said. 'It can mean only one thing.'

'You mean he's a spy!'

'And therefore, despite his charming appearance, a dangerous man. Now, why don't we—?' He stopped in mid-sentence. He must be mistaken. But, no. His heart sank. The black cloud of his guilt enveloped him anew.

'Rafiq? You look as if you've seen a ghost.'

She could have no idea how close to the truth she was. 'I see Prince Salim has unexpectedly graced us with his presence,' he said flatly.

'The Bedouin who stole your father's horses!'

'The Bedouin who *won* my father's horses,' Rafiq corrected her, touched by Stephanie's misplaced loyalty. 'You will excuse me,' he said. 'I was led to believe that he would not be present today, but it seems my information was inaccurate. I must pay my respects. Wait here, where I may keep an eye on you.'

Stephanie did as he bade her, watching apprehensively. Meeting the man who had stolen—won—his father's horses, the man who had taken the Sabr from Bharym, was obviously a daunting prospect for Rafiq. She would have wanted to turn tail and run in the opposite direction. He was a great deal more honourable than she.

He was gone only a matter of moments. When he returned, his princely expression was firmly in place, but he was walking like a man marching into battle. 'The fair is drawing to a close,' Stephanie said brightly, 'I think we should go.'

'Don't you want to wait and see who bought your favoured horses?'

'Rafiq, I'd prefer to leave,' she said anxiously.

'If there had been any change at the stables, Fadil would have sent someone.'

'Rafiq! It is not your horses I'm worried about.'

'Then what are you worried about, Stephanie?'

She didn't want to upset him further, but he would be much more upset if…

'Elmira,' she blurted out. 'I am afraid that Princess Elmira's tribe may be here after all. If your information regarding Prince Salim was wrong, then it's possible that your information regarding Princess Elmira's tribe is inaccurate too, and I don't want you to have to face them.'

'It is too late for that, I'm afraid,' Rafiq said grimly. 'Prince Salim is Elmira's father.'

Neither of them had spoken since they left the horse fair. Fortunately for Stephanie, her camel needed little encouragement to follow Rafiq's across the desert, for her mind was reeling. Rafiq had married the daughter of the man who had wrested the Sabr from Bharym. Why on earth would he do such a thing? She could make no sense of it. Time and again, she opened her mouth to formulate a question, and time and again, one glance at the stiff-backed figure on the camel in front of her had kept her silent. She couldn't begin to imagine what he was thinking.

The sun was sinking when they halted at a small oasis which she recognised from their outward journey. It was no more than a few palm trees, some scrub, and a small pool, beside which was pitched a Bedouin tent which had not been there this morning. There was no sign of life, no camels, no horses, and though the fire was set, it had not been lit. 'I wonder where the occupants are,' Stephanie said.

'They have just arrived.' Rafiq clicked his tongue, and both camels immediately dropped to their knees, allowing them to dismount, he infinitely more adroitly than she. 'You said that you wanted to escape. "Out into the desert, to breathe the night air" were your exact words, I believe.'

'You remembered,' Stephanie said, pulling off her *keffiyeh*. 'I can't believe you remembered.'

'I remember everything you say. Even the more unpalatable comments,' Rafiq said drily.

She recalled the context of her words now with dismay. 'The harem. I must have sounded terribly ungrateful.'

Rafiq pulled his headdress off, running his fingers through his hair. 'As ever, Stephanie, you force me to look afresh at things. When we return, you will find the locks removed and guard gone. You may enter and leave your rooms without being observed. If you prefer, I will have a suite set aside for you in the main body of the palace.'

'Oh, no. I did not mean—you didn't have to go to so much trouble.'

'As to the palace, I have had a plan of the rooms drawn up for you. Aside from the obvious exceptions of servants' quarters and my own, you may consider it entirely at your disposal.'

'Rafiq, I didn't mean—you didn't have to…'

'Stephanie, this is my world. I am so accustomed to it that I do not question our ways. Many of our traditions serve a sound purpose. Some of them are no longer valid. It was never my intention to confine you to the harem.'

'No, you wished only to protect me. And you did not want to compromise me, or yourself.'

He smiled crookedly. 'You do understand me, despite what you say. That is what you meant this morning, wasn't it? That I do not trust you enough to confide in you, that by refusing to confide in you, I deny you understanding?'

She was so surprised, she could only nod.

Rafiq pushed her hair away from her face to kiss her forehead. 'As a prince, I have been raised to remain aloof, to steer clear of exchanging confidences. But as you did not hesitate to point out, I am also a man. I don't know if I can—how much I can—but I will try, Stephanie, to break the habit and explain a little. For you, and you only.'

Rafiq hobbled the camels while Stephanie lit the fire. The front of the tent formed an awning propped open by two wooden poles. Thick luxuriant rugs, soft blankets and huge cushions were strewn across the floor. This was a Bedouin tent fit for a prince. They sat by the fire on a heap of cushions which she had set out. They drank the tea which she had made, picked at the selection of breads, salads and cold meats which, as ever, appeared wherever Rafiq commanded them to be. Above them, the sky was indigo, the stars turning from twinkling pinpoints of light to incandescent silver discs.

Rafiq set his tea glass to one side. He was sitting cross-legged, his feet bare, his cloak and belt discarded. His night-black hair was dishevelled by his headdress. The day's growth of his beard was a bluish shadow on his chin, accentuating his absurdly perfect bone structure, giving him a rakish air. Beside him, Stephanie pretended to sip at her tea, sneaking glances at him under cover of her fringe. She daren't think about what this meant. She daren't allow herself to imagine that it could mean anything.

'My father never forgave Prince Salim for shaming him by defeating him,' Rafiq said, picking up from a conversation he must have been having with himself, 'even though it was his own fault that the defeat had such catastrophic consequences. As a result a permanent rift developed between Bharym and Prince Salim's tribe while my father was still alive. I tried to bridge it when he died. It was a slow process, but I was prepared to be patient.'

'Because Prince Salim's horses were the direct descendants of the stallions you had lost? And because not only were they the best and therefore likely to secure victory, but by owning them you would restore the pure Arabian bloodline that had been broken.'

'Precisely.'

'And in doing so, restore the honour of your family name, your own bloodline.'

'It seems I left my impenetrable cloak at the horse fair! You are absolutely right but there is even more to it than that. That is—that is what I am attempting, rather poorly, to explain to you.'

'Elmira,' Stephanie whispered. Not because she understood, but because it was the only possible link. 'Elmira's father won the race. Elmira's father sold you the new bloodstock.'

Rafiq stared into the fire for a long time. When he spoke it was slowly, carefully. 'He did not sell them to me, Stephanie. He gave them to me. Sufficient stallions to replenish my stables, and all guaranteed descendants from the Bharym stud.'

'But you said—I thought—today—you said the stallions cost you more than I could imagine, and now you tell me that they were given to you...'

'At a price.'

'What price?'

'Can't you guess?'

He waited while she worked it out for herself, and when she did, she couldn't disguise her shock. 'That you marry Elmira!'

'I had no choice,' Rafiq said harshly. 'Prince Salim would not sell them to me for any amount of gold. He coveted the power and political influence that would result from an alliance with a kingdom such as Bharym. It was not only the opportunity to establish the stud, the first vital step on the road to reclaiming the Sabr, it would heal the rift between Bharym and the most influential Bedouin tribe. I had no choice, Stephanie.' He shook his head wearily. 'At least that is what I thought. I had no idea then—if I had realised—but I was blinded by my ambition.'

'Your people's ambition.'

'No, I will not allow you to excuse me. I am their

Prince and I have a duty to them, but I cannot deny the strength of my own ambition. I told you how, as a child, I dreamt of riding the winning string of horses one day, how that dream turned to ashes when my father burned down the stables. It was very important to me, but important enough to marry for? Because make no mistake, that is what I did, Stephanie. I married Elmira solely for her dowry.'

'She was a princess. Her bloodline—you said Prince Salim was happy with the match…'

'Oh, it was a good match, one my Council also heartily approved of.'

'There, you see! It all makes perfect royal sense.'

'Royal sense?'

'A bride with the appropriate pedigree. Stallions with the appropriate pedigree. An end to the feud your father started.'

'Royal sense,' Rafiq repeated dully. 'You're right, everyone got what they wanted, especially me. Everyone except poor Elmira. That is why my horses are plagued.'

'That is what you meant when you said that the sickness was your fault, when you said that your misfortune was all your own making? Rafiq!' Stephanie shook his arm. 'Nature is to blame for the sickness, you must see that. It would have struck whether you had married Elmira or not. Whether you loved her or not.'

'I did not love Elmira.'

For the first time when Rafiq spoke of his dead wife there was sorrow in his voice. It twisted at Stephanie's heart for reasons she was reluctant to explore. 'It is not a crime, in an arranged marriage, not to feel true love.'

'There are other crimes, which must be atoned for.' Rafiq shivered and stared into the fire.

'Are you cold?'

'A little.'

Stephanie was at a loss. He had clearly not told her everything, but he had told her a great deal. He had trusted her. The significance was not lost on her. She pulled his arm around her neck and rested her head on his shoulder. 'Thank you.'

Rafiq laughed gruffly. 'For revealing the flawed man lurking beneath the perfect Prince?'

She kissed his hand, snuggling closer. 'When I told you about Rupert, my biggest fear was that you would think me gullible, that you would judge me as harshly as I judged myself. You told me then that your opinion of me was based on what you knew of me, that what I had done in the past couldn't change that.'

She pressed another kiss on to his hand. 'It is the same for me. I know you for an honourable man. A man who wants desperately to do right by his people and his kingdom. A man who has sacrificed a great deal to make good on a pledge he made. A good man, Rafiq. One who, like me, may regret what he did, but who is determined to atone for it. You judge yourself far too harshly.'

'No.' He removed her arm gently and got to his feet. 'It is not possible to do so.'

'But...'

'No.' He held out his hand to help her up and pulled his boots on. 'It is a beautiful night, and I brought you here to walk in the desert under the stars, if you still wish to do so? We have dwelt long enough in the past.'

She tucked her arm into his. 'Then let us inhabit the present. Just us, just now.'

Stephanie was curled up inside the tent, sleeping under a mound of blankets. Rafiq fed the fire, listening to the sounds of the desert. They had walked for an hour, talking of little or nothing. The names of the insects which buzzed around the oasis. The constellations above them. No mention of horses. No Sabr. No Elmira.

Today was not his first meeting with Prince Salim, but it was the first time he had encountered him unexpectedly. At the time, the Prince had received the tragic news of Elmira's death with the phlegmatic resignation of a seasoned despot with a coterie of eligible daughters. A point he had been at pains to reinforce earlier today.

Rafiq groaned, dropping his head on to his hands. He didn't need to feed his guilt with the realisation that Elmira meant as little to her father as she had to him. But he fed it all the same, adding another branch to the towering pyre.

Were all men so heedless of the effect their actions had on women? Why did not more women rebel? Stupid question. He could not imagine Elmira speaking to him the way Stephanie did. He could not picture Elmira standing up to Jasim. Could not envisage her demanding he pay her more attention, spend more time with her. Because she was happy with her cosseted if cloistered lot? Or because she was afraid to?

The question made him feel quite sick. Confiding in Stephanie had only served to make him feel more guilty for having made a partial confession. The urge to tell her the whole of it was there, like a hand in his back, pushing him over a precipice. Madness. Pointless. Not that it mattered, whether he lost her good opinion of him or not, because she was only the Royal Horse Surgeon. She'd be going back to England in a few months.

No, it was far too late to pretend that he didn't care what Stephanie thought. Which meant it would be folly indeed to tell her the whole unpalatable truth. Sighing, he banked up the fire, for they would require coffee before they started out for the palace in the morning. Earlier today he had promised her there would be kisses tonight. Nothing had turned out as he had planned. He should have known better than to plan anything that involved Stephanie!

Rafiq pulled off his boots. He was far too overwrought to sleep. He would sit in the doorway of the tent and watch the stars. Stephanie sighed in her sleep, throwing an arm out of the cover. She had taken off her tunic, and wore only her pantaloons and camisole. He didn't want her to get cold. Kneeling down beside her, he tried to tuck her arm back under the covers. She pushed the blanket away. He really didn't want her to get cold. He lay down beside her, just for a minute to warm her up, curling himself into her back, and pulled the covers over both of them. He kissed the nape of her neck. He closed his eyes. She was so soft and warm. He had never slept the night with a woman before. But he wasn't going to sleep. He was simply keeping her warm. Rafiq closed his eyes, just for a second, enjoying the comforting presence of her quietly breathing form.

Stephanie awoke to find herself held in the tight embrace of a soundly asleep Rafiq. His breath was soft on her neck. His arms were wrapped around her waist. Her bottom was curved into his groin. And his fully aroused manhood was snuggled against her bottom. It was the most delightful feeling. More intimate in a way than any lovemaking, and arousing in a drowsy, sleepy way. If she turned around, he would kiss her and they would make proper love. How wonderful it would be, to be woken in this way every morning.

Her eyes snapped open. She eased herself out from his embrace, grabbed her tunic and headed for the icy waters of the oasis. By the time Rafiq awoke, she had dressed and reminded herself very firmly that there were a strictly finite number of mornings left to her in Arabia. She wasn't going to be waking up on any of them with Rafiq lying by her side again.

'I have made a decision regarding the Sabr,' Rafiq said, as she handed him a cup of the bitter, thick black coffee Mama had taught her to make. He was smiling. He made no mention of their night spent sleeping together. Perhaps like her, he thought it better to ignore it. Though that would be to assume he cared, as she did. Not that she did. Stephanie gave herself a little shake. 'I know, you said at the horse fair that Bharym would compete and you expected to win.'

'Yes, but it's not the decision I was referring to.'

'What, then?'

'I'm going to compete in the Sabr myself. I will be Bharym's rider.'

'You!'

'Don't you think I am up to it?'

Stephanie threw her arms around him, knocking his coffee flying and toppling them both over backwards into the tent. 'I can think of no one better suited, or qualified. When you first told me the story of the Sabr I pictured you on the back of one of your thoroughbreds, riding like the desert wind towards the finishing post.'

'Bareback,' Rafiq said, laughing.

She was sitting on top of him. He had washed, but he had not shaved. What was it she had been telling herself when she woke up? She had the logic all wrong. She shouldn't be avoiding intimacy with Rafiq. What she should be doing was making the most of the opportunity while she could. She ran her palm over the rough hair on his chest. 'Bareback. That will be quite a spectacle.'

Rafiq laughed again. She felt his chest rumbling. 'I was referring to the horse, as well you know.'

She settled herself on top of him. 'You slept with me last night.'

'I didn't intend to.'

'I'm glad you did, I liked it.' She leaned over, letting her hair tickle his face, and kissed him lightly on the lips. 'I was thinking, there are only a dwindling number of days left, before I return to England.'

'Four months is not an insignificant amount of time.'

'If you intend to ride the Sabr, you will need to dedicate yourself to a rigorous training regime. There will be precious few opportunities for us to spend time together.'

When she kissed him again, he put his arms around her waist and pulled her down. 'When you put it like that.'

'Precisely. And there is the small matter of the promise you made me yesterday.'

'I promised you kisses, and I am a man of my word.' His beard was rough on her skin. It made his mouth seem so much softer in contrast. He slid his hand up her side, to cup her breast. 'I did kiss you last night, but you didn't wake up.'

'You can't have kissed me properly, else I would have.'

He teased her nipple into a peak. She could feel the ridge of his arousal between her legs. 'Do you want me to kiss you properly now, Stephanie?'

'Yes, I do, Rafiq,' she whispered, nipping his ear. 'I want you to kiss me very, very properly.'

He did. Pulling her on top of him, he kissed her. Rolling her on to her back he kissed her, and she kissed him back, pulling him against her, wrapping her legs around him. Wild kisses that lacked all the control of their other kisses, as they snatched at each other's clothing, tearing buttons, tugging themselves free, kissing themselves naked.

His beard grazed the tender skin of her breasts, and she shuddered. He took her nipple in his mouth, tugging and teasing, making her moan. She arched under him, shuddering at the hard silky length of him between her legs. 'Rafiq,' she urged, clutching at the taut muscles of his buttocks.

'Wait.' He was breathless. His chest was heaving. 'Wait.'

'No.' She pulled his mouth to hers again, savaging him with a kiss. 'We've waited long enough.'

'Stephanie, I want this to be—wait.'

'I don't want to wait, and I'm pretty sure that you don't want to either.' She smoothed his hair back from his brow and kissed him deeply. 'I want to. I am very sure. I promise you. Very, very sure. Now, can we stop talking? Didn't you tell me that actions—?'

He cut her words short with a kiss. Then he kissed his way down, to the valley between her breasts, to the dip of her stomach, licking into her navel, then down, but this time it was no slow wooing. This time he sensed her urgency. This time when he licked into her, it was not teasing, but purposeful. She forgot to protest that it wasn't what she wanted. She didn't care whether it was his mouth or his tongue or his fingers which brought her straight to the edge, which made everything inside her tense, which sent her spinning out of control with a wild cry.

Then his mouth covered hers again. And his tongue touched hers. And finally he entered her, slowly, smoothly, the pulsing of her climax drawing him higher. She shuddered as he moved inside her, a slow withdrawal followed by a slow, delicious thrust back inside her. Another kiss. He slid his hands under her bottom, tilting her upwards, and she instinctively tightened her legs around his thighs. When he thrust into her this time, it was faster, higher, and this time she thrust back in rhythm, seeing the reaction on his face, feeling it inside her. She thought her release was over, but it was building again. She moaned, gripping his shoulders, kissing him urgently, sliding her legs up around his waist, moaning again when he slid higher, and again as she tightened around him, and again as his final thrust tilted her over the edge, sending him over too, pulling himself free of her with a harsh cry.

She was sprawled on a tangle of cushions and blankets. She was completely naked, and she was completely sated. She felt utterly wanton. Lying at her side, Rafiq looked just exactly as she felt, his eyes dark with passion, his cheeks slashed with colour, his chest heaving, his skin damp with sweat.

'I am a harlot and a brazen hussy,' Stephanie said, leaning over him to kiss him languorously. 'I find it is a very delightful thing to be.'

Rafiq smiled. 'Delightful,' he said.

'Was it? Truly?'

'Stephanie. Truly.'

## Chapter Ten

After the euphoria of their lovemaking, the melancholy that settled on her like a wet blanket took Stephanie unawares as they made their belated way back to the palace, leaving one of Rafiq's army of invisible servants to retrieve the tent. She couldn't understand it. She didn't doubt that Rafiq had found the experience every bit as pleasurable as she. She had known it would be pleasurable, but she hadn't dreamt it would be quite so—magical?

The word brought with it a sense of foreboding. No, not magical. Magical implied all sorts of the wrong things. Lovemaking was a physical experience. A sensual experience. A delightful, delicious experience. But it was not a magical one. It simply *felt* magical compared to the first time. But she couldn't remember the first time now. She didn't want to try. Her ambition to replace that memory had been fulfilled.

Glancing over at Rafiq, she felt her sense of foreboding increase. She didn't want to replace her memories of him with any others. Most likely she wouldn't have to. When she returned to England, she would have to be very careful of her reputation. Another melancholy thought. England. Grey skies. No Rafiq.

'Oh, no, Stephanie Darvill,' she muttered under her breath, making the camel's ears twitch. 'You would not be so foolish.'

No, she would not! She would not forget what she was here to do. She would not forget that when she had done it, she was going back to England. She would not forget that he was a prince and she was a farrier's daughter. And even if she was so incredibly foolish as to forget all these things, she would remember that she was a fallen woman, and that, ironically, the downfall which had freed her to play the harlot would be her downfall, because no man, and especially not a prince, would actually marry a fallen woman. Dally with her perhaps, but marriage would be out of the question.

All of which should reassure her, yet as they approached the palace, Stephanie could not recapture her elation. Perhaps it was *because* they were returning to the palace. Rafiq would turn back into a prince, and she would once again be his veterinarian. Yes, that could be it. Then there was the fact that he was going to start training for the Sabr, which was bound to leave him with even less time to throw off his princely mantle than before. That also, was a sound reason.

They arrived at the stables. Rafiq helped her down.

'I will leave you to your duties, you will no doubt be anxious to check what has transpired in your absence,' he said, making straight for the palace.

Not a trace of the turmoil she was feeling. It had been a pleasure for him, but no more. 'What more could there possibly be?' Stephanie muttered under her breath. She knew the answer, but she refused to countenance it. She would content herself with what she had. It was a great deal more than she could have imagined a few months ago, the promise of a future where she was no longer a burden, where she had the freedom to do what she loved best. She wasn't going to jeopardise it by giving way to feelings which had no future at all.

As she handed the camels over to one of the stable hands, Stephanie was about to head to the harem to take a bath, when Fadil accosted her. 'If you please, Miss Darvill, could you take a look at the new foal? I don't think it is the sickness but there is something wrong.'

Rafiq lay in his bathtub. In his bedchamber, his man would be laying out his formal robes for the Council meeting he had called this afternoon. In his office several secretaries would be cancelling, delegating, rearranging his official engagements from now until the date of the Sabr. Another team of secretaries would be in charge of the Sabr itself. This year, his people would throng to the race. The celebrations would have to be arranged well in advance. He would not allow himself to think of failure. He would meet with Jasim in half an hour's time. A meeting of extreme import to discuss Rafiq's personal training regime and the progress of his crack team of horses. A few months ago, a few weeks ago, he wouldn't have dared hope. Now, he was relying on it.

Actions spoke louder than words. Stephanie. He sank further into the hot water, draping a wet flannel over his face. Such actions. He had known from the moment they first kissed how it would be. It had been better. Better than he had imagined. Better than any other time before. Better than he had thought possible.

She was so bold. There were no half-measures with Stephanie. When he touched her, she made no attempt to disguise the effect he had on her. And when she touched him—the way she looked at him, as if she were trying to read his thoughts, as if every thought mattered. Wanting to understand him.

Rafiq sat up, snatching the flannel from his face. They had made love—that was all. It had been highly satisfying, but that was all it had been. A distraction. A very pleasant distraction. But none the less, a distraction is what it was. He had no time to be wallowing here reliving it. He had a race to win.

The foal had been born while Stephanie and Rafiq were away at the horse fair, suffering its first seizure the day they returned. She was not surprised when he suffered a second seizure at eight days old, and although it left the beautiful young creature exhausted, she and Fadil had been able to prevent him doing any damage to himself. She had seen such seizures occasionally afflict thoroughbred foals during her time at the Newmarket stud. They were not fatal and the foals eventually grew out of them naturally. 'A watchful eye to manage him through any further seizures, guard him carefully if they occur, just as we did just now, and with a bit of luck, when he is a year, eighteen months at the most, he will mature into a fine, healthy stallion,' Stephanie told Fadil.

But someone must have informed Jasim, because he was waiting for her when she arrived at the stables the next morning. 'Why are you wasting my men's time on a weakling?' he demanded.

They were in the middle of the courtyard and quite alone but Stephanie knew that every single stable hand, the men she had worked so hard to win over, would be watching. She stepped forward. 'You should not be here,' she said.

As usual, Jasim's long fingers were working incessantly at a set of worry beads. As usual, his expression was one of contempt. 'These are my stables. The foal is under my jurisdiction. I am affording you the courtesy of informing you personally before I have my orders carried out.'

'What orders?'

'To have the foal destroyed. This is a stud farm, Miss Darvill. We breed thoroughbreds as a business. Sentiment has no place here. We do not harbour weaklings.' He eyed her up and down disdainfully. 'Nor the weaker sex. It is not long until the Sabr. Then your presence here will be nothing but an unpleasant memory.'

Jasim snapped his fingers, and one of the stable hands appeared. The tall, surly one, Stephanie noticed, the one who was always lurking. He was carrying a gun. 'No!'

The man looked to Jasim. 'Do as I instructed and despatch the foal.'

'No!'

Jasim turned away. The stable hand began to make his way inside. 'No!' Stephanie rushed at him, grabbing the gun. Taken by surprise, the man loosened his hold on the weapon, but before she could grab it, he had recovered. 'No,' she cried out. 'Why won't one of you help me? I will not let you…'

He let go of the gun so suddenly that Stephanie fell backwards, clutching it. Fortunately, it did not go off.

'Are you hurt?'

The reason for the man's sudden compliance helped her up. 'Fadil came and fetched me. He seemed to think that you needed help. You *are* hurt,' Rafiq said, seeing her tear-streaked face. 'Stephanie…'

'No, no. *I* am perfectly fine, but—Rafiq, it is the foal. The one born eight days ago, to Dameer. He has been having seizures. I have seen it before, it is something which affects thoroughbreds, a problem with the bloodline, but the foal will grow out of it. There is no need to have him shot.'

'Stephanie,' Rafiq said gently, 'you must know that sometimes it is better to put an animal out of its suffering, especially if it is liable to hurt itself.'

She drew herself up to her full, short height. 'It is my vocation to prevent suffering, but it's also my vocation to save lives, where possible, and I think this foal's life should be spared.'

'Your Highness.' Fadil stepped forward, trembling but determined. 'Miss Darvill has—she is right, Your Highness. The foal is perfectly healthy, save for the occasional seizure, which she has shown me how to deal with in such a way as to avoid injury. There is no reason why he will not make a fine addition to your stables. In effect, Your Highness, I would endorse Miss Darvill's suggestion.'

'Thank you, Fadil,' Stephanie said, quite overcome by this brave testimonial.

'Very well,' Rafiq said to Stephanie, 'it seems you have spared a life, though why I must be summoned from my breakfast with such urgency…' Frowning, he turned to Fadil. 'Who gave the order to have the foal put down, if not you?'

'I did, sire.' The Master of the Horse had been lurking in the shadows of the main doorway. Now he came forward, making a bow. 'I was forced to come to the stables personally, in order to ensure my orders were implemented, Your Highness. When I was informed that Fadil had fallen under the spell of this woman…'

'You have been given specific instructions to remain at the training grounds. Your only concern for the present is the Sabr horses.' Rafiq spoke in his soft, icy tone that made everyone shrink back. 'Why have you seen fit to disobey me again?'

Jasim dropped his worry beads. 'Your Highness, my own orders were being disobeyed. My own Head

Groom had the nerve to suggest that I—*I,* the most respected trainer in the whole of Arabia, should pay heed to what that—that woman suggested. To imagine that a woman, that she could think to know better than I! These are my stables. My own Head Groom…'

'My stables, Jasim. My Head Groom, Jasim. You have not answered my question. This is not the first time I have had occasion to speak to you. Why have you seen fit to disobey me?'

The silence which followed was terrifying. Stephanie was afraid to breathe. Only Rafiq seemed unaffected, waiting still as a statue, his eyes hooded, the slight thinning of his mouth betraying his fury.

When Jasim spoke, it was in a broken whisper. 'It will not happen again, Your Highness.'

'No, it will not,' Rafiq said curtly. 'Pack your things. I will have one of my secretaries arrange to pay you what you are owed.'

'Highness! I beg of you—you cannot mean this.' Jasim threw himself to the ground. 'You cannot have thought—the Sabr…'

'Three times, I have warned you. I have granted you considerable leeway because there is no doubt as to your horse-training expertise, but you have gone too far. Now get out, your services are no longer required.'

'Rafiq,' Stephanie said urgently, 'truly, you don't need to take such drastic action on my behalf.'

'I am taking action on my own behalf. Long-overdue action. Now, I had not finished breakfast. You will come back to the palace and share a cup of coffee with me.'

'But...'

'Stephanie, the entire stables are watching us.' Rafiq detached her hand from his. 'You are now in sole charge,' he said to Fadil. 'Miss Darvill?'

'Coffee?' Without waiting for an answer, Rafiq poured Stephanie a cup from the silver pot. It was a fresh pot, he noticed, though he had not ordered one. Which of his servants had observed their return? Which had anticipated that he would return here, to the Courtyard of the Fountain? And who had known to place two cups on the tray where there had been only one before? He took such things for granted. He had only recently started to notice them, truth be told. Stephanie again.

He handed her the coffee, stirring in the sugar which she preferred, and which he loathed. It had not been on the tray earlier, either. 'You asked me once if I had a team of servants dedicated to the lighting and dousing of lamps in the palace.'

She smiled faintly. 'You couldn't answer me.'

'I enquired. It seems I do.'

She put her coffee down on the table under the lemon tree untouched. 'Rafiq, you can't put victory in the Sabr at risk. Jasim is the best trainer in Arabia, there is no doubt of that. Much as it goes against the grain to defend him—you simply can't sack him.'

'It is already done, Stephanie.'

'This is my fault,' she said wretchedly, wringing

her hands. 'I should have informed you that there was likely to be an issue, but you have been so busy. I thought that he would see reason, I didn't think for a moment he would simply go ahead and order...' She shuddered. 'That man. That gun. If I had not been there...'

She was pacing by the fountain. She had lost the scarf which bound her hair back in her scuffle with the stable hand. Her tunic was blue stripes today, the one that reminded him of a blending of the Arabian sea and sky. A week since they had returned from the horse fair, and their glorious morning in the tent. He had missed her terribly.

'Stephanie, come, sit, drink your coffee.'

She sank on to the cushions under the lemon tree beside him. Her hands were shaking as she picked up the delicate little cup. Her cheeks were streaked with tears. 'You can surely find some other way to discipline him,' she said, setting her cup back down. 'You can't risk the Sabr, Rafiq, not now.'

He emptied the dregs of her coffee, refilled the cup and stirred in another spoonful of sugar. She was right, it was a risk, but he could not regret it. He felt—lighter? Yes, he felt lighter. 'I should have rid myself of the man long ago,' he said. 'I knew he would never tolerate you. There is a pattern, after all. If I had acted the first time...'

He took a sip of his own coffee and set his cup down with a weary sigh. 'As you pointed out your-self, he should have realised that we are all on the same side. But he never would acknowledge that. I should have known better. It makes me wonder—but that is pointless.'

'Do you mean Elmira?' Stephanie asked softly.

Rafiq closed his eyes, leaning back against the trunk of the lemon tree. 'Interfering in the smooth running of the stables, that was what he told me she was doing. Then it was undermining it. And finally it progressed to contaminating it. I didn't question him. Now I'll never know.'

'Could you—do you want to tell me about it, Rafiq?'

'No, Stephanie, I don't. Suffice it to say that I am relieved to be rid of the man.'

She smiled at him, and he felt the tension in his shoulders ease, at the same time as her smile set off a different kind of tension. He took her hand, kissing her palm.

She curled her fingers around his, and settled down by his side, resting her head on his shoulder. 'How is your own training progressing?'

He laughed sardonically. 'Painfully. The running changeovers from horse to horse are the most technically difficult element. I seem to spend the greater part of the day sprawled on the ground.'

'Poor Rafiq. Are you terribly bruised?'

'Very.' Her hair tickled his chin. He slid his arm around her waist.

She lifted her head. 'Would you like me to kiss it better?'

'Yes.' He gazed into her big brown eyes. 'Oh, yes.'

She kissed him gently on the lips. 'Where is it painful, Rafiq?'

'Here,' he said, kissing her again, more deeply. 'Definitely here.' She tasted so sweet. He could drown in her kisses. He had been longing for those kisses all week. He ran his fingers through her hair, kissing her eyelids, her salty, tear-stained cheeks, then her mouth again, laying her gently down on the cushions, kissing her again and again. 'I can never have enough of your kisses,' he murmured. 'Never.'

Her fingers were tangling in his hair. 'Where else, Rafiq? Where else do you hurt?'

'Here,' he said, pulling his tunic over his head to bare the bruises on his chest, pulling Stephanie on top of him.

'Oh, poor you.' She kissed him softly, her hands fluttering over the purple-and-yellow bruises. 'Poor you.' More kisses. Her tongue licking over his nipple. His chest was heaving. He was achingly hard. Her touch was soothing and arousing at the same time. More kisses, tracing the curve of his ribcage. Her tongue dipping into his navel. She was setting him on fire. 'Better?'

'Not yet.' He pulled her tunic over her head. Beneath the filmy fabric of her camisole, her nipples were alluring circles. He stroked them, feeling her shudder on top of him. When their lips met again, their kisses were deep, slow, drugging.

On and on and on their kisses went. She was lying on her side. He untied the sash of her pantaloons and slipped his hand inside her. She moaned. He ached for her. When she fumbled with his belt, he yanked it open. Pantaloons and trousers were discarded.

'I want you so much. So much.' Was that his voice?

More kisses. She was so hot and wet and tight. More kisses. 'I want you more than words,' she said in that husky voice that gave him goose bumps.

He lifted her to straddle him. He slid into her so sweetly that he thought he would come instantly. 'Wait. Wait.' Deep breaths. But the sight of her on top of him was too much. 'Stephanie.'

He pushed himself deeper inside her wet, tight, heat. She moaned. He lifted her. She needed little encouragement. Moving on top of him. The *frisson* of her clinging withdrawal, the tightening when she sank on to him, drawing him inside her, arching her back, making him gasp at what it did to him.

She rode him, faster, held him tighter, until the first ripple of her climax set him over the edge, and with a hoarse cry he lifted her free just in time, and spent himself, pulsing, shuddering, shaken.

Afterwards, he reached for her blindly, pulling her close. He could feel her breathing slowing with his own. Only then did he realise how near he had been to losing control completely. What was he doing? What was he thinking?

Rafiq rolled himself free. He picked up his tunic and pulled it over his head. He couldn't look at her. He couldn't risk looking at her. 'I'd better get out to the training grounds,' he said more brusquely than he meant.

'Yes, of course.' He could hear the rustle of her clothing as she dressed.

'Rafiq?'

He turned reluctantly.

'Thank you,' Stephanie said. 'For trusting me. For taking my side again.'

Her lips were swollen with their kisses. He curled his toes inside his riding boots, as if that would stop him crossing the courtyard to wrap her in his arms. 'Jasim gave me no option,' he said.

Her smile became brittle. 'Go and practise, you have a race to win.'

Stephanie tried to go about her business. She thanked Fadil for his courage and support, and discovered to her surprise that with a few notable exceptions, the stable hands were actually relieved by Jasim's dismissal. Their trust in Rafiq's ability to win the Sabr for them with or without Jasim was unquestioning.

She was restless. Her emotions were simmering just below the surface, waiting to erupt. She kept a lid on them by keeping busy. She had no right to be upset by Rafiq's abrupt departure. She would be a fool to read too much into their lovemaking. Simply because it hadn't been planned, because there had been no pretence that this was another experiment in pleasure, did not mean that it was profoundly different.

Unable to find anything in the stable to occupy her, she wandered through the cool of the palace in the heat of the afternoon, using the map which Rafiq had had drawn up for her. So many rooms, some guarded, others not. So many confusingly similar names. The Courtyard of the Princes, for example, which was a simple space containing a plain fountain and nothing else. The Princes' Courtyard, on the other hand, was like the harem, an enclosed suite of rooms which, Aida informed her, had in the distant past been the domain of the unfortunate sons of the reigning Prince's concubines. Here, the poor boys were confined for the duration of their lives, for it was thought too dangerous to allow them to leave the palace, lest they attempt to usurp their father. So legend had it, Aida had said.

Though she tried to hide it, Aida resented the removal of the harem's lock and sentry. In Princess Elmira's day, it would have been unthinkable to expose the future mother of the royal family to the risk of intruders. When Stephanie pointed out that any intruder would first have to pass through the fortress-like walls of the palace, Aida stubbornly refused to accept that it made any difference. The harem was a secure place. She never could understand why Princess Elmira wished to spent so much time at the stables. Though towards the end, the Princess had embraced the sanctuary of the harem as a princess ought.

Stephanie pushed open the door of what, according to her plan, was the Royal Banqueting Hall, only to find herself in yet another courtyard. This one looked abandoned. The water in the fountain was foul and stagnant. Weeds grew up through the cracks in the mosaic floor. The avocado tree had grown so tall that it reached over the courtyard wall. Withered green fruit and brown pits were strewn around its circumference.

Elmira, the Bedouin nomad, had learned to love the harem, according to Aida. Stephanie wasn't convinced. She had heard some of the mystique of the Bedouin for herself at the horse fair. They considered themselves the aristocracy of the desert. Like Rafiq's horses, the ancestry of each tribe could be traced back to a single person. As Rafiq had told her, they had a strict and unique code of conduct, and they prided themselves on being answerable to no one, though willing to co-operate with all, on their own terms. The desert was the Bedouin's heart and soul, freedom to roam the desert defined him. Elmira was a true blue-blooded Bedouin. How could such a woman readily endure the confines of the harem?

Stephanie perched gingerly on the edge of the mossy fountain. The surface of the fetid water was alive with strange little swimming insects.

*'She paid the price for contaminating the stables,'* Jasim had said.

But this morning, Rafiq had been unquestionably on Stephanie's side. Or had he simply been acting to protect his authority? *'I should have rid myself of the man long ago,'* he had said. *'There is a pattern, after all. If I had acted the first time...'*

What price had Elmira been forced to pay? And what crime had she committed that required a price be paid?

Stephanie slapped at one of the swimming insects, which landed on her arm. Its long proboscis had pierced her skin, drawing blood. The bite was already swelling up into a hard lump. She stood up, thinking that she had better find her medical chest and get some ointment, when something else Rafiq had said popped into her head. Something about biting insects and water.

'The stallions' oasis!' Forgetting all about treating her bite, Stephanie ran for the stables.

'Are you sure?' Rafiq looked quite incredulous.

'I know it's difficult to believe, but it's the only explanation,' Stephanie said.

'Biting insects, who hitch a ride in my stallions' manes for the whole journey between the oasis and the stables, and who then leap from the stallion on to the mare which it is covering.'

'That's it exactly.'

'It's—unbelievable.'

'Yes, but, Rafiq, nature…'

He held up his hand. 'I know how wonderful nature is, and how ignorant we are of it. How can you be sure? Why don't the insects bite more of my stallions?'

'I think they probably do, but you see, your stallions are accustomed to them.'

'Accustomed?'

'Immune. In the way that milkmaids are immune to smallpox, because they are regularly exposed to cowpox and somehow this allows their bodies to resist the effects. You see…' She launched into an ex-

planation that was far-reaching and all-encompassing.
Rafiq, seated behind a large desk on the first proper
chair Stephanie had seen since arriving in Arabia,
listened attentively. 'But ultimately,' she concluded,
'I can't prove it, without forcing one of the insects
to bite one of your mares, or a mule, and even in the
name of science, I couldn't bring myself to do that.'

'So what do you propose we do?'

She smiled at him. He smiled back. He was still
dressed in the clothes he wore to the training ground.
His white shirt was dusty, open at the throat to re-
veal a smattering of hair. His chin had the bluish
shadow of the day's growth. This morning, when he
kissed her, he had been freshly shaven. His tunic had
smelled of lemons.

'I am asking my Royal Horse Surgeon a question.'

She got the message. 'The insects thrive in stagnant water,' Stephanie said briskly. 'I found the larvae in several pools at the stallions' enclosure. They
do not seem to like the fresh water of the oasis itself.
I suggest that we have the pools cleaned and drained,
all traces of the larvae removed, and that we continue
in the meantime to keep the stallions separate. Now,
if that is all…'

'Stephanie.'

'There is something else?'

He got up from his chair and crossed the room towards her. 'If you are correct, you might have stumbled on a significant scientific breakthrough.'

'I hadn't thought of it in those terms.'

'Then you should. You should write it up in a

paper. Present it to the Royal Society in London, which is so famous.'

'I don't think that Sir Joseph Banks—he is the President—I don't think he'd accept a paper from a woman.'

'Not even a woman of genius?'

She wished he wouldn't smile at her like that. She wished she could remember that he was a prince. 'I'm not a genius. It was simply a matter of observation and deduction.'

'As modest as ever, Stephanie. I think you are a genius. Congratulations. And thank you. I owe you a great deal.'

'You owe me nothing but the recompense you promised me, Rafiq.'

He grimaced, taking her reminder to herself as a reprimand directed at him. 'Forgive me. I find it increasingly difficult to remember—to distinguish between my Royal Horse Surgeon and Stephanie. If I appear—after this morning, you understand, I am merely attempting to remind myself of the rules of engagement.'

'There is no need to concern yourself, Rafiq. I am perfectly well aware of the rules, nor am I under any illusions. No one cares if a man goes to his marriage bed innocent, but every man wants to wed a virgin, and for a prince it is a necessity. You could not marry me even had I a pedigree to rival one of your thoroughbreds. Not even if you fell wildly, passionately in love with me.'

'Stephanie…'

She blushed violently. 'Not that I am suggesting for a moment that my thoughts have inclined in such a direction. Either direction. Any direction. I merely wished to reassure you that they had not.'

'Stephanie…'

'Excuse me. If you accept my strategy, I have a huge amount of work to organise.'

She fled, slamming the door behind her and running, careless of her destination, along a maze of corridors. Finally, panting, she found herself in the Hall of Campaign, and headed for the Pool of Nymphs. Tempting as it was to throw herself in, she had never been a fan of histrionics, so contented herself with rolling up her pantaloons and dipping her feet and her hands in the cooling water. The bite which was the inspiration for her breakthrough throbbed beneath the dressing which covered it. She would put more ointment on it tonight. Perhaps she ought to capture it on paper, like—like Archimedes' bath. If she could draw. Which she couldn't. No, what she would do instead was draft a paper for Papa to present to the Royal Society. Papa would be wildly proud of her discovery, and he would need some persuading to present her work as his own, but when he realised that if he did not it would not see the light of day—yes, he would do it, and that would be her gift to him to make up for all the pain her downfall had caused him.

This very satisfying idea distracted her for a few moments, and her plans for the morning distracted her for a few moments more. She must make a list of all that was to be done to make the stallions' paddock safe, and then…

A dry sob seized her. Stephanie dropped her head on to her hands. What a fool she was! The unavoidable truth which she had been steadfastly refusing to face all day could no longer be denied. Despite every check and balance she had put in place, she had fallen in love with Rafiq. What an absolute fool she was.

Leaning back on the tiles, Stephanie gazed up at the desert sky. The sun had set, but the moon had not yet made an appearance. The air felt sultry, as if it might be contemplating rain. It had not rained since she arrived here more than six weeks ago. And she was procrastinating.

She loved him so much, and it was so very different from the last time as to be futile to attempt a comparison. It was Rafiq's absurdly handsome face that had attracted her, but it was the man she had fallen in love with. She loved him because he respected her, and because despite the fact that he was a prince, he tried to treat her as an equal. He did not shy away from pointing out her faults, but he never failed to recognise her achievements. She loved him because he listened to her, and because he understood what she meant, even when it wasn't what she actually said. She loved him because he wasn't just playing the Prince, but because he was a prince in the true sense of the word, an honourable man who wanted what was best for his people. She loved him because he put those people first, even when his instincts were to act otherwise. And she loved him for the way he agonised over that fateful choice, even though his agonising pained her.

This morning had been magical. It had been magical, because she was in love. The fierce attraction which had drawn them together from the moment they met might be nothing more than that for Rafiq, but for Stephanie—oh, what a fool she was not to have noticed the way it had subtly changed, from physical experimentation, to powerful mutual pleasure, to a communion of their bodies, to an expression of her love. Because that's what it had been this morning.

Thank goodness Rafiq had not guessed. She would have to make very sure that he continued oblivious, because love didn't change a single thing between them. She wasn't that much of an idiot. Pushing herself upright, she shook her feet dry. She was a silly fool, but no one need ever know. In a few months' time she would return to England and get on with her new life.

Beneath her bandage, the insect bite itched. Stephanie stopped short in the act of scratching it. She had found the cause of the sickness. The terms of her appointment were for six months, but she had found a cure. The cure was prevention. Her work here was, in theory, over.

Her stomach lurched. It was too soon. Far too soon. She was not ready to return to England yet. Besides, there was still work to do. Until it was done, she refused to think about it.

# Chapter Eleven

'What happened?'

Stephanie quickly scrubbed at her eyes with her sleeve. 'Rafiq. I'm so sorry.'

'Sherifa.'

He stood transfixed. The mare was still on her feet, but only just. Her beautiful glossy grey coat was matted with sweat. Her flanks were quivering, her nose was streaming, and her cough had that unmistakable harsh, hacking sound. 'It started about four hours ago,' Stephanie said. 'I've been with her ever since. I sent for you immediately, but…'

'I was otherwise engaged. How bad is it?'

'Bad,' Stephanie said, unable to prevent her voice from wobbling. 'We have to keep her standing. I have been trying to keep her cool, keep her nose clear, but her heart is racing, and she is struggling to breathe. It is—it is bad, Rafiq. I am so sorry.'

'It's not your fault. Your theory— It was always— Well, now we have the proof, unfortunately, that you must have been wrong.'

'No.' She mustn't cry. She mustn't wallow in self-pity. 'I'm afraid that Sherifa is proof that my theory was sound. You see, I— When I went out to the stallions' oasis, I…' She caught herself on a sob. 'I took Sherifa, Rafiq. I rode Sherifa out to the oasis. I didn't take her into the paddock, I left her tethered outside, but she was there. And those biting flies—when I was collecting samples, it is mostly likely that one of them landed on me, then transferred to Sherifa and— and you see there is no other explanation. It was six days ago, well within the boundaries of the usual incubation period. Sherifa is my proof, and if she dies, I will never, ever forgive myself. I am so very sorry.'

Her tears had begun again in earnest, but she ignored them. 'We have to keep her on her feet Rafiq, and though Fadil is desperate to help, he has not your skills. Do you think…?'

'Anything. Just tell me what to do. Anything.'

He went to the mare's head and began to murmur to her. The slow, hypnotic tone calmed her, allowing Stephanie to cool the sick beast, but she was under no illusions. The sickness was affecting Sherifa to a far greater degree than it had Batal.

Through her tears she worked tirelessly, cooling, checking, decongesting the mare in a strict, endless sequence. She had seen Rafiq in passing over the last few days, but they had been like ships in the night. His training was relentless, her work at the stables exhausting. That the first time they were together since she admitted to herself that she loved him should be under such tragic circumstances was too awful to contemplate. Yet here they were together, with his dead wife's precious mare fighting for survival, and if she died it was Stephanie's fault.

She picked up the empty wooden bucket to fetch more cold water, but Rafiq took it from her. 'I will do it. Sherifa is calm for the moment. You need to calm yourself, Stephanie, or you will be of no use to either of us.'

'It's my fault. If I had thought for a moment…'

'You have proved beyond doubt the source of the disease. Even if we lose Sherifa, it means we won't lose any others.'

'But we can't lose Sherifa. I know how much she means to you.'

He did not deny it. Stephanie wanted to throw herself at his feet and beg forgiveness, but that was hardly constructive. By the time Rafiq returned with fresh water, she had herself under control. 'Thank you. If you can persuade her to drink a little, that would be very helpful, but the main thing is to…'

'…keep her on her feet.' Rafiq's smile was ghostly.

'Exactly. And tell her that she's going to make it,' Stephanie said firmly, 'because I'm determined not to lose her.'

Stephanie worked with a grim resolve which seemed to increase the more the mare visibly weakened and Rafiq's confidence fell. Though he kept up his murmuring, he was losing faith fast, and in the early hours of dawn, when Sherifa fell to her knees, despair set in. 'We are losing her.'

'No.' They got her back up, thanks mostly to Stephanie's sheer effort of will. 'I'm sorry,' she whispered to the mare, 'but it's not time for you to join your mistress just yet.'

He tried to block them out, but the memories took hold as he and Stephanie fought what seemed to be a losing battle to keep Sherifa alive.

Elmira putting Sherifa through her repertoire of tricks the night of the feast to celebrate the signing of the marriage contract.

Elmira riding Sherifa through the gates of the palace ahead of the train of stallions on their wedding day.

Elmira's tears of joy when Sherifa gave birth to her first foal.

Elmira's tears of sadness when Jasim took the foal away. Far too early, Elmira claimed. It had been early, but Rafiq had been reluctant to intercede on her behalf. The foal was a fine stallion now, one of their Sabr racing string, in fact.

Sherifa's knees buckled again, and once again Stephanie refused to allow her to fall. 'Shouldn't we—isn't it cruel to prolong her suffering?' Rafiq asked, his voice cracked.

'I am prolonging her life. Don't give up on her, Rafiq. Please don't give up.'

He had given up on Elmira. He wouldn't give up on her mare. 'Come on, Sherifa,' Rafiq muttered, in the language he had learnt as a child, in the language that Elmira had always spoken to her beloved mare. 'Your mistress would want you to show your true Arabian spirit.'

The hours passed in a daze. At times he could sense Elmira's ghost watching him, alternatively accusing him and pleading with him. If Sherifa died, it would be a damning judgement on him. He wasn't sure he could endure it. Would he still have the heart to enter the Sabr, far less win it?

'Rafiq.' A gentle hand on his shoulder roused him. Daylight streamed through the high window. He blinked. Silence. No wheezing. 'Is she…?'

'See for yourself.' Stephanie's smile was strained. 'A miracle,' she said.

Rafiq rubbed his eyes. Not a miracle, but an exhausted horse with a soaking wet coat and a streaming nose settling down for a long-overdue sleep. 'Sherifa.' Rafiq scrabbled to his feet. The mare tossed her head and attempted a wheezy whinny.

'She's made it. I'm not sure if she'll ever be fit for breeding again, but…'

'She's alive.' Rafiq ran his fingers along the horse's back. 'You saved her.'

'We saved her,' Stephanie said.

He caught her to him, hugging her tightly, burying his head in her hair. 'Thank you. You can have no idea how much this means.'

'I do.'

'No, you don't.' He staggered. The stable floor began to tip and tilt. 'I killed her, Stephanie.' His legs wouldn't hold him any longer. He slid down on to the floor, dropping his head on to his hands. 'I killed Elmira.'

'Rafiq!' Stephanie wrapped her arms around him. 'Rafiq, you are overwrought. You don't know what you are saying. Elmira died in her sleep. Aida told me.'

He was so tempted to agree. He was so tired. But it was said now, there was no taking it back. He lifted his head. 'Aida told you what everyone believes. Only I know the truth.'

He felt light-headed and heavy-witted at the same time. Elmira, Sherifa and Stephanie had become confused in his fevered dreams, he remembered that. Looking at Stephanie now, dark shadows under her eyes, her hair lank, her skin sallow, her tunic stained, he felt something inside him stir. An odd feeling. He didn't know what it was. He was too exhausted to work out what it was.

'I thought she was here,' he said. 'Elmira. She was a permanent presence here, in the stables, in the early days of our marriage. Haunted them,' he added with a dry laugh. 'That's what Jasim said. She certainly does now.'

'You didn't kill her. You're not capable of killing her. I know you, Rafiq.'

'You didn't know me then, Stephanie. I was obsessed.'

'You told me that. And I told you…'

'…that my marriage made perfect royal sense. I remember. It's no excuse. Though Elmira was happy at first, would have remained happy if I had been the husband I should have been. But even on our marriage day, I was more interested in the bloodstock that was her dowry, than my wife. I put her in the harem, I ensured she had all the clothes and jewels she desired, and I—I left her there. I visited, because it was my duty to visit for the sake of an heir, but I didn't visit often, and I made no effort to get to know her. Elmira was my wife, but she was a stranger to me, Stephanie.'

He slid a glance at her. She didn't like what she was hearing. Not surprising. She was trying to disguise it, but subterfuge was one of the few things at which Stephanie did not succeed. 'Her only pleasure was the stables, the horses, Sherifa. But not only Sherifa. She had a way with horses. She could charm them, much better than I could. She didn't like Jasim. She thought his methods harsh. She said he didn't love them. You and Elmira—you would have agreed on that. You would have probably—you'd probably have liked each other. If I had taken the time, I'd have liked her. But I didn't take the time.'

His head ached. His vision was slightly blurred. He narrowed his eyes. 'Stephanie?'

She touched his hand. Only fleetingly, but he knew it was her. 'Did you take a fall yesterday during training?' she asked.

'Never a day goes by without me taking a fall.'

'I think you are mildly concussed. Look into my eyes.'

'You won't like what you see.'

'Rafiq, I think…'

'She tried to talk to me, you know. She tried to tell

me that she was lonely, but I didn't listen. Perhaps she wasn't persistent enough or vehement enough. No, that's no excuse. I didn't listen to Elmira, but I did listen to Jasim. He told me she was interfering with the running of the stables. I asked her not to. He told me she was still interfering. She wanted to help with the training, she said. Impossible. Jasim would never permit it. I told her that she had to keep out of his way. She said she would, but she didn't. I thought it was because—Bedouins, horses, I thought it was that. Perhaps it was. Perhaps it was all Jasim's lies. Look what he did to you. I should have recognised it as a pattern, but I didn't.'

'You did, Rafiq. This time, you did. And you acted.'

'Too late for Elmira.' He closed his eyes. Darkness hovered. The floor beneath him shifted, like the deck of a ship at sea. He opened his eyes. 'I took his side. He told you that. He didn't tell you what he told me though, that Elmira had betrayed me with her groom. I didn't believe it, not at first. I confronted her and she didn't deny that she enjoyed his company, the attention. She said it was my fault for neglecting her. She said that she was lonely. She said that she only ever felt alive when she went out riding. And I told her she was forbidden to go out ever again.'

'What about the man?'

'Jasim sent him packing immediately. I didn't question that. It was the right thing to do. I could hardly have questioned the man myself, for if he confirmed it, I would have been forced to divorce Elmira.'

Rafiq grabbed Stephanie's wrist. 'Ever since I told you half the story, in the tent, it's been worse, not better. She's taken up residence here,' he said, touching his forehead. 'So now I have to tell you all of it, do you understand?'

She shook her head. 'I think you need to rest, Rafiq.'

'Soon. When I am done unburdening myself. I told myself I was protecting her honour by confining her to the harem, but I see now, I was actually protecting my own interests. I didn't want to send her back to her family. I needed her dowry, Stephanie.'

'She was unfaithful to you.'

'Was she? Her flirtation may have been quite innocent. It doesn't matter whether she was unfaithful or indiscreet or both. She was truly miserable, and it was my fault. My fault that she took solace in another man's company—whatever form that took. My fault that she withered away in the harem quite alone, a nomad confined within four walls, unable to protest because I didn't visit her, and because I didn't visit her, I didn't notice. I didn't see her interest in life itself ebb away, and I didn't notice when she eventually decided it was not worth living.'

Stephanie paled. Her hands fluttered to her breast. 'She took her own life?'

He was feeling nauseous. 'Poison. A powerful sleeping draught of some sort. I found her lying here with Sherifa, who was expecting a foal.'

'But Aida said that she died in her sleep.'

'She did. I tried, for what seemed like hours to rouse her, but to no avail, and so I took her body back to the harem.'

'Does Aida know what happened?'

'No, Elmira must have drugged Aida and the guard. The other maidservants slept apart. Aida discovered Elmira dead in her bed when she went to summon her for breakfast. The guard—well, it wasn't in the interests of a guard to admit to being asleep on duty.'

'You protected her honour, even in death.'

'I did little else for her in life. Elmira lost her life in the pursuit of the Sabr. I have to win it back for her. It's the only way.'

'Atonement,' Stephanie said.

'If I don't, she will always be here, haunting my every step.' His voice cracked. His chest heaved. A sob racked his body. He tried to struggle to his feet, ashamed, appalled, desperate to get away before his emotions overwhelmed him completely but Stephanie wrapped her arms around him, holding him tight, refusing to let him go.

She held him until he stopped struggling. Then she held him as he surrendered to the racking dry sobs that were the result of two years of pent-up emotion. Then she held him as he slept where he lay, utterly exhausted, stroking his hair from his brow, listening to his breathing become even, deep, as he settled his head on her lap. She held him for hours, easing herself gently away only to check on the sleeping mare, and then returning to Rafiq, holding him, stroking him, her heart aching with love for him.

Stephanie did not sleep. She replayed his tortured words over and over in her head. She couldn't reconcile the picture he painted of himself with the man she knew. He had not loved Elmira, but to hear him describe, from his own lips, his callous disregard for her, was shocking. Yet her own love for him was undaunted, undented.

She so desperately wanted to help him. Her sordid little story could not compare to his tragedy, but she had learned a great deal here in Arabia about leaving the shadows of the past behind. If there was any way she could use that newfound knowledge to help Rafiq then she would. Nothing could change what had happened, but there had to be a way to make him see that his past had shaped him into the man of honour he was today.

Rafiq slept deeply. He awoke slowly. His eyelids flickered, then opened. He gave a dazed smile when he saw Stephanie, then a tiny shake of his head, and then a firming of his mouth, and he jerked himself upright as he remembered.

'How long have I been asleep?'

'A few hours.'

'Sherifa?'

'She's fine, she's been sleeping too.'

His throat was working. He was horribly embarrassed, struggling to look at her in the dim light of the stall, shaded from the sun by the shutters. 'You saved her. I am extremely grateful. I fear I was a little—you must excuse my...'

She caught his hand as he made to get up and leave. 'Please don't go.'

She wanted to tell him that she loved him, but those three little words were guaranteed to send him running as surely as her assuring him even princes were allowed to cry. 'I want to talk to you, Rafiq,' Stephanie said, striving for calm. 'I want you to consider what will happen if you don't win the Sabr.'

'It's unthinkable.'

'But it's a possibility you can't afford to ignore,' she said earnestly. 'I understand why it's important to your people. You promised them a victory and you are a man who honours his promises. I understand that it's important to you, to restore your father's honour, and to win in Elmira's honour too. But you believe it's more than that, don't you? You believe that winning the Sabr will somehow rid you of all this terrible guilt you bear for Elmira's death and I am afraid...'

She caught herself on a sob. She must remain calm. 'I am so afraid, Rafiq, that you are wrong, and I can't bear to think of you suffering for another year, another, another, until you win—if you win. You have pinned all your hopes on this race, you are living your life in limbo until you win, but you don't have to.'

'What do you mean by that?'

'Nothing can change what happened in the past, Rafiq, but you can stop it ruling your life.'

'I fail to see how,' he said heavily, 'but I'm willing to listen.'

Stephanie laced her fingers together, frowning down at them. 'I admit, I was shocked by what you told me. There is no denying that you neglected Elmira, that you contributed to making her very unhappy, but what you haven't taken account of is her role in this.'

'Stephanie, you know I only married her for her dowry.'

'You married her to make good on the pledge you made to your people, and to heal the rift your father had made. You put your kingdom first when you made that marriage, not yourself.'

'And I put Elmira last, Stephanie.'

'Why did she marry you?'

He looked confused. 'It was her father's wish.'

'But if she hadn't wanted to marry you, could she have refused?'

Frowning, he picked up a piece of straw and knotted it. 'Salim has several daughters. If Elmira had been against the match, then I expect one of her sisters would have taken her place.'

'So she wanted to marry you? And she knew what that entailed—the harem, the life that she would lead, it was not a shock to her?'

'No, of course not. It was one of the few things we did discuss before the contract was signed. I know how the Bedouin are, I know how much they value their freedom, it was why I agreed that Elmira could take her horse out into the desert every day, provided she also took an escort.' He stared down at the knotted straw, his frown deepening. 'I had forgotten that.'

'So Elmira knew the risk she was taking if she abused that freedom?'

'But was she abusing it?'

'If she had been completely innocent, don't you think she would have said so, Rafiq? She had far too much to lose.'

'She was lonely, and that was my fault.'

'Elmira was a grown woman with a mind of her own. Did she tell you how lonely she was? Did she tell you she was unhappy?'

'Stephanie, most women don't have the courage to speak their minds as you do. Besides, that's not the point. I was her husband. I was responsible for her. I should have been aware of her unhappiness.'

'Yes, you should have, but she should have spoken to you. You take too much of the blame on yourself.' Stephanie took a deep breath. 'It is the same with her death.'

He flinched. 'It's true, I did not administer the sleeping draught, but...'

'You assume that Elmira took her own life because she was lonely, because she was effectively a prisoner in the harem, because you made her unhappy, but you don't actually know for sure, do you?' Stephanie laced her hands more tightly together. She couldn't risk crying. She couldn't risk any emotion. Beside her, Rafiq was distractedly tying another knot in another piece of straw. 'If you had had any idea how desperate she was...'

'How could I? I never visited her.'

'And she never asked for you. Did she speak to Aida?'

'No.' He cast the straw aside. 'No. I couldn't ask her directly without betraying Elmira but—no.'

'It's my impression too, that Aida thought her content. Whatever drove Elmira to take such extreme action, she was determined to keep it to herself. It is one of the most tragic aspects of her death that the act which she saw as putting an end to her suffering made you suffer so much.'

'I deserve to suffer.'

Was she imagining it, or did he sound less convinced? 'Do you think that Elmira wished you to feel so guilty?' Stephanie asked. 'She went to great pains to escape the harem that night, drugging Aida and the guard.'

'She wanted to be with Sherifa.'

'Of course, but do you think it's possible that she also wanted to make someone other than you feel guilty?'

'I don't know what you— You mean Jasim?' Rafiq looked as if he had taken another blow to the head. *'Jasim?'*

'It is Jasim who stopped Elmira going to the stables. Jasim who accused her of interfering. Jasim who accused her of having an affair. Jasim who sacked the man who, if he was not her lover, was at very least her closest friend. You cannot know what was lies and what was malice, but Elmira knew. And Elmira chose to die in the stables.'

'Stephanie, it is too much. I don't—I can't...'

'Grant me a few more moments, please?' She waited for his nod. 'Elmira took her own life, Rafiq, and whatever her reasons, the act itself was hers, not yours. What you did do afterwards was protect her honour and that of her family as you had when she was indiscreet. No one knows that she died by her own hand. You have borne all the guilt of that, spared her family that scandal. And you spared them the shame of a divorce too.'

'Because I wanted to keep the horses.'

'Do you think Elmira would have been happier, returned to her family a divorced woman, than she was confined to your harem?' Stephanie touched his arm gently. 'I know, an impossible question, but you must think about it. Much more importantly, what you need to think about is how much this tragedy has changed you. The man I know, the honourable, caring, thoughtful man sitting beside me, is not the man who married Elmira. When you marry again—' She broke off, blinking furiously. She couldn't fall at this last hurdle. 'When you marry again, you will be a very different husband. You may even encourage your wife to be honest with you, for you will need someone to do so when I am gone.'

'Stephanie, you are unique.'

'No. I am simply the first of my kind you have encountered. Given a little encouragement, you will find that most women will speak their minds as I do.'

He took her hands, unlacing her fingers carefully

before kissing her fingertips. 'Speaking your mind, as you have done, takes a great deal of courage.'

'I want you to be happy, Rafiq. You deserve to be happy.'

He kissed her hand again. 'I will settle for making my peace.'

'Don't settle for that,' Stephanie said fiercely. 'You deserve more than that.'

He sighed. 'You have given me a great deal to think about. I need time—I have no idea—I need time.'

'Of course you do. But please, Rafiq, you will reflect on what I have said?'

He got to his feet, pulling her with him. 'I promise.' He kissed her softly. 'Thank you.'

*Two weeks later*

The training paddock was north of the palace, a large natural arena in the valley created by a huge red rock in the shape of a horseshoe. The hard-packed sand was an ideal surface for the racehorses, although the Sabr team were also taken out to train on the course, in order to acclimatise them to the different terrains. When Stephanie had pointed out that this must give the home team an advantage, Fadil had been insulted, informing her that any team from any kingdom was welcome to use the course.

At the far end of the grounds, in the shelter of the rock at the top of the horseshoe, were the stable buildings and temporary accommodation. She dismounted near the entrance to the arena, tethering Sherifa in the shade and fetching her a bucket of water. This was the mare's first outing since her sickness, and though it was a short ride, Stephanie was taking no chances.

Rafiq had invited her to come today to watch the training. She had seen very little of him since his confession. Though she was desperate to know whether her heartfelt arguments had changed his thinking, she was determined to give him the time he had asked for.

There was no sign of him. Two horses were being schooled over high hurdles in the centre of the arena. Three yearlings were being put through their paces on the course over at the far end. There were five or six more in a pen nearby, with a mule companion.

Out on the course, four horses were being brought out. Each had a rope bridle and reins but no saddle. Three mares and one stallion, and all were very frisky, their handlers struggling to hold them. Rafiq emerged from the stable building, and Stephanie's heart leapt. He was dressed in his usual riding clothes: leather breeches, long boots, white shirt. He scanned the arena, and when he spotted Stephanie with Sherifa, he smiled and waved, and her heart leapt again.

There followed an intense discussion between the men which she could not hear, presumably over the order in which Rafiq would ride. She knew from Fadil that this was one of the trickiest decisions on the day, particularly if the race was close. It was not uncommon for a horse to bolt without his rider, or for a horse to refuse to stop for the change. Riding bareback without stirrups made it even more of a challenge for the jockey to control a runaway or a rearing horse. Fadil had recounted many instances of what sounded to Stephanie terrible injuries, with some relish. Seeing her horror, he had been hasty to reassure her that the horses were rarely hurt. It didn't occur to him that she would be far more concerned about Rafiq than his thoroughbreds. But that was most likely because it didn't seem to occur to a single one of Bharym's people that their Prince could do anything other than triumph.

The order was decided. Rafiq leapt on to the back of the first horse, an impressive feat in itself, for the black mare was refusing to stand still. Stephanie watched, her heart in her mouth, as he set off around the circuit of the track. The yearlings had been returned to their pen. A storm of dust and sand blew up as Rafiq galloped at full tilt, sitting forward and straight on the mare, his body swaying easily with the horse. He made it look effortless. Stephanie knew, because she had tried it only the other day, that it was incredibly difficult.

He was approaching the change now. The other three horses were fidgety. The change horse was being led out. The handler for the current horse was crouched, ready to dash forward. A thundering of hooves. Surely Rafiq would slow down. He did, but only yards before the change. Stephanie watched through her fingers as he leaned forward on to the neck of the horse, pulling on the reins to slow her, then throwing one leg over, hovering half on, half off, as the change horse was brought up, then sliding to the ground, running without breaking stride, and leaping on to the fresh horse as if he had springs on his heels, then he was off again at a gallop.

It all happened so fast. The other three horses, one panting, two fresh, were straining at their halters. The next change went more slowly, Rafiq's fresh horse rearing up before thundering into a gallop. At the third change, his foot slipped on the sand, but by a miracle or superb muscle control, he managed to regain his balance.

The fourth change was to the stallion. Stephanie's jaw was clenched as she watched him bucking and tossing his head. He was much bigger and considerably more powerful than the mares. A higher leap would be needed to mount him, more strength to control him, and he had a vicious temper too, by the looks of it. But the change was safely made. The last circuit was complete. Rafiq was reining in when the stallion took umbrage and reared. Stephanie held her breath as man and horse fought for supremacy. She exhaled as the stallion was brought under control. And she screamed when he bucked, hurtling Rafiq on to the ground.

By the time she reached him, he had picked himself up and was dusting himself down. 'Are you hurt?'

He grinned. 'No more than usual. You brought Sherifa. She is the dam of Lameh, the beast who threw me. He is the fastest horse in the team, but he does not like to be mastered. I am glad you came.'

'I am glad you asked me.'

He ushered her over to the shade, where they sat

down together behind a rock, not wholly hidden from the arena, but sufficiently out of view to afford them some privacy. 'Four weeks until the Sabr, and my changeovers are still not slick enough. I started training too late.'

'Fadil has been telling me all sorts of horror stories about the race. I had no idea it was so dangerous.'

'It's only dangerous if you don't know your horses. Ours are in excellent fettle. I think we have a good chance of winning.'

'Only a good chance?'

He smiled. 'An excellent chance, but as you have pointed out, there are no guarantees. It is a long race. So much can go wrong. All it takes is one lame horse. You see, I do listen, Stephanie.' He leaned back on his hands, stretching his legs out in front of him. 'I hadn't allowed myself to consider the possibility of losing. I was so set on winning, so focused on that one goal that I wasn't thinking rationally at all. Unlike my Royal Horse Surgeon.'

Stephanie blushed. Rafiq smiled at her again. 'You see, I have also learned how to pay you the kind of compliments you like. You want to know if your rational thinking has had any effect.'

Stephanie nodded. He seemed different, but that didn't mean...

Rafiq leaned over to kiss her cheek. 'It has. It has taken me a great deal of time and effort—two years' worth of guilt is a lot to come to terms with, but I think I finally have.'

He sat up, crossing his legs. 'When Elmira died, I

came very close to giving up. I wouldn't have taken such dramatic action as my father did, but I would have sold the horses, closed the stud. But then it would have been futile—my marriage, her death— and so I vowed to win the Sabr for Elmira. I still want to race in her honour, but I see now, thanks to you, that winning would not assuage my guilt. It is all I can do to atone, but it won't actually make me feel any better about what I did. It took you, and your very impressive brain to point that out. Clever Stephanie.'

'It is merely that I have had some experience myself, at coming to terms with my mistakes, Rafiq.'

'And now I'm benefitting from what you have learned. I am very fortunate.' He kissed her again, this time on the lips. 'I will never know what drove Elmira to such a terrible act. I wish with all my heart that she had not, but I do see now that it was her act, not mine. I cannot in all honesty say that I don't feel guilty, because guilt defies logic, but I believe it will fade. And in your own words, much more importantly, I have changed. Not only because of that dark time, but more recently because of you.'

She was blushing again. 'You mean you know now that there are some things a woman can do every bit as well as a man, such as tend to horses.'

'You *have* made me realise that my thinking has been very traditional, but that's not what I meant. Your refusal to grant me the deference I deserve,' he said wryly, 'has made me see how much I have taken for granted. Your description of my palace, a place for everyone, and a guard to keep everyone in their place, it shocked me, but what shocked me even more was the discovery that I do the same with my life.'

Their lips met and lingered. Her eyes drifted closed, as his tongue traced the line of her lower lip. When they broke apart, when she opened her eyes, sunspots dazzled her. 'Rafiq, I...'

'I want you too,' he said, misunderstanding her meaning, saving her from a most ill-judged declaration. 'I want you so much, but I'm afraid I'm going to have to remain here for the next four weeks, until the Sabr. It is vitally important that I dedicate the little time I have to doing all I can to obtain that victory. So I'm going to be living out here with my team until the race. You understand?'

'Of course I do.' Afraid that her feelings would show, Stephanie got up, shaking out her tunic, picking up her headdress. 'I will see you at the starting post on the day of the race.'

## Chapter Twelve

*Four weeks later*

The race, as tradition dictated, started as dawn broke. In this centenary year, a record twenty-five teams had entered. By the time Stephanie arrived at the starting post, the crowd was enormous and in high spirits. Children screamed and shouted, men called to one another, women gossiped behind their hands. Each rider wore their traditional colours, and the spectators showed their allegiance by sporting that colour too. Bharym's flag was emerald-green with a white band. Stephanie's tunic and headdress were emerald-green, her cloak and the scarf which tied her keffiyeh were white. The same colours worn by the vast majority of the spectators. The whole kingdom of Bharym seemed to have turned out to watch.

Fadil ushered her through to the enclosure, where the starting horses were held. The air here was thick with dust from pawing hooves, redolent of horse and sweat, the atmosphere tense. Rafiq was consulting with his team of handlers, but when he saw Stephanie he fought through the crowd to join her, and Fadil discreetly left them alone, joining the Bharym team.

'I'm glad to see you have made your allegiance clear. Nailed your colours to the mast, so to speak,' he said with a smile.

Like hers, his tunic and headdress were green, the *keffiyeh* band white, though he wore his usual riding breeches. She was on edge, seeing him for the first time in four weeks. He had lost weight and developed muscle. He was even more ridiculously handsome than ever. 'I didn't know there would be so many competitors,' she said inanely. 'I didn't know it would be so—there can't be a soul left in the city.'

'There will be more crowds at each of the staging posts.'

'Are you nervous?'

He shook his head. 'Our horses are already highly strung. It is better for them, and for me, if I remain calm.'

'You're going to win, Rafiq. I know you are.'

He grinned. 'Even though you've been at great pains to point out that I might not?'

'Hush! Don't let anyone hear you suggest such a thing. You're going to win. I am certain of it.'

His face became serious. 'So am I.' One of his team was calling to him. 'The race is about to start. Tomorrow will be a day of celebration if we win, most likely a day of mourning if we lose, but whichever,

I intend to absent myself as soon as I possibly can. We can celebrate or commiserate in our own way. Together. Alone. If you wish?'

'Oh, I do wish, Rafiq, very much.'

'Wish me something else, wish me luck.'

She wanted to kiss him, but it was impossible. The eyes of everyone around them were watching. 'You don't need it, but good luck anyway. I will be waiting here at the finishing line tomorrow.'

He pressed her hand, under cover of her cloak, then he left her. The crowd parted for him, cheering and shouting their support and encouragement. Fadil appeared at Stephanie's side, guiding her over to the enclosure, to a privileged space where the starting line could be clearly viewed. A ladder was placed against the Sabr tower, and the crowd grew silent as they watched the man bearing the starting flag climb to the top, the tension sharp as a blade. On the starting line, twenty-five horses pranced and strained, their handlers keeping them on a tight rein, beside them stood the riders, waiting nervously.

Rafiq was in the middle of the line, which was ordered according to the results of last year's Sabr, with the outer positions given to the highest placed, the middle occupied by those who didn't finish or didn't run. The worst place to start because of all the jockeying for position, the bumping and boring, but Rafiq would claim no home advantage, as host. He fixed his headdress over his face as the starter reached the top of the tower. All eyes were on the flag raised high in the sky, Bharym's royal insignia fluttering in the light breeze, and then the flag was dropped, the Sabr began, and the crowd erupted as the horses galloped into the desert a cloud of dust.

It would be at around ten hours before Rafiq completed his first lap of a hundred miles around the stamina-sapping desert course, all being well. Though most of the spectators had brought supplies and seemed set to settle down where they were for the duration, Stephanie rode back to the stables. It was unnaturally quiet, with only one guard on duty. She entered the little room which had become her office, opened her instrument case, closed it again. It was stiflingly hot today. The Sabr riders would need to have a care their horses didn't overheat. The laps would have to be run at a measured pace.

Quitting her office, Stephanie wandered aimlessly past the stalls, stopping to feed Sherifa some dates before heading back to the palace and the empty, unlocked harem. How long since she had discovered the source of the sickness? Seven, no, eight weeks. Eight weeks, since she had found that deserted courtyard and the stagnant fountain. Eight weeks since she and Rafiq had made love. Eight weeks since she had realised that she was in love with him.

Tomorrow she and Rafiq would make love again. For the first time she would make love with the man she loved in the knowledge that she was in love. A love that must remain undeclared. The dull sensation which had been following her around all day began to crystallise into an inescapable conclusion.

One she didn't want to acknowledge. She wandered out to her courtyard, dipped her feet in the cool waters of the fountain. It really was stifling. She really didn't want to face up to where her thoughts were taking her.

But in the still of the late morning, in the still of the palace, it would not be ignored. Her work here in Bharym was done. These last four weeks, while Rafiq had been training, she had been waiting. As she carried out her diminishing duties, the time had lagged, stretched, stood still, yet all she could do was wait. Now the waiting was over. Tomorrow she and Rafiq would make love. And then she would leave.

There it was, the image she didn't want to conjure, Bharym and Rafiq disappearing into the distance as she rode away, heading back to England, to a future which should be bright and gleaming, but which had lost its lustre, for it was bereft of love. She could remain here another week, another month, another three, but to what purpose? Her work was done. Her future was hers to claim. And Rafiq's own, very different future awaited him. A bright one free from guilt. Yes, there was satisfaction to be had in knowing she had helped him open the door to the possibility of happiness. A great deal of satisfaction. And there would be satisfaction too, in making the success of her own life she was determined to achieve, and in repaying Papa with his Royal Society paper

on insect-borne infection. She would find content-
ment, once she had recovered from the heartache of
leaving. But she had the long journey from Arabia to
England in which to do that.

The decision was made. The deed would be done.
Telling herself firmly that there was no time to be
wasted on tears or regrets now, Stephanie headed
back out to the stables to begin preparations for her
departure.

The first lap took just nine hours, the early pace
fast. Rafiq made no bid for the lead, content merely
to remain in the pack with the front runners. Ten of
them were grouped together as they made the fifth
change of horses at the starting line, the gathering
gloom pierced by the hundreds of bonfires lit to keep
the spectators warm. There were eight of them still
together at the sixth and seventh changes. And then
only four at the eighth and last. Lameh was as determined as ever to prevent Rafiq from leaping on
to his back, but Rafiq was in no mood to tolerate the
stallion's customary defiance, and Lameh, for once,
seemed to sense this, and was quickly brought to
the bridle.

Twenty-five miles, and three riders to beat, one
of them sporting Prince Salim's colours. Lameh was
eager to pin his ears back and gallop flat-out, but
Rafiq reined him in. This last leg was the hardest,
rocky underfoot for the large part, with some steep
climbs and treacherous descents before the home

straight. On the first lap, several horses had fallen to their knees on those descents. Rafiq had no intentions of allowing Lameh to do so.

'You must do this for your dam,' he whispered to the stallion, 'and I do this for her mistress.' It was astonishing, now that he no longer needed to win, how confident he was about winning. There was still a great deal at stake, but it no longer felt like he was racing for his life. For Elmira. For his people. For his kingdom. But not for his life. That belonged to him.

Eighteen hours into the race, every muscle and sinew ached but on he rode with grim determination. Two miles to go, the final and steepest descent safely accomplished, and there were only two of them left in contention, he and Salim's man. 'Let's show them that Bharym breeds the best bar none,' he said, crouching over the thoroughbred's neck, urging Lameh into a final gallop.

Though he had never doubted, his heart was pounding as the finishing line came into sight. Close behind him, he could hear the thundering hooves, the panting breath of his competitor, but Rafiq did not look over his shoulder. He was dimly aware of the crowds, the flags, the cheering as he raced by, but his entire being was focused on crossing that line first, on the trophy that he would claim for his people and for Elmira. As Lameh galloped across the line to record the narrowest of victories, Rafiq reined him in. As his entourage crowded around him and his subjects roared their approval, Rafiq saw her standing quietly by the enclosure, waiting for him, beaming, clapping. Stephanie. His own and very personal prize.

Rafiq was paraded in state on camel back, astride his father's monstrous, throne-like saddle, all the way from the finishing post to the city, bearing the huge gold Sabr trophy. His people were ecstatic. The festivities which his secretaries had planned so meticulously for just such an outcome would last for days, all across the kingdom.

He stood on the podium which had been set up in the city square. There were a number of faces at the window of the royal viewing gallery. He knew one of them was Stephanie, but he could not make out which. He summoned Prince Salim on to the podium. He lifted the gold Sabr trophy high. 'Today I raced in honour of your daughter, the Princess Elmira. It is appropriate therefore that I bequeath the trophy to you to keep in perpetuity. It is time to put the past behind us. Next year there will be a new Sabr, open to all horses of any breed. Fresh blood, my people. A fresh start for all of us.'

Stephanie decided to wear the pink gown for the first time, to mark her last night with Rafiq. It seemed appropriate somehow, as it was something the old Stephanie would never have dared wear. The bells tinkled on the matching pink slippers as she paced the terrace by the Pool of Nymphs, waiting for him. When she left the city, he was still being besieged by milling crowds. He had underestimated their enthusiasm and their desire to include him in their celebrations.

The flambeaux were lit, and all the lanterns too. Finally her straining ears heard the sound of the connecting door from the Hall of Campaign being opened, and she made her way swiftly inside to await him. He would have crossed the poolside to the terrace, surprised not to find her there, as she had told him she would be. Then he would have noticed the open door to the library. And then the open door to the changing room. And finally the *tepidarium*. And now...

The door of the Great Bathing Chamber opened and closed. The steam dispersed. 'Stephanie?'

He was wearing a white silk tunic. There were slippers on his feet. His hair was damp from his bath. He was freshly shaved. When he saw her waiting by the marble table, he smiled at her. His sinful smile. Her heart ached with the love for him she must keep hidden.

'Stephanie.'

No one would ever say her name in that way again. He swept her into his arms, and she let her kisses say the words she could not utter.

'I am sorry I could not get here sooner.'

'You are here now, that is all that matters.'

More kisses. She wanted more kisses, and more kisses, and more. A lifetime's store of kisses in one night. Tearing herself free, she began to unfasten the buttons on Rafiq's top, kissing his throat, his chest. 'Take it off,' she said.

He did as she asked, pulling the tunic over his head, the movement rippling through the toned muscles of his stomach, his shoulders, his arms. 'Now you,' he said.

But Stephanie shook her head. 'Not yet. First I want to thank you for all that you have given me, all that you have taught me.'

His eyes gleamed. He kissed her hard on the mouth. 'How do you plan to do that?'

'Take off the rest of your clothes, and I will show you.'

Another kiss. His hand on her breast. She was so desperate for him that she almost succumbed, but she could wait. She wanted this to be special. The gift of her love. Actions would speak louder than words. She disentangled herself, and undid the sash that held his trousers. They slid to the floor. He was already aroused. And so was she.

'On the table,' she said, kissing him. 'On your back.'

That slow growl of a laugh that made her shiver, and then he did as she bid him. She kicked off her slippers. His gaze was riveted on her. She undid the sash which held her robe in place, and let it fall to the ground. Next, the buttons, each one undone slowly and deliberately, and her robe joined the sash on the floor. Rafiq's eyes were dark with desire. His chest rose and fell in shallow breaths.

Her camisole was pink silk. The steam was making it cling to her breasts. She peeled the garment from her body. Next her pantaloons. His face, his body, made it clear how much her actions aroused him. His response made her confident. Her body delighted Rafiq. Now she would show him how much his delighted her.

She picked up the little vial of oil and stepped on to the table, kneeling between his legs. She leaned over him, allowing her nipples to brush his chest. The rough hair made them tingle. When she kissed him, his erection pressed into her belly. Their kiss was savage.

She trickled the oil on to his chest. As she worked it in with smooth strokes of her palms, his muscles rippled, his breathing quickened, her own excitement mounted. Sweeping strokes with soothing oil. When she leaned over to kiss him again, their bodies slipped and slid together. She sat back. She worked her way down. His hard belly. A muscled flank. The other one. His eyes never leaving her. Colour slashing his cheeks. More oil on her hands, sliding them up the inside of his thighs, drawing a deep moan from him. Then more oil, and she cupped him carefully, tenderly, feeling him tighten, watching his member swell.

And then more oil. 'Let us test ourselves,' she whispered, using his own words, smiling his sinful smile. She circled the silken length of him, stroking up to the tip slowly, feeling him pulse beneath her, relishing his groan, the way he bit his lip, the way his eyes were still fixed on her.

Another slow stroke. And then another. And then his hand gripped her wrist. 'Stephanie,' he said hoarsely, 'I think I might fail your test.'

She shook her head, smiling, but she let him go. 'Not a test, Rafiq. A new experience for both of us, something you once told me sounded tempting.'

His eyes widened. His smile was positively wicked as she faced him, lying back on her hands, slipping her feet on to his shoulders. '*Love's Fusion*, Stephanie?'

'*Love's Fusion*,' she agreed. Love. Fusion. She couldn't think of anything more apt.

He lifted her on to him. She was so aroused that when he entered her, she could already feel the first tensing prelude of her climax. 'Let us test ourselves,' he said, holding her still.

Stephanie tightened around him. 'No. Let us forget ourselves.'

They moved together, and *Love's Fusion* drew Rafiq high inside her. She shuddered. Again, and she cried out. But *Love's Fusion* did not allow her to kiss him. *Love's Fusion* was delightful, but it was about pleasure, not love. Fusing.

'Not this,' she panted, sliding her legs down. 'I want…'

'Kisses,' he said, pulling her on to his lap.

'Kisses,' Stephanie said, wrapping her arms around his neck.

Love. Fusing. Lips and tongues and drugging kisses. Her breasts crushed against his chest. Rafiq inside her, around her, pulsing, pushing, thrusting, kissing, stroking, until her climax shook her, making her cry out, spiralling out of control, forgetting herself, barely noticing that he did not, lifting her free as his own release drew a harsh cry from him. A cry in the form of her name.

They lay on the table wrapped in each other's arms for endless moments. Rafiq's heart was pounding, yet he felt weightless, a mindless pleasure, a floating sense of peace suffused him, a feeling he could not put a name to. He was here, where he was meant to be.

An odd thing to be thinking. It was most likely the result of the day. The culmination of so much. The Sabr was won. He had made his reparation. His people thought him a hero. And right now, he couldn't care less about any of it. After the euphoria of crossing the finishing line, all he had cared about was finding Stephanie. And here she was, curled up in his arms smiling that smile of hers, and, yes, that's exactly what he was feeling. He was here, where he was meant to be.

He kissed her lingeringly. The perfumed oil was heady. It made their skin slick. Parts of them were melded together in a very delightful way. A fusion. *Love's Fusion*. His heart lurched for no apparent reason. Stephanie's smile was languorous. She looked now exactly as he had first imagined her, sated, her lips swollen with kisses, her eyes heavy with passion. He kissed her again.

She sighed softly. 'Rafiq? Surely you can't…'

He ran his hand down her side, to the sweet indent of her waist, then back up to the voluptuous curve of her breast. 'Stephanie.' She arched up as he grazed her nipple. His shaft, lying against the soft flesh of her outer thigh, stirred. 'Stephanie,' he said, 'I think I can.'

She laughed. A throaty sound that spoke of invitation and expectation. 'Rafiq.' She wrapped her arms around his neck and pulled him to her. 'In that case, I can too.'

He woke in the cold light of dawn on the terrace, alone. The lamps were still lit in the library, but there was no sign of Stephanie. They had gone for a swim, and then they had sat together on the cushions wrapped in drying sheets watching the stars. He hadn't meant to fall asleep, but the exertions of the race had finally taken their toll. Or perhaps it was their intense and prolonged lovemaking.

Rafiq pulled on a robe from the changing room and sat down in the library. Let us forget ourselves, she had said last night, and he so very nearly had. He had lost himself in her. Holding her, kissing her, touching her, it had felt as if their bodies were one. As he rocked them into a slow climax that second time, she had clung so tightly to him, he had pressed himself so tightly against her, they had been conjoined. Not Stephanie and Rafiq, but some new entity. When she came, when she called out his name, such a fierce need to spill himself inside her had gripped him as to almost overwhelm him. He had not, though it felt wrong, not right. And afterwards, holding her, his face burrowed in the nape of her neck, breathing in the scent of her, and of them, he had felt such a profound tenderness envelop him. He had wanted to hold her like that for ever. He hadn't wanted to let her go.

He would have no option but to let her go when her appointment was over. Three more months, and then there would be no Stephanie in his stables, no Stephanie in his palace, no Stephanie in his bed, no Stephanie in his life. The ground tilted. His heart lurched. But he had always known she would leave, that she would return to England to claim her precious independence, leaving him to—how had she put it?—grasp his own future. Which he could do now—thanks not to winning the Sabr, but thanks to Stephanie.

He didn't want to think of his life without Stephanie. There would be a gap, a huge gap, which no one else could fill, which he didn't want anyone else to fill. Stephanie had forced him to confront his past. Stephanie had shown him that past not in a better light, but in a sharper, clearer light. She did not absolve his faults, she was, as ever, painfully honest, but she had set them against the faults of others. He was guilty, but he was not wholly responsible. Stephanie had given him the power to vanquish his ghost. Yesterday, he had finally laid Elmira to rest. He would always regret, but he had ceased looking back. Stephanie had made that possible.

And so much more, he thought ruefully, thinking of his lamplighting team of servants as he snuffed out

the lantern, for the sun had come up. He was irrevo-
cably changed. He would be a better prince, thanks
to Stephanie, for she had taught him that a prince
was also a man. Indeed, must be a man, before he
can be a prince.

Three months, and Stephanie would be gone. He
didn't want her to go. Why must she go? Why couldn't
she remain here in Arabia, running his stables? She
could be his Mistress of the Horse as well as his Royal
Horse Surgeon. He would not lose his touchstone if
she stayed. He would not have to miss her. He would
not have to live without her. Rafiq smiled to himself.
He couldn't understand why he hadn't thought of it
before. It was the perfect solution.

Stephanie was in her office in the stables, packing her text books into their wooden travelling crate.
Last night had been everything she had hoped and
dreamed. It had been magical. Confirmation, as if she
needed it, of how much she loved Rafiq. Confirmation, as if she needed it, that she must leave him as
soon as possible. Another day, another week, would
turn pleasure into torture.

'What are you doing?'

Rafiq had been profoundly asleep when she had
kissed him goodbye. Now he was wide awake, freshly
shaved, and her heart jumped at the sight of him, then
sank at what she must tell him. 'I'm packing.'

He came into the room, closing the door behind

him, looking bewildered. 'There are still three months of your appointment to run.'

'My work here is done.' She couldn't look at him. She picked up another book, staring down at it sightlessly.

'But the appointment was for six months. Why would you leave earlier?'

She chose her words carefully, for she knew he would easily catch her in any lie. 'The sickness is cured. I am eager to—it would be sensible for me to—now that the Sabr is won, you will be eager to look to the future. All your plans for your kingdom, your people will embrace them now, Rafiq. My presence would only be a distraction.'

'Stephanie, why won't you look at me? Last night—did I…?'

'Last night was perfect, Rafiq.' She forced herself to set the book down. She forced herself to meet his eyes. 'One cannot improve on perfection.'

He flinched. 'You think the next time would be a disappointment?'

She swallowed the lump in her throat. 'I think that there shouldn't be a next time. I cannot be part of your life, Rafiq.'

'I came here to offer you a permanent position. The independence you crave, here in Arabia. You could manage my stables. You could even—now that the sickness is cured, now that it can be talked of outside the stables, your fame would spread. You could take on assistants, train others. You would be much in demand. I would not insist—you would be my Royal Horse Surgeon, but I would not confine you to Bharym, Stephanie.'

A tear escaped. She brushed it away hastily. She couldn't cry. She couldn't let him see how much she cared. 'That is an extremely generous offer, Rafiq.'

His expression hardened. 'But despite that, you're not going to accept it, are you?'

She shook her head.

'May I ask why?'

She stared at him helplessly. She loved him so much. 'Would I be your mistress, as well as your Royal Horse Surgeon? What would happen then, when you tired of me?'

'Stephanie, if that is what you are worried about!' He took her hands. He smiled at her. 'This morning, when I realised that in three months' time you would be leaving, I knew it was nowhere near long enough. I would never tire of you.'

She felt as if her heart was being squeezed. What would be so wrong with staying here, in a role that offered her everything, so much, much more than she could ever hope for in England, with the man she loved? What could be wrong with that? One very fundamental thing was wrong with that. 'Now that the Sabr is won, your people will expect you to marry again, produce an heir, won't they? You can't deny that's true. So my presence here wouldn't just be inconvenient it would be inappropriate, from both our points of view.'

He ran his fingers through his hair. 'You are not

an inconvenience, you are a necessity. I have no plans
to marry any time soon.'

'That changes nothing. I still can't stay.'

'Why not, Stephanie?'

'Because I'm in love with you!' The words echoed
in the stuffy room, shocking both of them. Rafiq
looked quite stunned. She wrapped her arms around
herself and glared at him. 'There, I've said it. I am
in love with you. I know it's preposterous. I have
no pedigree, no family, no blue blood—nothing that
would make me acceptable to your people even if I
were a virgin, which you know very well I'm not.
Even if all those obstacles could be overcome there
is one insurmountable obstacle.'

'Which is?'

'You're not in love with me, Rafiq!'

There was a long silence. Then he shook his head.
'It's not an insurmountable obstacle.'

'Don't be ridiculous.'

'Stephanie, I *am* in love with you.' He looked quite
as dazed as she felt. 'I love you. What is ridiculous
is that I sat in the library this morning and listed out
all the reasons why I wanted you to stay, and it didn't
occur to me, not once…'

'You're just saying that in order to persuade me
to stay.'

He shook his head vehemently. 'I love you, Stephanie.'

Her heart was making a very good attempt at es-
caping from her ribcage. 'You can't.'

'I can,' he said firmly. 'I do. I love you. I don't

want you here for six months or a year or even ten. I want you in my life for ever.'

'Oh, Rafiq.' Tears trickled down her cheeks. 'If only that was possible.'

'I wouldn't put you in a gilded cage, Stephanie. I would not try to change what I love most about you. You would be my wife, but you would also be my Royal Horse Surgeon, my Mistress of the Horses, whatever you wished.'

'Rafiq, I can't marry you.'

'You're not listening Stephanie. You would still be independent…'

'It's not a question of independence. It's a question of appropriateness. I don't have any of the qualities your people require from a princess.'

He gave an exasperated sigh. 'Bloodlines. Pedigrees. I am heartily sick of it. Yesterday, when I said that we must have new blood for the Sabr, I was thinking of our horses. The foal who had the seizures has a perfect bloodline, but there is flaw in that perfect bloodline which made him sick. History! Heritage! But what about my heart? I am sick of looking back at the past. It is time we looked forward, Stephanie. It is high time the Royal House of Bharym itself had an injection of fresh blood.'

He pushed her hair back from her eyes, kissed her forehead. 'You have every quality that I desire in a consort. You have honour and integrity. You are honest and you are brave. You are a remarkable person. Stephanie. Last night, when we made love, I felt at peace for the first time ever.' He smiled crookedly.

'As one, complete. And still, this morning, when I was thinking of us, of you, I did not realise what I was feeling was love. But I know now, that's what it was. I love you, and you love me.'

He kissed her gently. Tenderly. As if he was afraid she would break. 'That is what is important, Stephanie. We can shape our own history, we can build our own heritage, as long as our hearts are unbreakably entwined.'

Her lip trembled. Her heart really did feel as if it might escape her chest. 'I don't know what to say.'

He kissed her again. 'Say nothing, save that you love me.'

'Oh, I do, with all my heart.'

'And that you will marry me.'

'I want to, so much, but I— Rafiq, surely because you are a prince your bride's purity should be beyond reproach?'

'Why would my people question your innocence? What matters is that my bride is true to me, and that I am true to her. What matters is not the past, Stephanie. What matters is the future. Our future. Can you see it, waiting for us to grasp it? Don't you want to?'

'Oh, I do.'

'Will you marry me?'

'Yes.' She threw her arms around him. 'I love you so much.'

'And I love you. With all of my heart.'

He kissed her tenderly. She kissed him back, tasting her tears on their lips, pressing herself close to him. But then he let her go. Picking up the heavy crate of books, he set it against the door, and stacked another one on top of it.

'What are you doing?' Stephanie asked.

Rafiq's smile was sinful. His kiss was passionate. 'Ensuring that we are not disturbed while I prove that we can improve on perfection.'

\* \* \* \* \*

*If you enjoyed this story,
you won't want to miss these other great reads in
Marguerite Kaye's*
HOT ARABIAN NIGHTS *mini-series:*
*THE WIDOW AND THE SHEIKH*
*SHEIKH'S MAIL-ORDER BRIDE*

*And make sure you pick up this fantastic duet, also
by Marguerite Kaye:*
*THE SOLDIER'S DARK SECRET*
*THE SOLDIER'S REBEL LOVER*

## *Historical Note*

If you follow me on Twitter, you'll know my tongue-in-cheek tag for this book was #studsheikh. In writing Stephanie and Rafiq's story I had to get up to speed with all things equine, but although *The Sheikh's Mail-Order Bride* inspired me to take up star gazing, I assure all animal lovers out there, I've no intention of attempting anything veterinary—though I did harbour a childhood ambition to be a vet, inspired by the novels of James Herriot.

Anyone with any semblance of medical knowledge will know that I have made Stephanie somewhat ahead of her time in terms of her understanding of methods of infection and contagion. If you're interested in a general history of eighteenth-century medicine then I would highly recommend Wendy Moore's fabulous and highly readable biography of the anatomist John Hunter, *The Knife Man*, which inspired my heroine's dedication to the principles of observation and experimentation.

Veterinary science was very much in its infancy in 1815, when the army farriers were the primary exponents. I am very grateful to Dr John Clewlow of the Veterinary History Society for his help with all things veterinarian in the early days of the discipline. Richard Darvill really did serve at Waterloo as the Veterinary Officer for the Seventh Hussars, although the history I've given him is entirely of my own making. Thanks also to Peter Thomson for putting me in touch with Dr Clewlow, and for his advice on the preventative measures which Stephanie takes—in reality, sadly, based on Peter's own extensive experience during the foot-and-mouth outbreak in 2001.

As for the 'sickness' which Stephanie 'cures', it is African Horse Sickness, which rampaged through Egypt in the 1870s, killing many thousands of horses, mules and camels. The Arabian thoroughbreds at the famous stud farm owned by Ali Pasha Sherif, part inspiration for the Bharym stud, were saved only because they were sent into isolation, a tactic which Stephanie adopts.

The Sabr endurance race is entirely a figment of my imagination, though the spectacular changeover which Rafiq makes between horses is a key element of the Indian Relay. I read of the tradition of sending children out to be raised by Bedouin in a biography of Gertrude Bell.

Are you still with me and up for more? There's a comprehensive list of my reading on my website, *www.margueritekaye.com*. Enjoy!

# COMING NEXT MONTH FROM

# **H**HARLEQUIN®

# **H**ISTORICAL

## Available March 21, 2017

### THE COWBOY'S ORPHAN BRIDE (Western)
by Lauri Robinson

Orphans Bridgette Banks and Garth McCain are reunited after years of separation. Sparks fly...especially when the cowboy catches impulsive Bridgette telling everyone she's his bride!

### CLAIMING HIS DESERT PRINCESS (Regency)
*Hot Arabian Nights* • by Marguerite Kaye

Princess Tahira encounters a wildly attractive stranger on her secret escape into the desert. Christopher Fordyce's past makes any future together forbidden...but will he risk everything to claim his princess?

### BOUND BY THEIR SECRET PASSION (Regency)
*The Scandalous Summerfields* • by Diane Gaston

The Earl of Penford knows his passion for Lorene Summerfield is scandalous, but when he's accused of her husband's murder, he must clear his name—and win her hand!

### THE SPANIARD'S INNOCENT MAIDEN (Aztec)
by Greta Gilbert

Benicio Villafuerte buys Tula's freedom in return for her help discovering hidden treasure... As their dangerous days explode into sensuous nights, Tula embarks on her own quest—to capture the conquistador's heart!

---

## *Available via Reader Service and online:*

### CAPTIVE OF THE VIKING (Viking)
by Juliet Landon

Aric the Ruthless takes widow Lady Fearn prisoner for vengeance, planning to tempt her into his bed! Nothing like her cruel husband, Aric's seduction awakens her to new sensations...

### THE WALLFLOWER DUCHESS (Regency)
by Liz Tyner

Wallflower Lily Hightower is amazed to learn the Duke of Edgeworth wants to make her his duchess—and this formidable suitor won't take no for an answer!

---

SPECIAL EXCERPT FROM

**H HARLEQUIN**®
™

# ℍISTORICAL

*Hardened desert trader Tahar knows he could—and should—sell his new captive Kiya for a handsome price. But when a wild heat explodes between them, can Tahar find a way to keep Kiya as his own?*

*Read on for a sneak preview of*
*ENSLAVED BY THE DESERT TRADER*
by *Greta Gilbert*.

When she saw him unwrapping his headdress and stepping out of his long tunic she knew she had overestimated the power of her own will. He stood to his full height and gazed at her from the bank, and already she yearned for him. His luxuriant mane hung about his face in thick, wavy ropes, and it was the only thing he wore.

He was a man. That was clear.

Stunningly clear.

But as she appraised the whole of his body, she realized that he was also a god. Every chiseled bit of him radiated strength and masculinity. There was not even a hint of the softness of age or leisure, not a single inch of fallow flesh. He was as taut and ready as a drum.

And he was coming for her.

The strong sinews of his lower legs tensed as he stepped barefoot into the water. He began to walk toward her, and his upper leg muscles bulged and contracted, creating rings of small waves that radiated out from his body. Those waves traveled slowly across the pool, and when they crashed into her body they made her shiver.

If she had seen him among the tomb workers she would have thought him a loader. She pictured him bare chested and sweating in the sun, lifting some large boulder, his dense muscles flexing. He would have been the most irresistibly handsome loader that ever was.

And he wanted her—nothing could be clearer.

She had thought that she repulsed him. Now it seemed he was making the opposite known.

Just the sight of him made her heart thump wildly.

He continued toward her, his narrow hips sinking beneath the velvety water, his muscular arms stretching out to caress its still surface. With the moon above him, the contours of his massive chest cast shadows upon his pale skin. It was as if he had been carved in alabaster, a temple relief showing the picture of an ideal man. Only this man was real—very, very real—and he was advancing toward her.

*Don't miss*
*ENSLAVED BY THE DESERT TRADER*
*by Greta Gilbert, available August 2016 wherever*
*Harlequin® Historical books and ebooks are sold.*

www.Harlequin.com

HHEXP0716

# JUST CAN'T GET ENOUGH?

Join our social communities
and talk to us online.

You will have access to the latest
news on upcoming titles and special
promotions, but most importantly,
you can talk to other fans about your
favorite Harlequin reads.

Harlequin.com/Community

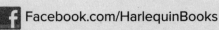 Facebook.com/HarlequinBooks

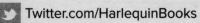 Twitter.com/HarlequinBooks

Pinterest.com/HarlequinBooks